Magic Eight Ball

Magic Eight Ball

Marion Douglas

Polestar Book Publishers

Vancouver

Polestar Book Publishers acknowledges the ongoing support of The Canada Council; the British Columbia Ministry of Small Business, Tourism and Culture through the BC Arts Council; and the Government of Canada through the Book Publishing Industry Development Program (BPIDP).

Cover artwork by Jan Wade
Cover design by Val Speidel
Printed and bound in Canada

Canadian Cataloguing in Publication Data

Douglas, Marion K. (Marion Kay), 1952-
  Magic eight ball

  ISBN 0-88974-063-1

  I. Title.
PS8557.O812M34 2000   C813'.54   C00-910006-7
PR9199.3.D584M34 2000

POLESTAR BOOK PUBLISHERS
An imprint of Raincoast Books
8680 Cambie Street
Vancouver, B.C. V6P 6M9
Canada
www.raincoast.com

5 4 3 2 1

Acknowledgements

I would like to thank the Alberta Foundation for the Arts for grant money received during the writing of this book. Barbara Kuhne, thanks for your valued editorial help. Also, thanks to Ginny Ratsoy, Roberta Rees, Eric Savoy and Jim Ellis for their support and encouragement. To my children, Carla and Eric, thanks for being who you are. And a special thank you to Susan Bennett, gal-pal extraordinaire.

Contents

1

Late in spring, the day after her eleventh birthday, Lois abducted Mrs. McCracken. Stole her, in other words. Left the tiny chenille bedspread Julia had made — at great personal risk — all plumped up on the pink plastic bed to create the impression of a slumbering-yet-present doll. Which worked until Julia got an uneasy feeling around bedtime and checked in on the McCrackens, the miniature and not very life-like family that had come with Julia's dollhouse several Christmases ago. Such was the power invested in Mrs. McCracken that her absence could prevent sleep, raise suspicions about Lois Wilde, make you think, if only for a moment, the Big Dipper had flipped itself upright.

Julia was outside in her pyjamas,

trying telepathy. When it was late, past nine-thirty, and she needed to speak to Lois, this sometimes worked, and Lois would call. In Lois's house, where very few rules applied and none consistently, phone calls after nine were sometimes icily received. Here at the Raine house, with its mealtimes and bedtimes and "now you're old enough to work in the greenhouses," people were welcome to phone whenever. Not that they did.

To begin telepathy, you need deep, percussive thoughts, thunderous messages broken into syllables. *Call Ju-li-a. Call Ju-li-a.* There went the telepathic waves, undulating across the fields as in a science filmstrip, over Millicent Creek, until they could actually see the lights of Flax. Lois didn't live in Flax; she, too, lived in the country, but closer to the village. This proximity increased her confidence, or so Julia had concluded. There had to be a reason why the teacher regularly commented that Julia needed to develop more confidence, while Lois was a very confident young lady.

Any minute now Julia would hear the phone. It was a humid Ontario summer night. Every window in the house was open, so the ring would vibrate its pleasure into the yard and beyond the trees, past the falling-down barn and into the weeds. Perhaps the goldenrod and thistle would experience a quiet joy, a goosebumping of the leaves when they heard the telephone. It would jangle the quiet with its chain of messages: someone has thought about you, planned to call, approached the telephone, dialled, and now this — ring, ring. Glad tidings. If the call was for her, Julia sometimes shaped her mind into that of a busy executive or important movie agent. This was 1964; a girl could be whatever she wanted. "Yes?" she liked to answer, instead of "Hello."

Why had Lois not called? Apparently telepathy didn't know the meaning of urgent. Now it was nine thirty-five. She would have to take the risk and call. Her parents were watching television in the living room. They didn't know Julia was still up, skulking around as they would call it. The phone was in the kitchen, but you could stretch the cord into the pantry, push the door shut for privacy and dial from there. Here's hoping Mrs. Wilde didn't answer.

"Hello." It was Lois.

"You took Mrs. McCracken."

"Well actually it was a jail break."

"This isn't a jail. She lives here."

"I know. I know. Sorry. I wanted her to come home with me and tell me to cut my hair."

"Cut your hair?"

They both had braids, started in the second grade and long now, with bangs the ideal length.

"I knew I wouldn't be able to do it without Mrs. McCracken, so I brought her here. I went in the bathroom, stood her up on the little shelf beneath the mirror and she said, 'Oh for heaven's sake, it's just hair. At least it grows. Look at this plastic mat I'm saddled with.' So I cut it. Two big snips right through the braids."

"Did your mom see?"

"No, she's at a class. She won't be home till at least eleven. And my dad's on the road."

"But now we won't have the same hair."

"I know. That's OK. Mrs. McCracken thinks we're getting too similar — it'll be good to have different hair for a change."

"Yeah, I guess you're right," Julia conceded, sounding very unlike an executive or movie agent, who probably would have said, in the voice of Fred McMurray, *"Now wait a minute here, Lois Wilde."* Oh well. She supposed it was only fair that Lois have Mrs. McCracken and her demanding personality all to herself occasionally. *"Who's ever going to notice if you cut a little corner off your chenille bedspread?"* Mrs. McCracken had goaded Julia a week ago. *"If it's a corner that's against the wall, who's ever going to notice?"* *"Well, maybe my mom when she washes it."* *"She'll just think it got torn in the agitator."* *"OK then."*

Getting back to the matter at hand, Julia said, "Bring her to school tomorrow, then you can come here on the bus, OK?"

"Yeah, OK."

No matter what, hanging up was exhilarating: people walking away from one another in separate houses, more than three miles apart, two diminishing parallel whirs of thought. How could you know for sure that it wasn't telepathy? How could you be certain those wires carried the voices?

~ ~ ~ ~

"**Don't let my** mom see you," Julia warned as she and Lois snuck with the finesse of secret agents from school bus to tree trunk to tree trunk, past the row of greenhouses (a self-propagating species, Julia was certain, through an underground root system — seemed every other month another one appeared), into the house and upstairs to the playroom. If they managed this without being seen, they were free until dinnertime. It was as if, on a day-to-day basis, Mrs. Frances Raine didn't recall Julia's existence until she entered her field of vision. Later, in university, when Julia first read Piaget, she surmised that her mother had suffered from frequent lapses of object permanence.

This was the routine, at least for now. "Thank god for those trees," Julia said from the comfort and perspective of the playroom, with its second-floor view.

"I know," Lois responded. "If it weren't for those trees, the McCrackens probably never would have been invented." And that was the beginning, the key in the door. Then they were gone. Julia might catch glimpses of her parents in greenhouse number one, especially now that they wore new white smocks, spectral and brisk. "They just bought those lab coats. Got them from a uniform store in London. They think they're doctors or something, so I guess that makes me a nurse." *You're old enough now, Julia, almost eleven, you can help out in the greenhouses. That's what older children do.* Ha. Not true. Only older children unlucky enough to live with greenhouse operators.

The playroom was the best part of the house, the one bedroom nobody used for sleeping. Julia's parents, Abraham and Frances Raine, occupied the large and gabled room facing the road. Julia had the little one with the chandelier, and the playroom belonged to Julia and her best friend, Lois Wilde. As if it were territory adults had forgotten or never learned about in the first place — or as if they were afraid of its power to undo — Mr. and Mrs. Raine never entered the playroom.

Outside the playroom walls, Julia and Lois had come to expect microscopic seams of cause and effect to hold events in place, binding them to their school and their little town of Flax. Tiny, tiny threads, they stuck like spider webs on your face wherever you went. But not in the playroom. Through some cosmological oversight, the playroom had escaped the vast and containing web of worldly sense. If you wanted, here you could make your own family tree, a pastime of Julia's when Lois was not around. Using pictures from magazines and her own bad drawings, Julia had constructed a line of descent including Alice the Goon and Popeye, Dale Evans and Roy Rogers, Elizabeth Taylor, several Mouseketeers, Walt Disney and, occupying the place of great-great-great-grandmother, a smiling Hayley Mills.

When Lois came to visit, the McCrackens — with their history and bickering and insatiable material needs — came to life. There had been an inheritance, large sums of money were involved, and when the metal house with the trompe l'oeil furniture was no longer adequate, the McCrackens had moved into the playroom. The place desperately needed redecoration, but Mr. McCracken was a tightwad. "You can't get blood from a stone," Mrs. McCracken said. They would have to improvise. First, a sideboard, which Lois and Julia assembled from bricks and planks. Then an occasional table with a pink lace tablecloth from Lois's mother's trunk. "It's a beginning," said Mrs. McCracken, "but we need more colour."

Now they had a series of bright bowls filled with leaves and chestnuts and crabapples, a card table supporting an old kettle and a cracked blue-and-white platter, and one armchair with white stuffing forever bursting from its cushions. And there was an original masterpiece, the Mona Lisa, lifted from one of Eugenia Wilde's art history books. "I had to have it," Mrs. McCracken said. "I don't care what Mr. McCracken says, it was worth every penny."

With the art and the family tree, the walls were covered and the floor space gradually consumed with cast-off pieces of dusty-smelling junk. But never mind, Mrs. McCracken couldn't actually see or smell. The interior decorating was nearing completion — negotiations were underway to obtain an elegant, yet dangerous, hot plate from Mr. Wilde's garage — when the first abduction occurred. To Julia's thinking, that affected the design of things in a way not apparent to the naked eye. Yet had she been asked to explain the change, Julia would have said it was more the result of the hair cutting than the theft. The hair-cutting episode had seemed a little like Mrs. McCracken taking sides, trying to form an opposing team or construct a rival playroom.

For several days Julia remained vigilant, always looking sideways or beneath the bedspread or into Lois's impenetrable mind. Nothing happened. Then, a little over three weeks after the first abduction, another disappearance. This time Julia skipped the telepathy and dialled briskly: the executive was annoyed.

"She asked to come with me," Lois said. Not even a hello. "She's thinking of opening an art gallery, so she wanted to look at my mom's art books."

"You can't really have an art gallery."

"Oh, as if I don't know that."

Silence, both parties wishing the wires to be sliced, accidentally downed by a horrifyingly large flock of crows. *They just came down from the south there and all decided to roost on that one wire. No way she could hold up that weight,* a watchful farmer would say.

"It just ruins everything when you take Mrs. McCracken," Julia said. "It should be out of bounds, is what it should be. It's like we're both in a TV show, but all the time we're there, you're thinking about another show you're going to start up someplace else. An art gallery at your house should be out of bounds."

"Not according to Mrs. McCracken."

"Bring her to school tomorrow," Julia ordered. "And goodbye." She hoped to leave Lois with a hive of thoughts, a swarm buzzing in a funnel cloud above her head. Unlikely though. Probably Lois was already looking at pictures of famous art with Mrs. McCracken again, swarmless and happy.

After that phone call, Mrs. McCracken didn't talk as much. She developed migraines and sinus problems, and one day Julia thought she overheard her mumbling about packing it all in, Mr. McCracken was such a good-for-nothing. Which was probably why Julia wasn't surprised when she arrived home from school one day late in June to find the McCrackens' metal house on the downstairs kitchen table, the family and all of their furniture stuffed into a paper bag. Maybe this had been coming, like a telepathic dart from wherever Mrs. McCracken got her passport. Still.

Upstairs in the playroom, all the decorations and artwork had been removed, piled up like so much refuse. The walls were freshly papered with images of the seven dwarfs, unwelcome and menacing figures heigh-ho-ing their way to work. On the floor, awaiting assembly, lay Julia's old crib. "I'm pregnant," her mom said. "You're going to have a little sister or brother. A very little brother or sister. You'll be almost twelve when it's born."

The possibility that her mother might become pregnant had never occurred to Julia. Her mother was so unlike other mothers who routinely became pregnant, mothers whose bodies were round and cushiony, where developing babies might be curled up beneath generous rolls of fat. Frances Raine was straight and without hiding places. Julia understood that her mother had given birth to her in the same way she understood Bible stories — as an unlikely tale the adults expected her to believe.

That very day at school, in health class, Julia had read about a woman in the United States who lost all her hair. Apparently the shock of arriving home from church to find her house burned to the ground had been too much for her scalp to endure. If only Julia's body could communicate such eloquent ruin. Standing in the doorway to the playroom, she pulled at her brown braids, willed each of the follicles to clench itself shut and free her hair in protest. No visible change.

Julia picked up the pieces of her family tree and arranged them on her bed. This could easily find new life on the bedroom walls, but the McCrackens would require something more drastic. She carted the dollhouse out to a dark and musty shed, then brought along the family and their effects as well. For the time being they would have to share space with a cement mixer, garden tools and junk Mrs. McCracken had never wanted brought near her.

Then Julia called Lois Wilde with the news.

~ ~ ~ ~

A couple of years passed with the McCrackens and all their fur-nishings languishing in darkness. The shed they were in was used as a repository for items to be kept out of the way and eventually auctioned off. When this might happen was never made clear. "Someday that'll be worth something to somebody," Julia's dad would say of a broken pulley or a garden hose that had sprung leaks. He would open the door to the storage shed and sequester the item in question until it was miraculously invested with value. Occasionally, Julia liked to sit there and enjoy the pleasing melan-choly of objects growing older. Despite the mess and the earth floor, the McCrackens were well suited to this environment. Mrs. McCracken had a rare, unappreciated quality to her, and now here she rested, becoming more exceptional with each passing day.

It stood to reason that the McCrackens, having squandered their inheritance, would need to sell their house. When Julia knew she was alone and nobody could possibly hear her, when her mom and dad and her new brother Stephen were away in London or Mesmer, she entertained herself auctioning off the McCrackens' home. She replicated sounds she had heard from auctioneers: "Who'll give me ten, ten, ten... this is a beautiful piece of workmanship! Who'll give me ten thousand dollars for this exquisite dollhouse? It came over from the old country. Ten thousand. Who's going to make a bid? Come on, somebody start us up here. Come on, you stupid people." Julia had no patience for them. "You stupid, stupid people."

The bidders' lack of interest in the dollhouse invariably forced Julia to move into oration. What she sought, really, was to position herself in front of a crowd, exhorting, upbraiding and urging people not to be so complacent. She would shout about the dangers of nuclear destruction, describing in great detail the nuclear winter awaiting them. "Have you not eyes to see? Ears to hear?" she demanded, easily making the shift from auctioneer to television evangelist. "Nuclear weapons will kill us all. Show me that you're willing to shake off the evil prejudices of the cold war, the yoke of nuclear power. Stand up and renounce their evil hold upon you. Stand up, you cowards," Julia said, almost becoming abusive. Then the shed door opened and there stood Lois Wilde. Yikes.

"What are you doing?" asked Lois, so very normal and sunlit.

Julia's humiliation was caused only in part by her ridiculous behaviour. What was unbearable was to be discovered by Lois Wilde. Had it been Barbara White or Lesley Munro, the other two girls in their seventh grade class, she would not have cared so much. Barbara and Lesley were chemically bound, a boring atomic team, one of those blue or red knob-headed representations found in their science text. On the way home from school, they planned what colours to wear the following day. To herself, Julia called them the molecule.

But Lois mattered. The unfortunate truth was that in grade

17

seven neither Lois nor Julia had a best friend. They had been friends; it seemed logical they should continue to be, but now they weren't. What could possibly be the problem? Julia imagined groups of puzzled adults discussing and analyzing the situation. Why don't the Wilde and Raine girls spend more time together? they asked one another over cards.

And then Julia's ears turned red because she knew the answer: she was in love with Lois Wilde. She was in love with Alexander Mast, too, an Amish boy (a safe choice in his suspenders and black vest, his cultural harness), so she knew what the word meant. She had given the subject considerable thought and even composed a few definitions, this being an area in which Julia Raine excelled. Had she been given the job of Minister of Education, she would have made definitions a subject area.

What Is Love? Julia asked the inside back page of her math scribbler. Love is a slightly bad feeling and causes worry, like stretched-out elastic from old underpants. Love is poached eggs, a little raw, that you have to eat because your friend's mom prepared them. It brings on a fear of gagging. Love is *Lady Chatterley's Lover* and all the reasons it is not to be taken from the shelf at home. Love is your eyes turning on like the headlights of a car when Alexander Mast comes into sight.

Julia could have gone on and on. If she wanted to magnify and grow the warm Pablum of love she carried deep inside her, she had only to walk close to Alexander at recess or goad him into teasing or chasing her. If he grabbed her arm, the feeling rose from her stomach to a place between her ears from which a dozen imperatives issued forth: run, touch him, kiss him, don't even think such a thing, wrestle with him, go and see what Lesley and Barbara are doing, make him chase you, go inside the school. If she went inside where it was dark and sat at her desk for a while, she could control the feeling.

With Lois, the feeling, although similar, existed outside Julia's body. It was like a poltergeist but not frightening exactly; a natural phenomenon, a comet, the northern lights, swamp gas, UFOs. If Julia went looking for it, she might see it; if she didn't, she wouldn't. It was at Lois's house, in Lois's clothing, and also in her mother's car. It hovered over her desk at school and was buzzing slightly within the McCrackens' house. Groups of scientists from the National Research Council would have been hard pressed to iden-tify it, much less explain it.

Flax Elementary School had only two classrooms, one for the first four grades, the other for grades five to eight. The grade seven class was small and occupied a single row of desks. At the beginning of the year, because of her inability to see the board, Julia had been seated in the very front desk. By spring, she had glasses with a beige case and a gold clasp, the opening and shutting of which made her feel important, glamorous even, as if she might have connections to Hollywood. Julia removed her glasses, snapped them into their case and massaged the bridge of her nose at least twenty times a day. Lois, seated two desks behind, easily became Hayley Mills, passing by from the set for *Pollyanna*. The voice of the teacher, Miss Brilz, became that of Agnes Moorehead, suggesting, insisting, that Lois and Julia were twins, separated by feuding parents.

Thanks to her optometrist, Julia spent the final weeks of sev-enth grade in an extravaganza of daydreams, all of which cast Lois Wilde in leading roles. And even though they were not officially friends, sometimes didn't even speak for days at a time, when Julia anticipated the long summer days ahead, Lois was included in the plans forming in her head.

So it was not surprising that Lois appeared that day at the shed door. With all the unstoppable talk that's heard on the skin, in the abdomen, at the back of the throat and inside the knees — Lois must have picked up on the general murmur. She had just decided to ride her bike over. No reason, really. And then she thought Julia was being hurt — what else was the yelling about? "I'm fine," Julia said, and offered no further comment. Frankly, Lois was too cute to be expected to suffer long-winded explanations, especially since she had begun to wear her dark hair in a style identical to that of the shorthaired twin in *The Parent Trap*. Like her, she wore jeans and T-shirts. Lois did not follow trends: stretchies, for example. Tight nylon stirrup pants were not her style. She would have looked as ridiculous in stretchies as Alexander Mast would.

"The McCrackens!" Lois said as soon as she realized Julia was unhurt and merely behaving like Billy Graham. "They've been in this shed all this time. We have to bring them out. They'll be turned into albinos by now. We should make them some little sunglasses. Do you have any black construction paper? If you don't, I can go home and get some from my mom."

"Actually, I think I do."

And for the remainder of June, in the long evenings, the McCrackens made several trips from the shed to the slanted daylight beneath the big, half-dead elm tree. A little disoriented, they donned their paper glasses and adapted as best they could. Their house had been sold to a collector, Julia told Lois. They'd have to leave it in the shed.

~ ~ ~ ~

That summer, the summer Julia turned thirteen, she and Lois moved the McCrackens and their furniture into a corner of one of the greenhouses. Because Lois was not required to be home until midnight, they stayed up late, playing until five minutes before her curfew. Then she left in a hurry on her CCM, out the laneway in the standing position, bobbing with that piston quality, like a boy. As Julia watched, she imagined the walls and rooms of air Lois was passing through, one minute warm and full of insects, then mysteriously cool by the stand of dead elms. The hair on her arms stood up.

They made a net hammock for Mr. McCracken out of an onion bag and four knitting needles, sharp ends sunk in pots of sand. The effect was pyre-like. They both knew he could not get out of there and was likely starving, but oh well. Mrs. McCracken had stopped making meals anyway. The kids fended for themselves. Everyone was still in sunglasses because of the brilliance of the lighting. Lois said, "We can't see them but there is an audience outside watching us, people sometimes halfway up the hillside, depending on the size of the house." She talked that way because of her mother, who had connections to theatre.

Julia asked Lois if the Stanton twins were in the audience.

"Most nights," she answered. "They see better in the dark, so some nights they like to waddle out here."

The Stanton twins were two old fellows from the village whose sole occupation was people watching. Seated on the bench outside the Flax hardware store, they watched; that was the work they did. A strange choice, this watching, since they were blinded from cataracts. Their eyes, cloudy like bits of ice in a glass of Pepsi, seemed always to drip and melt with a tender enthusiasm when Lois and Julia came into view. Whether alone or together, they elicited comment: "All by yourself today? Where's your little friend?" Or, "Aren't you two the happy pair?" Around the Stanton twins, Julia could always feel her love for Lois bunch up in her hair like a gnarly tat.

One night Julia said to Lois, "I really wish the Stanton twins weren't in the audience."

"You can't make people stay home," Lois said. "But with their night vision they probably can only see the people around them in the audience out there. The greenhouse is likely just kind of a blur to them. I seem to have heard that they hate it when the street-lights come on at night because then everything goes blurry for them. Everything's opposite for them." Lois had a way of seeming to have heard important bits of information.

Julia moved her transistor radio into the greenhouse and roamed the myriad band widths of North America, sometimes as far away as Texas. With the radio balanced on an overturned clay pot and the aerial at a forty-five degree angle, south-southwest, a signal from Chicago came in loud and clear. Suddenly, that's where they were living, in an apartment next door to the McCrackens. It was apparent that Lois had a job and Julia kept house.

"A man jumped in front of the train today," Lois said one night. "I think I've seen him before. I tried to save him, tried to talk him out of it. 'Don't you want to live any longer?' I asked. He jumped anyway. There was nothing anybody could do."

Despite Julia's auctioneering and Hollywood fantasies, despite adoring Lois, she was ill at ease with this type of pretending. She could imagine the Chicago apartment and picture the two of them in it, but she couldn't comfortably play along. Instead, she contributed by drawing floor plans and arranging and rearranging the furniture. "We need to get a trilight lamp," she said, having taken inventory.

Lois began to bring a jackknife and whittle pieces of wood. She made lawn chairs for the balcony. The street was always busy. The McCrackens made a lot of noise next door.

Mrs. McCracken dropped in like a character in a situation comedy, making preposterous announcements. She wanted to hop the train to New York — there were some important auditions she didn't want to miss. She was in a hurry; she had a coffee date with a senator. She wanted to get out of this damn blue skirt; she hated it. Lois agreed to whittle off the plastic pleated skirt Mrs. McCracken had never been without. She whittled until Mrs. McCracken's entire bottom half was Band-Aid-coloured, while her top half remained blue. She carved a V-shaped notch for legs.

"Do you have a pen?"

Through the yard, the single bulb atop a pole casting an unnatural shadow beneath the dying elm. Why was it only at night the branches moved so abruptly and creepily, like a bad puppet show? Inside, Julia found a pen on the kitchen counter and raced back.

With great concentration, Lois drew a little triangle of hair on Mrs. McCracken, then leaned her against a small pot. There she was, transformed. Julia experienced an odd feeling, like too much pudding, but not in the stomach, lower.

After that, Mrs. McCracken always visited half nude. When Lois wasn't around, Mrs. McCracken had to be hidden in a pot of vermiculite. If she were found, the Stantons would have something to talk about that would make their sinking eyes light up. Julia began to make sure she was in the greenhouse before Lois arrived, with Mrs. McCracken already out of her hiding place. She wanted Lois to know that things went on between Mrs. McCracken and her when Lois wasn't there.

~ ~ ~ ~

In the fall of 1966, Mr. McCracken slipped into a coma for all eternity. The story was that in the move from the greenhouse to the barn, Mr. McCracken had caught a chill that rendered him vulnerable to a form of dust virus, several of which infected the barn. The possibility of disease and fire made the barn dangerous, but the greenhouse had become too public. "We live in a glass house and we do throw stones," Mrs. McCracken had complained. "I need some damn privacy." A move was absolutely necessary.

The upstairs of the unused barn offered quantities of hay and straw, housed there since the dawn of time in two dizzyingly attractive lofts. The straw was stored in hard-edged and urine-coloured rectangular bales, which they set to arranging. First, they constructed a sort of palliative shrine for Mr. McCracken, using three bales off in a darkened corner. There, wrapped in toilet paper, suspended in his hammock, safe from the threat of rats and mice, he rested in peace.

In the barn, no effort was made to replicate the greenhouse floor plan; instead, they created a version of the upstairs of the Raines' house. They made the walls as high as they possibly could, four bales up. Then, with the help of an overturned box, they settled bales above the entrances to make doorframes. The McCracken children were immediately quarantined in separate bedrooms because of the dust virus. Being less than three inches tall, they were easily kept from harm in Mason jars covered with two layers of cheesecloth secured with elastic bands. And there they stayed, indefinitely. Very little was known about the dust virus; the experts were not in agreement on the period of quarantine.

This left Mrs. McCracken, Lois, and Julia to make a life for themselves. There was a small coma pension from Mr. McCracken's former employer, but this barely covered the rent. With her nudity — "Yes, I'm naked. So? You are too under those cheap clothes" — there were some barriers to employment. Then Julia hit upon the solution of a television broadcast from the apartment. Mrs. McCracken was so worldly wise she could provide advice. "Ask Mrs. McCracken" would be the name of the show. Julia imagined herself with an executive position, someone in charge of research.

By chopping off the plastic mirror of the dollhouse bedroom vanity, Lois created a desk. With this and a piece of ink-blue bathroom tile from a Wilde family home renovation project, they created a studio for Mrs. McCracken. Behind her, they propped a map of the world, glued to cardboard. The barn was wired. They found an outlet near the stairwell and used an extension cord and a gooseneck desk lamp to create studio lights. Julia was in heaven. Mrs. McCracken, the studio, Lois Wilde, the straw with its smell of museum-quality dust — all of it created a perfect miniature world, like the intricate model of the township's future the Flax village reeve had brought to school one day, with its groups of plastic trees and Monopoly houses.

The first few broadcasts were slow. Then, Mrs. McCracken found her stride.

~ ~ ~ ~

Eugenia Wilde, Lois's mother, was third-generation Mercury Township, and from a successful farming family. When she and Allister married, her parents, Margaret and Harold Favell, retired into town, allowing Allister and Eugenia to move into the farmhouse. Eugenia needed space. The land was rented to a neighbouring farmer.

Not long after Lois was born, Mrs. Wilde began a Bachelor of Arts degree. Now she was nearing completion of a Master's degree in philosophy from the University of Western Ontario. The front seat of her car held a permanent collection of books and papers and cardboard boxes. "It's my locker," she said, "don't touch anything. There is some organization here. It's just not visible to the untrained eye." When Eugenia drove them anywhere, Lois and Julia cleared a space in the back-seat debris of candy wrappers and coffee cups.

Lois's mother sought ever-expanding circles of acquaintanceship, and she liked entertaining. People from the university visited, frequently staying overnight — it was such a lovely spot. Mr. Wilde never seemed to be there. His work took him away on business trips, and he was an avid hunter. Maybe he, too, fell ill with a dust virus and was consigned for periods of time to a pyre in the garage. Hard to say where Mr. Wilde was much of the time.

In a small community, the Wilde situation, as it was called, generated talk with a nuclear proficiency. This gossip mill fuelled Lois's own personal cold war. Still, she had an exaggerated notion of the locals' censure of Eugenia Wilde. "They think she's a floozy. They think she's a drug addict. They think she has crackpot ideas," she told Julia up in the barn.

"They like her plays," Julia said. Eugenia also more or less ran the Flax Little Theatre. "My parents liked the last one. Everybody applauded, didn't they? What more do you want? Nobody ever jumps out of their car and applauds my parents' perennials."

"Do you think your parents would let me live here if I worked for free in the greenhouses?" Lois asked.

"I honestly don't know," Julia said. Her mom most likely would; her dad, maybe not.

Ask Mrs. McCracken. There were a host of unanswered questions. It began with the magic eight ball. The pyramidal floating body inside a black ball of viscous liquid yielded up its oracular messages: *Outlook not so good*; or *It is decidedly so*; or *Cannot predict now*. This quickly reached its limits and, by her own account, bored Mrs. McCracken to tears.

The medium idea was Lois's, from a movie she had seen at the drive-in. This was the format. "I read your question," Lois instructed, "and you shake the eight ball and read the answer. Then you read my question and I shake the eight ball. That way we both get to be the medium." Or the voice of Mrs. McCracken. Until, that is, Julia proved her inadequacy as a clairvoyant with the first question she handed Lois.

"Will Alexander Mast ever run away from the Amish?"

A vigorous shake of the eight ball. *"Ask again later,"* Julia read, relieved, thinking that settled that.

An expectant look from Lois was Julia's cue to continue, but she stalled. Her face reddened, her thoughts milled in directionless groups.

Lois, who had inherited some of her mother's directorial talent, jumped in. "Look at Mrs. McCracken. Let everything else blur. Empty your mind and answer the question."

"The answer is," Julia intoned in the low monotone she felt befit the brainwashed or the living dead, "the answer is *'Ask again later.'*"

"No, that's not the answer. You're Mrs. McCracken. She's not a zombie. She's way more than just the magic eight ball. OK. Listen. Watch. Read the question."

Julia obeyed. "Will Alexander Mast ever run away from the Amish?"

Mrs. McCracken absorbed Lois's gaze as if it were light and she was colour. Her small plastic frame changed, became animated,

Julia would have sworn to it. And then, in a voice of authority, Lois began to speak.

"As I see it, no. Of course Alexander Mast will never run away from the Amish. Think about it. What's he going to run away with, or to? He has to quit school the minute he turns sixteen. He doesn't have one non-Amish friend, except Julia Raine. Cuteness does not equal running away. Look at Lorne Hogan. He's not Amish and he's certainly not cute, but _he_ ran away."

"How does Mrs. McCracken know Lorne Hogan?" asked Julia, suspicious.

"Why wouldn't I know him? I've lived here all my life, ever since I came from Eaton's."

Now the voice of Lois. "All right. Read my question to Mrs. McCracken."

Julia read, "Is Allister Wilde really the biological father of Lois Wilde?" She had no idea this was the sort of question they would be asking Mrs. McCracken.

The eight ball was unambiguous. _"Yes,"_ Lois read the watery message, then continued: "Don't be ridiculous. People talk nonsense, especially here in Mercury Township. You've got to understand people have nothing better to occupy their minds. Lois Wilde and Allister Wilde have the same hair and eyes: that's genetic proof. Whoever started that talk about Lois Wilde being the possible daughter of somebody else has shit for brains. People talk nonsense here in Mercury Township."

Who started that talk? Julia would have asked, had she not already asked one question beyond her allotment. And anyway, when their eyes met, blink, the spell was broken and Lois was no longer a medium. The authority exiting Lois had entered Julia, wiring her insides with a jumble of cables and current and volume control, like a drive-in movie, with a speaker attached to the car door.

"Maybe we should check on the kids," Julia said, by way of

diversion. "I don't think they're all that sure the dust virus can't get through cheesecloth."

Lois saw no reason not to.

Later, Julia would return to the barn alone, hold the eight ball in the lamplight and await the arrival of the medium. But nothing of the kind happened. Then she picked up Mrs. McCracken and, lying on her back, placed her in the space between her non-existent breasts. And it was as if she had found the reverse gear on her crushes; she could feel their warm knowledge backing into her, parking, brake lights on, then off. If it were possible, she would have grown a layer of skin over Mrs. McCracken and kept her there. So what if she made a weird lump.

~ ~ ~ ~

"Ask Mrs. McCracken" was broadcast Saturday nights. Throughout September and October, Julia kept an eye on the little barn window with its partitioned moments of late evening sky, a blue that seemed, like Alexander Mast's shirts, to slowly fade to grey. By the time the sky had darkened to the indigo of Mrs. McCracken's studio floor, it was eleven o'clock and Lois was expected home.

Once daylight-saving time was over, however, it was as if they moved east against the sun's progress, into a much later time. Lois adjusted her watch to whatever hour she wanted. "So much for the curfew," she said. The McCrackens' lived in a time zone someplace over the Atlantic, an island where night was darker and the sky the colour of waves most people never see. And this, for reasons Julia could not articulate, was good.

They had to use the barn's overhead lighting — two old bulbs from the time when electricity was first invented — which cast an inspirational mood. "And with just the flick of a switch," Lois liked to say when they arrived.

November temperatures were a problem, so Lois supplied blankets. Eugenia Wilde didn't pay much attention to domestic details. Entire pieces of furniture probably could have gone missing without comment, and Julia marvelled at this. In her home, any effort to traipse off to the barn carrying blankets would have been observed from a greenhouse and stopped. "Julia, what are you doing with those blankets?" "Nothing." "Then nothing them back inside right now."

Mrs. McCracken was a little moodier, so time had to be taken before the show to assess her state of mind or just give her the stage. "Be careful," Lois might say in the voice of the medium. "I've got a damn hangover. It's not easy being mom and dad to a couple of ungrateful kids in jars." Or "Stop staring at me like you've never seen a half-naked person before. Get me my magic eight ball; I want to ask it a question."

"Is Mr. McCracken ever going to come out of his coma?" Lois asked impatiently. And immediately came the resolute answer, *"Don't count on it."*

"Are the kids OK?"

"Most likely."

"Will somebody, someday write a play about my life and will it be a big Broadway hit?"

"Signs point to yes."

Mrs. McCracken had a right to her mood swings, she said, because they asked so many questions. They — meaning Lois — now asked whole strings of questions requiring strings of answers.

"Is Eugenia Wilde now having, or has she ever had, an affair with that Professor Byrne she keeps talking about?"

"It is decidedly so," Lois reported from the eight ball, then expanded. "What do you think they were doing that time he came to stay for the weekend and Mr. Wilde was in Winnipeg? They weren't playing checkers, I assure you. You saw them kissing when you came back from the greenhouse one night — thank god we got out of that fish bowl — and they were embarrassed, as well they

should be. But it's not such a huge deal. I've stepped out on Mr. McCracken a couple of times. Well, can you blame me?"

"Does Mr. Wilde know?"

"*Yes definitely.* Next question."

"Well does he care?"

"*As I see it, yes.* Mr. Wilde does and does not care. Eugenia Wilde talked him into that open marriage agreement, and he tries to make the best of it. Once he had an affair with a woman in a motel in Ottawa. They were at the same motel, so it just kind of happened. He felt bad but also a little good, because it cancelled out Professor Byrne."

"But didn't Eugenia like Professor Byrne?"

"*Signs point to yes,* but why I don't know. Professor Byrne looked like Ed Sullivan, all hunched over in a suit. I guess there's no accounting for taste. It's marriage that's the problem anyway. No offence to Mr. McCracken, but marriage is silly. Don't ever get married. God, you two are making me tired."

"What about Julia's mom? Has she ever had an affair?"

"*My sources say no.* Julia's mom is not interested in an affair. She's interested in greenhouses and money."

"Julia's dad?"

"*No.* Julia's dad isn't interested in affairs either. He's also preoccupied with greenhouses and getting the meals on the table. Julia's parents are not the types to have extramarital affairs. They don't wear caftans or make frequent trips to Toronto."

"If Eugenia and Allister Wilde were killed in a car accident, would the Raines adopt Lois Wilde?"

"*Most likely.* They need somebody to help out in the greenhouses and Lanny Shepherd is no good to them."

"Hmmm," Lois said, skeptical. "Do you know the Stanton twins?"

"*Don't count on it.*"

"Do you know the Stanton twins?"

"*Without a doubt.*"

"What exactly is wrong with them?"

"They have cataracts, that's why their eyes look the way they do. And they don't ever get away, so they have nothing better to think about than everybody's business."

"Do the Stanton twins talk about Lois Wilde?"

"Cannot predict now."

"Yes you can. Come on. How come when Julia and I ... I mean Lois Wilde ... weren't friends, they said to me once in this sissy voice, 'Why aren't you friends with the little Raine girl? You both stick to yourselves too much.'"

"I think I just answered that with my previous comment about not ever getting out of Flax. Plus, the Stanton twins like to see everybody in pairs, like they are."

"Except now that we are friends, I mean Julia and Lois are friends, when they see us together they make a sound like hussy hussy. Why?"

"Cannot predict now."

"Why?"

"Oh, I don't know. I'm tired. I don't have an answer to every-thing. It's hard having a husband in a coma."

"Do you know the Stanton twins?" Lois asked with renewed intent, shaking the eight ball again, in need of a more fruitful response.

"It is certain."

"Well then give me an answer. When the Stanton twins see us together, why do they make a noise that sounds like hussy hussy?"

A deep sigh from Mrs. McCracken. "The Stanton twins live in a dream world. They make everything up. When they were children, they spoke their own language and had to go to a special school for the first two years. After that, they had a tutor. Mr. and Mrs. Stan-ton were too old to cope. They just let the twins go until they were driven to an early grave. Nobody even knows which one is Russell and which one is Berty. So who knows what hussy hussy means. It

31

could mean the square of the hypotenuse is equal to the sum of the squares of the other two sides, or it could mean, I think you're a little hussy, hussy — twice because there are two of you."

It was Julia's turn to ask a question. "Are the Stanton twins homos?"

"As I see it, yes."

"How do you know?"

"I just know. I've lived in Chicago long enough to be familiar with such things. There are signs."

"Like what?"

"They walk and talk like sissies."

"I could have told you that," Julia interrupted. She was the technical director, she had a right to interrupt. It had been her idea to turn off the overhead lights for the broadcast. That meant Lois climbing down the ladder, out of the mow and switching off the lights, then returning to the cosy, dusty gloom of their straw house, their triangular party hat of lamplight. Although the best place to be was behind the lamp, on the blankets, in the space where the light was kept in grey abeyance. It was there, that night, Julia first asked Lois didn't she think Alexander Mast looked a little bit like Hayley Mills.

~ ~ ~ ~

In the eighth grade Julia and Lois were introduced to "the new math." The new math was a representation of a future that people such as mathematicians and space explorers knew was on its way. It started with binary notation, base two. Everything could be made to be understood in a series of zeros and ones. $111010=58$. So futuristic. Julia worked on converting the alphabet to binary code, tried to translate a poem by Archibald Lampman, covered an entire page of foolscap with ones and zeros, all to the enthusiastic approval of Miss Brilz.

Then they turned a page in the mathematics text and there was algebra. It almost made the binary system seem like a cheap gim-mick. Julia loved algebra. Let X = the unknown. Let X = Hayley Mills, she wrote in her notebook. Alexander Mast = X. Lois Wilde = X. Therefore, Alexander Mast = Lois Wilde.

Late November and Julia was waiting for Lois out in the barn. She had had to schedule an emergency session with Mrs. McCracken because of developments at school. Julia was the one with ques-tions, for a change.

Lois's mother had volunteered to stage the Christmas concert, a situation Miss Brilz approved of, because then she could continue to devote herself fulltime to academic instruction. Eugenia Wilde had decided on a production called "Joy to the World," a musical revue offering jazzed-up versions of Christmas carols accompanied by interpretive dance. Eight grades, eight carols, eight dance routines. The student body, as Mrs. Wilde called them — an image of a forty-seven-headed ton of flesh sprang to mind — made up the choir, with the separate grades breaking rank for the dance portions.

As eighth graders, they should consider themselves privileged to have the opportunity to perform the finale and title piece, "Joy to the World." Alexander Mast was not allowed to dance, but the four girls were to wear flapper-style dresses for a 1920s number. Lois fomented resistance, but Barbara and Lesley loved the idea.

The more complicated costumes would be sewn by the retired high-school home economics teacher, Miss Maudsley, who visited the school to take measurements. Even in retirement, Miss Maud-sley wore the white nurse's uniform she had worn during her teaching years, a uniform that implied domestic science, hygiene and professionalism. One by one, she took the students behind the piano, her tape measure in hand.

Miss Maudsley had an overbite, and she breathed loudly. The acoustics behind the piano amplified the problem with her nasal passages, creating the effect of telephone-breathing in a suspense movie. "Raise your arms," she said, manoeuvring to find Julia's bust line. Then came the instruction "Raise your skirt." Julia took a moment to admire the blond wood of the piano, then looked out at the grade eight class. Not one girl was wearing a skirt. Had she asked them to lower their pants?

Miss Maudsley was creaking to her knees. "Raise your skirt," she repeated. To wrap the tape around Julia she practically had to rest her cheek on her right hip. Thank god, thank god Julia was wearing leotards. She had considered taking them off at recess, since it had warmed up. Pulling the tape tight, Miss Maudsley leaned forward to read the numbers above Julia's pubic bone. Worse than when a dog sniffed you there and everyone watched. OK. Julia dropped her skirt and managed to walk to her desk as if nothing had happened. Lois was watching.

"She practically squeezed my tits back behind the piano," Lois said at lunchtime out on the playground. "She had the tape measure like this," Lois began an imitation of the breathing, "and she's fiddling around trying to get it right at the spot where my tits are biggest and she kind of rubs her hand there. Did she do that to you? Oh right, you don't have tits yet. I keep forgetting."

"No," Julia said, "she didn't do much. Just measured. It was kind of creepy being back there with her."

~ ~ ~ ~

Since the start of the Christmas concert rehearsals, Mrs. McCracken had been drinking, for no particular reason other than she felt like it. Her drink of choice was the vodka martini. Lois had had several questions in the past couple of weeks about other kids' views of Eugenia Wilde and their thoughts on "Joy to the World: A Musical Revue." She even had requests for predictions. Will people laugh at me in that flapper-girl dress? Is there any possible way I might be able to get the dust virus before December 21?

Mrs. McCracken was friendly when intoxicated and kinder in her judgements. "Who cares what the other kids think? Chances are they aren't thinking anything. And as for Barbara and Lesley, they love the idea of showing off in those trashy dresses. They adore your mother for giving them this opportunity. They're both certain a talent scout will show up for the concert and that by January 2 they'll have been signed up with the June Taylor dancers. Stop worrying. If anyone should be worrying, it's me. Look at the family I have: comatose and quarantined. I think it's time we moved out of this damn barn; it's been nothing but trouble."

Lois had made a few changes to the set. Now a little martini glass stood on the end of a swizzle stick, entering the straw like a sceptre. Tiny rectangles of paper, like those of a TV broadcaster, lay on the desk. Lois had even made a small but still disproportionately large typewriter from cardboard, and this sat on a brick at right angles to Mrs. McCracken's desk. The brick also supported an empty two-ounce vodka bottle from Mr. Wilde's most recent flight to a convention in Ottawa.

When the overhead light went off, Julia knew Lois had arrived. She clicked on the studio light and there she was. They wrapped themselves in the blanket and got ready to roll. Julia had her questions ready.

"Do you know Miss Maudsley?"

"Definitely."

"How much difference to a pattern would skirt material make?"

"What?" Mrs. McCracken had never before sought clarification.

"How much difference to a pattern would skirt material make?" Julia repeated. "Why did she have to ask me to raise my skirt when she was measuring me? Couldn't she have measured me without that having to happen?"

No visible reaction from Lois. No disgust from Mrs. McCracken. Just the usual smooth transition from question to answer. "She's an old home ec teacher who probably wanted to be famous. She probably wanted to be a famous designer, or maybe she thinks she is one, so she has to do things the right way, like a famous designer

35

would. You'd be amazed how many people go around thinking they're movie stars or Liberace."

"What do you think she was thinking about when she said 'Raise your skirt'?"

"Thinking? I would suggest she was thinking next to nothing. It's a big effort for her just to breathe. She's got some kind of problem like adenoids that never got removed or a blockage like that flap at the back of your throat — I seem to have heard hers was enlarged. Thinking about breathing takes up a lot of Miss Maudsley's mental energy. You can imagine what that must be like."

After a short while Lois said, "Let's lie down. We can tuck in with the blanket." And they did, Julia lying in front on her side and Lois behind. They curved themselves around the studio lamp, a crescent shape of girls, the dark side of the moon. Lois put her arm around Julia and it was as if Hayley Mills had just dropped by and they were directors, watching the action behind the lights. Lois had a couple of half-hearted questions about her dad's trip to Ottawa. Then there was quiet and the loft filled with a familiar happiness, as if Julia's crushes were out driving around together, turning on their headlights, sweeping down one side of the river bank and up the other. If she lifted her shirt — raise your shirt, Julia thought spookily — she was sure to see a glow behind her skin. If she stood, the lights shining from behind her ribs could have illuminated Mrs. McCracken's set.

Which was when Lois kissed the back of Julia's neck, twice. And whoa, Julia's mind said to itself — this was more happiness than her body could contain. It leapt out of her onto the straw in yellow and green grasshopper-sized fragments of light. Then on came the overhead lightbulbs, ruining everything, and her dad's voice. "Julia? Is Lois up there?"

"Yes," Julia said, reaching out to extinguish the studio light, as if the whole set was wrong. They weren't supposed to have an extension cord in the barn. The wiring was no good.

"Her mother called. She wants her home. They have company."

"I forgot the damn Hubbards were coming over."

In her room, Julia stayed up late doing algebra homework. How pleasingly the numbers and symbols moved back and forth across the equations. That night she made the remarkable discovery that Lois's name was practically a binary structure: 101s, she wrote. Lois Wilde was a girl of the future.

~ ~ ~ ~

Two weeks before the staging of "Joy to the World," Mr. Wilde learned he was being promoted to a junior executive position in Winnipeg. The Wildes would be moving. Julia repeated this statement to herself as if it were a paradoxical formula, the new math at its most innovative. An actual moving van would arrive at their front door on December 31. Atlas. This was the sort of thing that happened to Hayley Mills and girls who had been to Hollywood. So Lois did equal Hayley Mills, after all. Algebra did not lie.

Lois began to speak of junior high school — an institution foreign to Mercury Township. She made reference to the visits with Mrs. McCracken as mental. Julia returned to the studio a couple of times alone, climbed the ladder in the dark smell of tinder-dry alfalfa and switched on the lamp. Not one question for Mrs. McCracken. She had nothing to ask. Instead she wanted Mrs. McCracken to ask her a question: How do you know Lois will never come back to the studio?

I just know, Julia said. She knew it the way an ant knew its way around the anthill. She could read it somewhere inside her. Not that an ant can read words, but maybe it can recognize certain ledges and bumps and familiar inclines.

Lois became increasingly irritated by the demands of the dance routine and the costumes they were to wear for the revue. She was looking for an out, and she made some headway by seizing on the definition of flapper. "Free from social and moral restraints," Lois read from the dictionary at one of the final rehearsals. "Do you really think it's a good idea to go ahead with this?" she asked her mother. "Do you think Barbara's and Lesley's mothers are going to be happy with their daughters dancing around up here free from social and moral restraints?"

"They don't care," Barbara and Lesley said in perfect unison.

"Well I care," Lois said at recess. "Only my mother would want to stage some crappy musical with flappers. She wants me to be just like her. She wants to raise me as a slut. Well you know what? I might be very sick the night of the concert. I might just be puking my guts out."

But of course, she wasn't. The revue was a success, the ovation, standing. Although as Lois pointed out, this was more or less meaningless because, in case you hadn't noticed, there was a standing ovation every year.

Then a surprising affair. In the social hour after the show, Julia's father invited the Wildes for dinner on the day after Boxing Day. Eugenia accepted the invitation with pleasure.

In the days that followed, Julia contemplated what was needed before Lois Hayley Mills Wilde could be permitted to enter her bedroom. This immature family tree should go. It had grown to the point where it now covered three sheets of Bristol board and included a woman from a Maidenform bra ad, Perry Mason and Della Street, Princess Anne, and Eric Burden and the Animals, to name just a few. Ridiculous, really. Very childish. But Julia didn't want to get rid of that or anything else, except the sissy jewellery box with the twirling ballerina, which she hid in her closet.

Julia's parents were busy with the Christmas poinsettia trade, and she was supposed to help, or at the very least watch Stephen. Instead, very inconveniently, she fell suddenly ill. Some sort of potentially deadly greenhouse virus, contracted from mistletoe, she told her father with all the drama she could muster. Five days passed, were viewed rather, as if on a movie screen suspended between Julia's eyelids and the spackled ceiling of her room. Through some assemblage of cameras and projection equipment, her parents made their debut, along with the thermometer, which appeared again and again, followed by enormous tumblers of ginger ale. Even the doctor, with his Pepto-Bismol breath, made a cameo appearance. Smellovision, Julia thought, just in time for the holidays.

Christmas morning, the gifts came to her bed, hydrofoiling above and around her feverish brain. Everyone stood and watched. Now they resembled people Julia had seen in a book of optical illusions, made to look large by being placed in a tiny room. Her brother came and went, came and went, until finally he had worn himself down to his regular size and demeanour. On the afternoon of the twenty-seventh, like the two-year-old he was, Stephen ordered Julia out of bed, and to her surprise, she found she was better. Her recovery had timed itself to accommodate Lois Wilde and her parents. What luck! Aging but vital groups of antibodies moved through her bloodstream, carrying streamers, throwing ticker tape: this was certainly the life.

Moments later, in the shower, for the first time Julia observed two small breasts in the making.

"Julia! Company's here," her mom was calling from downstairs.

Julia had just finished dressing, her hair looked great, and she was downstairs in a minute. The smell of turkey and stuffing and cooked turnip caused a hard shove to the lining of her stomach, but never mind. Before Lois had even begun to unbutton her coat, there was Julia in her harlequin-checked Christmas jumpsuit. "Do you want to go and see Mrs. McCracken?"

"No. I told you, that's mental what we were doing out there." First the pea coat, then the new yellow banlon sweater was hung in the hall closet. Lois was beautiful. Her response ricocheted off Julia easily enough, the way her occasional cruel comments no doubt bounced off the rubbery skin of the molecule. Briefly she saw herself with a blue knob for a head, much smaller pink knobs for breasts.

"What do you think junior high will be like?"

"How should I know?"

"I guess there'll be lots of rooms full of grade nines."

"I gu-ess," elongated with sarcasm.

"I wonder if you'll have more of the new math."

"That's really been on my mind, Julia."

There was nothing particularly wrong with this conversation, Julia observed. Lois was nervous about moving. She would be, too. Lois had always liked Stephen, so it made perfect sense that she would want to play with his new Tinkertoys. And Julia was still a little weak from the virus. Better for her just to relax.

It wasn't until they sat down to eat that Julia began to appreciate the difference between Lois's family and hers. Their clothing, for example. Lois's black dress had Julia planning to fling her red-and-green Christmas jumpsuit into the furnace the first chance available. Mrs. Wilde was in a purple velvet dress while Frances had on her stock pair of green plaid and slightly pilled slacks and a navy turtleneck. Both men wore white shirts and pants, but Julia's dad's were the kind that would never get him sent to Winnipeg. And when Julia tried to gauge what the Wildes might think of her parents, she arrived at a wordless void into which tumbled the certain knowledge that the Wildes were infinitely superior. Maybe they didn't know that, but she did. Why had she never noticed it before?

"Are you going to take Lois up to your room?" her mom asked after dinner.

Upstairs, they sat on the bed where Julia had just spent five delirious days growing breasts. Lois didn't ridicule the family tree; in fact she paid no attention to it. She was restless, she said, bouncing to her feet, she had to keep moving. And Julia was probably still quite sick, Lois thought. "Usually with these things there's some kind of relapse," she said.

"How about a game of Cootie?"

"Nah."

"Monopoly?"

"I might go look at Stephen's room."

Lois and Stephen busied themselves with his baby jigsaw puzzles. Julia, like a chameleon, took on the seven dwarfs pattern of the wallpaper. And then the Wildes were leaving, they had so much packing still to do.

The next morning, there was the yellow sweater in the hall closet. When nobody was looking, Julia moved it to her bedroom closet.

~ ~ ~ ~

In the final afternoons of eighth grade, Miss Brilz was allowing Julia to help the younger children finish their topographical map of Canada. While the grade fives and sixes sculpted and painted their way through eastern Canada, constantly consulting the Gage Canadian School Atlas, Julia single-handedly and grumblingly constructed the West Coast. As far as she was concerned, elevation was an irrelevant feature. Far from being the exemplary substitute teacher she was supposed to be, she spent large periods of time creating rows of pointed Dixie-cup breasts, flattening them and starting all over again. If she didn't get out of this damn kindergarten soon she'd go nuts.

And to add to her annoyance, Lois Wilde was coming to visit. She and her dad would be dropping by someday soon. Her junior high school ended in the middle of June; they were on a six-day cycle. Lois was now someone whose life conformed to another calendar, living in an altogether different galaxy with six-day weeks and perhaps an extra month thrown in. For the first time, Julia began to worry that the world awaiting her after grade eight might be more plastic than she could imagine or endure. Topographical maps seemed inadequate preparation for a future that might structure its years in binary notation.

The day the map was finally complete, Julia arrived home from school to find Lois and her dad already there. This was all wrong.

Julia had hoped for hours of preparatory waiting, ennui, utter boredom leading eventually to a coma of unresponsiveness much like that of Mr. McCracken's. Now the best she could do was to feign indifference, hoping to chill Lois to the bone. But Lois was not one to be chilled. She gave off a certain heat, in fact, an incandescence, like Miss Brilz on the topic of the Great Depression.

"I have something for you," she said.

"Oh yeah, me too. I've got your sweater up in my room," Julia said. Lois could follow her upstairs if she wanted.

"Thanks," Lois said, placing the yellow sweater on the desk chair where Julia watched it slide to the floor and pool in a square of sunlight. It was the colour of lemon pie filling, she saw for the first time, and much too bright. Hayley Mills would never have chosen such a garment.

"I've had some testing done at my school," Lois announced. "They're putting me in the enrichment class next year. They say I have a mental age of eighteen. Even though I've just turned fourteen."

"I know you're fourteen, you don't have to tell me."

Lois pulled some folded, ragged-edged papers from a pocket. "I brought this to show you," she said. It's from the *Reader's Digest.* I found it in the school library and ripped it out, it was so interesting." Then she looked at Julia the way Julia looked at Miss Brilz when she was busy with her rows of breasts, hoping she would and wouldn't notice. "Anyway, it's about ... you know ... that time in the barn when I touched you. Well, it has these graphs and percentages and it says that," and here she began to read with the confidence of the smartest girl at the science fair, "under age fourteen, a large proportion of girls might experiment with another girl, but by age eighteen, 70 percent will know for sure whether or not they're [very brief pause] lesbians." The enunciation of this word had obviously required some practice. It had the bulky self-consciousness of a Kotex pad worn for the very first time.

"But you're not eighteen, in real time," Julia said.

"I'm eighteen in mental age time. Which is just as real, if you ask the school psychologist. And I know for sure I'm not, and by the time I'm twenty-eight, I'll be 85 percent sure."

"But that's not what it means," Julia said, studying the array of bar graphs. "It means by age twenty-eight, 85 percent of the women in the survey who were that way said they knew."

"Well, whatever. I'll be in the 85 percent who know they're not, and I'll be 100 percent sure. Why don't you just read it yourself, little Miss Mathematics? It's you I brought it for. And anyway, I'd better see what Dad's up to. We're not staying for long."

Left sitting on the bed with her glossy sheets of statistical probability, Julia felt as if she had just made a visit to the doctor. And not the local doctor, no, she had seen a specialist, someone from farther away, paid to impart certainty. The yellow sweater lay on the floor, and Julia made no move to pick it up until after Lois had left. After she had sat in the kitchen talking to Julia's parents in her eighteen-mental-years-old voice, after she had waved goodbye and said adios, as if Spanish were the first language of those who live in Winnipeg.

Julia put the sweater in the suitcase under her bed, the suitcase where she had stored the McCracken family that spring.

The sight of Mrs. McCracken caused Julia to feel a sudden and odd desire: She wanted her back. She had to admit, she missed her. She even thought about taking her to school with her the next day, inside her pants pocket. Maybe she would stand her, if only for a moment, in those flour-and-water Rocky Mountains, facing westward to the ocean, like an explorer. She knew she wouldn't though. Too easily Julia could imagine the voice of Miss Brilz saying silliness and high jinks are one thing, but a miniature woman with ink-drawn pubic hair is quite another. Then Julia went looking for the masking tape and fastened Mrs. McCracken to the top of the family tree, a little above Hayley Mills.

chapter

2

In the late-

September Saturday afternoon heat of an unseasonably warm autumn, Julia's mother was redecorating the playroom. Using a jar and hose attached to the rear end of the vacuum cleaner, she was soaking the walls and tearing away groups of dwarfs in long satisfying strips. Like sunburnt skin, Julia thought as her mother said, "I guess the expensive paper's worth the money after all. You haven't had to scrape yet."

Yes, she knew that. And she would die if she did not get this window open. It had been painted shut for years, but here she was with a putty knife, so why not drive it between the frame and window with her dad's hammer and see what happened. Sooner or later it had to open. The combination of humidity, glue and the vacuum's dysentery-like spray action was threatening to close Julia's windpipe and cut off her oxygen supply. Damn the window. She was choking to death. If she were to fall to the floor, wearing last year's bright and floral home economics project — matching shorts and sleeveless blouse — would anyone notice? Not likely.

Nausea. She should never have read Sartre this summer. That book had managed to throw a pail of dirty dishwater over everything she saw. Or maybe she had mononucleosis. Something was making her sick. And her mother was not helping by wearing that outfit, her favourite work wear: a pair of her husband's overalls and a bra — white Maidenform cones, wholly visible and containing nothing whatsoever. Why? Julia wanted to ask. Why not wear a T-shirt and shorts, or a simple housedress? Earlier in the summer, her friend Jannette had dropped by to show off her driver's licence, and there had been Julia Raine's mother, in bra and overalls, working in the garden, waving hello. Staring angrily at her mother, Julia willed her to wrap her upper body in rhubarb leaves, or at least crouch modestly and attend to her weeding. But telepathy failed.

"Hello Jannette. How are you?" Oh dear god.

"Does your mom always do her gardening in a bra?" Jannette had asked later.

"No, just in the extreme heat of summer."

"You are a rural rube." That was Jannette's clever variation on rural route. She had sent a postcard from Vancouver addressed to Miss Julia Raine at Rural Rube Number Two, Flax, Ontario. Well, fine. Julia was born into a less-than-small-town family, now described as making-a-go-of-it. She had worked her way up through the social strata of Flax Elementary School and had successfully repeated the climb at Mesmer High. Her friends were all from town; Jannette's father was the pharmacist. The greater her social success, the more her windpipe threatened to close, the more her body threatened at critical moments to enter into brief trances of placid embarrassment.

"If you're not going to scrape you might as well go downstairs and peel some potatoes," her mother admonished.

Julia's body was a source of intense and detached interest, an important anthropological site she had recently discovered. She was surprised and thankful that it had developed a full and uncompromised set of secondary sex characteristics. Having read all three books on human physiology from the Mesmer High School library, Julia was familiar enough with the sex-linked chromosomal anomalies to know that a female mat of chest hair was not beyond the realm of the possible. And although at sixteen her physical development remained unremarkable, Julia continued to view her body as an unpredictable machine, manufactured from spare genetic parts. Chromosomes were radiators or fuses, mechanisms beneath the hood that could act up at any moment with no warning at all. Recombinant DNA, that's what it was called. In Julia's body, her parents had been recombined to create a female who was not certain she was all girl — normal on the surface, in her phenotype, yet compelled to express her inner disorder through the stirred-up mess of her genotype. What could you expect?

Still, Julia liked biology. Which was why she had flung up her hand when Miss Crombie, the health and physical education teacher, asked if any of the grade eleven girls would consider talking to the grade nine girls about menstruation. "Yes, Miss Crombie, I would be happy to do that." And within a week, there she was, disguised as someone with absolutely no worries about her secondary sex characteristics, saying: "Most of you probably already have your period, but for those who don't — and I didn't get mine until grade nine — one day you'll go to the bathroom and there it will be. Blood in your underwear. Not a whole lot, like from a cut, just some pinkish stuff. After that, cramps. And the worst part, a really uncomfortable belt and giant-sized pads."

Her friends had said, "It's because you're from a farm, that's why you're comfortable with that stuff. That's why you volunteered." As if her daily experience included mating horses, cows in heat, roosters mounting hens in every corner of the yard. As if, because she lived in the country, the vulgar snorting and puffing of reproduction were as routine, as unexceptional, as dandelions.

"Actually, I live on a greenhouse operation," she had replied, but no one cared.

During certain solitary moments such as now, as she chose the right potatoes from the bin in the cellar, Julia admitted that she could understand her friends' misperceptions of her social position. Since a portion of the barn roof had caved in during a summer windstorm, from the road Julia's home resembled a derelict farm, like the Caseys', where the electricity was forever being cut off and roosters and hens probably mated in unlit corners of the living room. Julia had considered dismantling the barn herself to improve the appearance of the place, but this was out of the question. Besides, the barn offered a safe refuge for masturbation.

"It's not safe. Don't go into that rundown shack," her dad had said. And so she experienced a double dose of guilt, since it went without saying she wasn't supposed to be masturbating.

Julia liked that statement, "It went without saying." In her biological musings, she had arrived at an understanding of the problem with masturbation. It represented a wasted orgasm. Orgasms were supposed to be saved and hoarded, or at least sold for a price. If you were going to have an orgasm, then you were also going to have a baby, and suffer, and be responsible for someone else for the rest of your life. That was the original plan, before people could walk upright or speak words. Masturbation tricked people's sex organs into believing they were being used for the good of the species. Julia would have liked to discuss this idea with Jannette, but there was a catch. She would happily discuss menstruation in front of a class of grade nine girls, but she was not about to mention masturbation to her best friend. Even if Jannette asked, she would lie and deny ever having heard of the practice. It went without saying.

And why was this? She didn't know. She gave up trying to answer her own questions and focused on the task at hand, peeling potatoes. There really could be nothing blinder than a potato. And this made her think maybe she'd have a couple of friends sleep over once the redecorated room was finished. Once her Great-Aunt Katharine had been and gone, the freshly appointed room with its new cast-iron bed and matching end tables and dresser would be all hers. She could put blindfolds on her friends to take them through the house, past the worn linoleum and faded oilcloth and the couch with its blanket throw and painful crunching sound of metal on wood when anyone sat on the middle cushion. She would convince them that blindfolding was a rural custom, a quaint social convention. Then, surprise! "What a great room you have, Julia!"

The only problem was they would have to be blindfolded again when they wanted to go downstairs to get a drink of water, and in the morning for breakfast when her mother sat by the radio listening to the news and smoking, her hair out of its braid and hanging in waves and tendrils like a witch's. Blindfolding was not a practical solution.

~ ~ ~ ~

The Raines were driving to the airport, or Malton as it was called, to pick up Great-Aunt Katharine. She was flying in from Calgary to spend a couple of weeks. The visit was unexpected and had precipitated the room renovation: Aunt Katharine was known to be fussy. Julia's mom had not said much about Katharine, her mother's sister, other than to express the hope that, despite her advanced years, she was not forgetful and could be left alone with the stove. She appeared to believe that in exchange for the lovely room, Katharine would assume all cooking duties.

"How come I've never met her?" Julia asked.

"You did once, but it was at a family reunion in 1955, so you'd be too young to remember. That was the last Morrissey reunion."

"Why was that the last?"

"Mom died the next year, and she was the one who always organized them. You have to have a certain temperament to organize family reunions. I'm the only daughter of the four Morrisseys, and I don't have the proper temperament, so the torch may be passed to you in due time."

The torch of duty? Julia's mind couldn't advance to a time when she might wish to reunite her family: that would be like Australopithecus furrowing up his brow to imagine 16-mm home-movie cameras. This family should really never have assembled in the first place, so once the parts had gone their separate ways, been cast asunder . . .

"There's a table there," her mother said.

"That looks just fine," her dad confirmed.

The picnic table stood in the long grass of a dried-out ditch, somewhere outside Georgetown. Since they were travelling more than a half hour's distance from Flax, a picnic lunch was required, complete with egg salad sandwiches, Kool-Aid, a tablecloth, plastic cups and road dust.

"Might as well make an event of it," Julia's father found any excuse to say. "Katharine's plane isn't due in until after three."

The presence of a garbage can provided some solace, reassuring Julia that they were indeed stopping at a designated picnic site and not eating from a piece of litter, an object formerly used in the slaughter of hogs or for god knows what kind of sexual pleasures.

"Julia, could you pour Stephen some Kool-Aid?"

"Sure, Mom."

"Stephen, don't touch the garbage can. You never know what's been in it."

"Do you think there's ever been a dead body in it?"

49

"No."

"But how do you know, Mom?"

"I don't know."

"Then it's possible."

"Anything's possible."

Other families, Julia knew for sure, had conversations about sci-entific advances and cures for cancer. Other families did not eat sandwiches in a ditch.

"You folks all right?" A passing motorist had stopped, a long-haired young man. A hippie, Julia realized with some excitement. This is what hippies did: they offered help in times of need.

"Oh no, we're fine. We're just fine. Would you like a sandwich?" her mother asked.

"No thanks. Just thought you might be in trouble."

"Well, that's very kind of you."

Julia waved a small and private wave, hoping to convey that she was all too aware that what qualified as an event for her family probably resembled a disaster to the average urban hippie. She waved again as he left, thinking she might be in love with him now, wondering if he might be going to the airport too.

Great-Aunt Katharine's plane was an hour late, causing Julia's mother to become grumpy and complain about time lost, never to be reclaimed. She was like that. Happy enough to go on an outing, but the minute the event surpassed a mysteriously pre-established time limit, she became vexed and impatient. The first round of complaints had to do with the never-to-be-reclaimed minutes or hours, as if time could fall from a cliff or high tower and be heard faintly screaming until it landed far below, shattered into millions of fragments.

If things went terribly wrong, a second alarm sounded deeper within Julia's mother's brain. Like the time they were Christmas shopping in Kitchener, and her dad locked the keys in the car. It was one of the coldest days of the year. The Automobile Association was backed up with requests to boost vehicles and wouldn't be able to get to them for three hours. Julia's mother began predicting financial ruin. It was their busiest time as greenhouse operators, the Christmas season, and with the Automobile Association taking so long, she didn't know how they would afford Christmas presents, how they would pay their taxes. Most likely the bank would foreclose and take the place out from under them, and just as bloody well.

When her mother's alarms started going off, Julia usually sought shelter in a voluntary trance, like the one she had entered now over by a luggage carousel. Stephen did too. Meanwhile their father said, "Oh don't be so dramatic. You make everything into a catastrophe."

And then, for an unknown reason, Katharine's plane was not so late after all. There was some confusion as to where they should meet her, and in her exuberance at actually having reclaimed more than half an hour, Julia's mother ran off to the information desk. She came back waving them all down to Gate 15, striding ahead, grinning like a prize-winner on a TV game show.

Katharine was already there, standing tall, resembling a pencil in her yellow jacket and terra-cotta hair arranged in an eraser-shaped bun. Julia wanted to laugh a little, but that impulse was wrestled back down her throat. In its place was the increasingly familiar whoosh of instant love, exactly what she'd felt with the hippie in the ditch.

Instant love was not the same as love at first sight or any other of the commonly recognized loves. It had its own evolutionary life, which Jannette and Julia had half worked out. They believed that a person's insides were much more old-fashioned than the exterior. The cruder and most essential of the body's functions — such as reproduction — were less highly evolved than more recent adaptations such as the body's ability to wear high-heeled shoes. As a result, hormones remained incapable of any sort of reason or discrimination, and travelled through the circulatory system in a condition of potent indifference (a term they had invented to imply drowsy hopefulness). On occasion, sometimes frequent occasions, the hormones were alerted to the presence of an attractant — Julia's word — which caught their attention and pulled them like hundreds of eyes to a window. The result was instant love: exactly the same sensation as running to a window expecting to see someone you desperately wanted to see. Regrettably, the hormones and circulatory system were so brachiopod-like in their development, the attractant might be anything — man, woman, horse, car, eighty-year-old great-aunt.

Like an adult, for the first time in her life Julia extended her hand and introduced herself: "I'm Julia." A logjam of words was forming in her throat, but just in time she realized she was not at the front of Miss Crombie's health class or any audience at all and would be better off being quiet and dignified.

Travelling home in the back seat of the car — her mom was driving, with Katharine in the front, and Dad was squished between Stephen and her — Julia spent some time examining the skin of her arms. It looked the same, despite the fact that the moment she had taken Katharine's hand, she felt an entire outer epidermal layer of childhood skin come away in one easy tear, like expensive wallpaper.

~ ~ ~ ~

Within a short time, Katharine had demonstrated beyond a doubt that she could be left alone with the stove, and she showed no signs of forgetfulness. "I've made you a list, but you won't need it," Julia's mom had said before they set off for the Flax IGA. "You've got Katharine. She's better than a list."

Now that Julia had her licence, the grocery shopping fell to her. She and Katharine were in the truck — she preferred the blue Ford pickup to the car — when they had their conversation, a word Julia capitalized each time she recalled it. Their Conversation. It began benignly enough, a simple and spontaneous exchange.

"What do they teach you in school now?" Katharine asked.

"The usual, I guess. History, English, Latin and different sciences. This year I have biology. Next year, physics, and finally, chemistry. In biology we're starting out with creatures of the sea. I guess you could call it marine biology."

"Ah, yes. Plankton and beyond. I'm assuming you know I taught high school for thirty-five years."

"I knew you taught, but not for how long or what subjects exactly."

"Sciences. Physics and biology, mainly. For thirty-five years. I have to repeat that because there's still part of me that doesn't quite believe it. Even though I quit in 1955, I still can't quite believe it. Anyway, that's boring to you, I'm sure. Young people don't like to hear old people speak in terms of thirty-five years. Once they hear that sort of talk, their faces assume a carefully guarded expression of disdain with which I'm very familiar."

"Well, mine isn't doing that," Julia said, relaxing the muscles of her face into what she felt certain was a statement of utter neutrality mixed with a hint of curiosity. She glanced into the rearview mirror for confirmation.

"I saw that," said Katharine. She really was rather difficult. "Anyway, you know what I mean. Once a speaker such as me moves beyond certain dates and times in her discourse, a listener such as you stops hearing the words and hears a whirring sound, or just substitutes some of her own thoughts, like I wonder how fast I can make this truck go."

"Oh, sorry. I didn't think I was going that fast."

"Hmmm. Who's your biology teacher? What's his name?"

"Her name is Miss Borbridge."

"Oh. Well, on Monday do me a favour and ask your Miss Borbridge if she's read this month's issue of *Science*. Ask her if she read the piece on trout. Interesting, fascinating really. Apparently trout have a structure in their noses that responds to magnetism and that's how they find their way to their spawning grounds. Some connection with olfaction perhaps, the proximal senses, although it's hard to say if reading magnetism would be considered proximal or distal. Do you know what I'm saying?"

"No, not exactly."

"Never mind. I'm sorry. I'm being a show-off. It's been a life-long propensity. I wanted to mention the trout business because I'm thinking that's why I came back here. Just a magnetic pull. Not that I've come back to Ontario to spawn, don't get alarmed — but there could be some ancient part of the mind that remembers mag-netic information. Point your nose in the air and it will lead you back to where you came from. Just like the trout."

Katharine's gaze remained forward, but Julia had the feeling, especially when she remembered the conversation later, time and time again, that every part but Katharine's eyes was watching Julia, awaiting a response to a parenthetical you-know-what-I-mean. Like her friends Rose and Annie were always saying, except with them, she always did know.

They were driving the back route, the concession with nothing but woodlots, passing through the tunnel of trees. "Oh, I might as well tell you. I hate all that ridiculous innuendo," Katharine said. "I lived for a long time with a woman named Gertie. She was a nurse at the General in Calgary, well forever really. I loved her, to make a long story short, and she died last year. December 29 was the day, to be exact. I thought I would be fine. I have friends, after all, but once Gertie was gone I made the startling observation that most of my friends, in fact all of my friends except Margaret, were dead. And Margaret can be such a cranky old bitch. Complains con-stantly about everything, really, but she's the only one of us left, and for that alone, I love her."

If only Jannette could be with them now, Julia thought, posi-tioned between her and Katharine. With her confident big mouth, she would know what to say. Jannette was more psychologically advanced than Julia was, as she had observed a couple of times. And Julia agreed. That was the advantage of having a pharmacist father.

"Oh," Julia said. Oh. A single syllable, a vowel sound. Surely she could do better than that.

"And I am doing OK, really," Katharine continued. "It's not a new story, after all. People die and they're buried. I just finally recognized I needed a change of scenery. I was becoming addicted to feeling sorry for myself. Every day I'd go to the cemetery and talk to Gertie, as if I couldn't talk to her elsewhere, and I began to realize I was getting some kind of cheap thrill out of this. I'd stand over her grave feeling melancholy and wondering how I looked, if you can imagine that. I'm eighty years old and still I'm wondering if somebody might be taking notice of this tragic figure in the graveyard. It's an odd thing, but there's some part of the human mind that refuses to accept the reality of its aging body. It has a photo album from at least thirty years earlier, and it refuses to update it."

Here was the end of the tree tunnel, the stop sign and the paved road. Julia was planning to accelerate very quickly, get from first to fourth in less than twenty seconds.

"So, I read the trout article one day, and that evening I called your mother. I haven't been back for so long, I'd lost touch. There were family problems because of Gertie — not with your mother — my sisters and your grandfather, to name a few."

Once she had the truck in fourth gear, Julia was prepared to comment. "I'm sorry about Gertie," she said. "I really am. My friend Patty's brother died last year in an accident. He rolled his car, over and over. It was terrible. He was all crushed. They had to keep the casket shut." Now that she was on the paved road she could go as fast as she wanted, no matter what Katharine said.

But Katharine wasn't listening to Julia; she was conducting a monologue, flinging all other commentary from the truck windows like so much litter.

"Your mother was always accepting of the situation. And your dad. They're live-and-let-live types, as far as I know. We never sat down and talked about it, no, you don't do that. That would cause so much spinning and friction of the mental wheels, your hair would catch fire. But the thing about your parents is, they did send a sympathy card when Gertie died, which is more than I got from your grandfather or Molly and Alma. I think Betty, your grandma, might have come around had she lived long enough. Had she had another twenty-five years to mull and stew and weigh her opinions and read up on things. She used to phone me once in a while and say something like, 'Are you sure this is what you really want? I just read a novel called *The Well of Loneliness* and those girls didn't seem very happy.'"

Katharine laughed. And Julia did too, because laughter didn't require even one syllable of thought. What was *The Well of Loneliness*? Julia was the wrong audience for this conversation. She was reminded of the time she went to Toronto with a group of ninth grade students to see Swan Lake. Julia had spent the entire performance wanting to leave the room, stand in the lobby of the O'Keefe Centre, walk back to Union Station or almost anywhere. She would have preferred a visit to the Noxzema factory they'd passed on the way into the city. She missed entire scenes of the ballet thinking of vats of white and soothing cream. If you worked on the assembly line and had a sunburn, could you burrow right in?

"Well, here we are in Flax," Julia said. "Not a lot of industry in the outskirts, like Toronto for example. Just the Vreelands' sawmill. Not much mystery there." Someone had to introduce a new topic. You couldn't enter a grocery store discussing lesbians, could you?

Had she said something wrong? Was Katharine one of those taciturn people inclined to combustion? Julia could feel Katharine's eyes on her, observing her park as if she were a natural phenomenon, a geyser or the magnetic trout perhaps. Julia would have been happy to flop out onto the sidewalk and lie there for a moment, gasping through her gills. The drive had been exhausting.

But she had the grocery list she didn't need, and Katharine was not
the sort to be kept waiting.

~ ~ ~ ~

Born at the right time: that was their motto. Not one of Julia's
friends would have fit in with the grade twelve girls, so civic-
minded and earnest about Students' Council, or the grade ten girls
with their anxieties over the correct brand of penny loafer. Only
Julia's select group of eleventh grade girls found the conventions
of high school absurd, laughable even, and consequently loved each
new day of school life. We really are too psychologically advanced
for this place, was their motto-in-waiting.

"Why do these Shakespeare records all sound the same?" Julia
asked Jannette. It was Tuesday, which meant a double period of
English and time to listen to an entire act of *Macbeth*, review, discuss, compare and contrast.

"Because the actors didn't even take a break between *Hamlet* and
Macbeth. They didn't even go home to change."

"But wouldn't they at least have to change costumes? Put on a
different doublet?"

"Costumes? They're standing around a microphone in some
studio wearing turtlenecks and jeans. There are no costumes.
These records are for high-school audiences only. My cousin Norm
is an actor. He does this kind of thing."

"Oh." Julia sat back, assuming the role of high-school audience.
Jannette had innumerable older cousins in all walks of life, and she
was the beneficiary of their collective wisdom. In each class, Julia
and her four friends occupied the same configuration of desks in
the centre of the room. Jannette was in the middle, Rose to her left,
Patty to her right, Annie in front and Julia behind. Julia's was the
best spot. She was in the best position to whisper to Jannette and
have Jannette swivel her head sideways and talk out of the side of
her mouth like an undercover agent. She could drift into a trance

while gazing at the back of Jannette's head, her chestnut-coloured Breck girl pageboy forever held in place through a miracle of genetic obedience. Jannette did not use hair spray.

Patty was the prettiest of the five, Annie the best student, Rose the richest — her dad owned the casket factory — Julia the boldest and Jannette had the best sense of style. She usually wore a shirt under a good wool sweater, and a co-ordinating skirt, straight or A-line. She wore tights as soon as the weather turned cool, and desert boots or loafers, but no ridiculous penny. Jannette owned only three or four of these ensembles, but the effect was one of understated plenty, of unassailable suitability. She could have been astral-projected to any high school in New York or Paris, welcomed and ushered to the desk in the epicentre of the most popular group of girls. Whereas Julia, in a similar position, would have elicited a puzzled response: "Oui, mademoiselle? It's probably plus mieux if you were to retourner to your school in rural southern Ontario immediatement."

And Jannette sang. She was always the girl chosen to sing the haunting solo lines at the Christmas chorale, prompting the audience to ask, "Who is that girl with the angelic voice?" Her two sisters sang, as well. Together, they were the Mesmer Three, performing at wedding anniversaries or during intermissions at a dance. Just last week in the change room after physical education, Jannette had led them all in the best Supremes song, with gestures and lead vocals, everyone stopping in the name of love. In her bra and underpants, the way her ribcage moved, the way her shoulder blades took on definition was an incredible sight. Heartbreaking, Julia thought, looking back on it. Heartbreaking.

Act 1, scene 5, said the record.

Heartbreaking? Julia's thinking stopped itself like a gymnast on the bar at the top of a rotation, when you don't know if she's planning to circle on around or go into reverse. (Jannette was good at gymnastics, too.) Why heartbreaking? Might as well be honest: Watching Jannette perform in the girls' locker room was painful because Julia

wanted to be Jannette. She wanted to wear her pale blue underpants, her skirts of heather wool, expertly sewn by her mother. She
wanted Jannette's pageboy hair and her blinking and reserved brown
eyes. Wanted to wait before she spoke, wanted to lead them all in
action songs and make them believe they were the Supremes. Julia
wanted to hear people say: Those Leary girls can really put on a show.

Julia wanted to be Jannette, and also she did not want to be Julia
Raine. She did not want ever to look down and see dirt under her
nails. Did not wish to observe that her bras seemed greyer and more
threadbare. Did not wish to own skirts made of synthetic material, or
blouses with even a hint of yellowed armpits. Julia no longer wanted
to be the bold one. The bold one was a running-after position, a repu-
tation made of what you did not have: inhibitions, rules, manners.
She was tired of being the bold one, and the only one who had ever
been mistaken for a boy. What a horrible day that had been.

Last year, before she'd started to grow her hair, when it was still
in the Prince Valiant cut, as Jannette called it, before her ears had
been pierced, she'd run into the drugstore one Saturday afternoon
to buy something for her mom. The clerk, a woman she didn't recognize, asked, "Aren't you Cynthia Snell's boy?"

"No, I'm actually Franny Raine's girl."

"Oh. Oh, I'm sorry. Guess I need my glasses. So you are."

"No need to be sorry," Julia had said, panic in her eyes, as if they
wanted to climb out of her head right there so as to get a good look at
herself from the other side of the drugstore counter. What would
they see? Someone in white shorts and a grey T-shirt, with medium-
sized breasts, legs that were perhaps a little too muscular from being
on the track team, eyebrows that were a little too dark and prominent.

She called Jannette as soon as she was home again. "Who's
Cynthia Snell's son?"

"Why do you ask?"

Julia had anticipated that. "My mom knows Cynthia Snell. We're
looking at the yearbook."

59

"Oh. I think it's Randy Snell. He's in grade nine."

"Great. Thanks." Julia hung up before Jannette could offer any opinions.

In the yearbook, Julia had hoped to find a feminine boy, one resembling Twiggy, with eyebrows barely visible, but Randy Snell was none of these. He was unmistakably a boy with dark hair and eyebrows and — the chilling part — a similar hairstyle. So there *was* a resemblance. For at least two weeks, every night before bed, Julia examined Randy Snell's yearbook photo while sensations of dread and reassurance backflipped from her stomach to her mind and back again. He doesn't look anything like me; oh yes he does. The drugstore clerk wouldn't have mistaken Jannette for Randy, even if she didn't have her glasses on.

Now Julia's hair was long and straight like millions of girls', and she wore dangly earrings in her pierced ears. She had tried to pluck her eyebrows but lacked the necessary fortitude. "It's not as if they look like caterpillars glued to my forehead," she had said to Rose, who assured her they looked fine just the way they were. Jannette went overboard with her sculptured lines of paint. Still, in the dictionary of antonyms, Julia Raine would not have been listed opposite Randy Snell; she would not. And why was that?

"Unsex me here," the teacher was saying. "What does Lady Macbeth mean by this? Julia?"

Even the teachers were onto something, expecting her to reveal some character anomaly, a mature understanding of the unsexed. Well, not this time. Julia would wait, take time to blink thoughtfully like Jannette did, and answer tentatively.

"I guess she meant she would prefer not to be female."

"And why would that be?"

"I suppose because it's considered unladylike behaviour to kill someone."

"Unladylike behaviour. An area of expertise for our Julia Raine."

There was no escape. Oh well.

"There's the bell, class. Make sure you've read act 3 for tomorrow."

"Hey, Jannette. You should come over sometime in the next little while. Drive out to my place. My great-aunt is visiting from Calgary. I'd like you to meet her."

"Great-aunt?"

"Yeah. She's really interesting."

"How old exactly? Is she all trembly?"

"She's eighty."

"I'll think about it. Old people scare me, as a rule."

"She's not scary at all."

~ ~ ~ ~

"That was before I took my stroke," Grandpa Corrigan said of most events. And of the recent past, "That was after I took my stroke." As if a remarkable geographical divide existed inside his mind, separating the two pasts, preventing communion between them. Three years ago a stroke had changed Grandpa for both the good and the bad. He had been depressed since his wife's death in 1956. No matter how many years passed, he could not seem to shake his anger over this injustice. The stroke had lightened this mood, allowed him to forget how to hang onto a single thought for years on end. At the same time, the brain injury seemed to have blown out a few of the inhibitory roadblocks of his mental functions. Grandpa Corrigan didn't say everything that entered his mind now, but much more so than he used to before he took his stroke. He'd tell you that himself. Which was why there had been some oblique discussion about inviting him to dinner.

"I don't know if we should have Dad for supper or not," Julia's mom commented twice, meaning, Grandpa Corrigan couldn't be trusted not to insult his sister-in-law, Katharine.

"Give him a call. I'd love to see him," said Katharine at least twice.

So Abraham Raine drove off to the seniors' home south of Killaloo, on the way to London, to fetch Grandpa, while Julia waited in a growing cumulonimbus of worry. She even checked the barometer, expecting it to provide some reading of her anxiety, but the hand pointed to fair. And fair it was, a beautiful fall day, almost Thanksgiving, but Katharine would be gone by then, so they would have a ham now.

Mr. Raine escorted Grandpa from the car to the front door, giving everyone time to stand on the step and watch. "Sometimes the left side just goes," he was saying, as he had said many times before. And then there was the confusion at the door, make way, and already he was saying, as usual, "Let's see if there's any of the pension left. Oh, lucky for you two. They let me have a little something out of petty cash before I left," and he handed Julia and Stephen each a five-dollar bill. "That's so you'll encourage your mother to invite me back." Now he was shaking Katharine's hand and they were all smilingly watchful. "Well, Katharine, still dressing like a man, I see. You're looking well, irregardless."

"Regardless, Dad," Julia's mother corrected. "There's no such word as irregardless. You know that."

"Aunt Katharine's a cowgirl," Julia said. "She's from Calgary. That's how cowgirls dress in the West." But Julia's words sounded dry and nervous, like the first sentence of a prepared speech. Maybe Katharine did dress like a man, in her shirts and jackets and trousers, a feminine man like Mr. Tregellis, the drama teacher. So what? There must be some other defence, other than this cowgirl line, if only Julia had more time to think.

"Well, speaking of dress, Joseph, maybe I'll get a chance to take you shopping while I'm here. I'm almost certain those are the same duds you wore to the reunion in '55. And I think I have the photographs to prove it."

"Still the smart-ass, I see. Is somebody going to get me a chair or are you all just waiting until my left side gives out? It's quite a show, I assure you."

As they all got settled, Julia wished there were more aunts and cousins present to distract Grandpa Corrigan from returning to the subject of Katharine. But Julia's mother had been an only child, because of the frailty of Grandma Corrigan's heart after she had rheumatic fever. There were the great-aunts, Katharine's sister Molly, who lived in the States, and Alma and her husband in Sudbury. They both visited occasionally, but not today. And the Corrigans were all too old and deaf to be of any help to Katharine. If they had been there they would only have made matters worse by insisting Grandpa repeat every comment at a higher decibel.

"Are we going to play some cards? Be nice to play with people who have all their faculties, who don't routinely trump their partners' aces." Well, certainly, they guessed there was time. Julia would keep an eye on the ham and vegetables while the adults played a few hands of euchre, women paired up against the men. But Grandpa Corrigan was not about to stop talking.

"I was thinking about this as I was waiting for Abe to pick me up. Not that I haven't thought about it before, but since I took my stroke, some ideas seem new again, like they got a dusting off. Hmmm. Quite the hand. I'll pass.

"Anyway, don't get all defensive on me now Katharine, but I was thinking as I was waiting that of the four Morrissey girls, my Betty was the only really normal one. Betty was the best of the lot, but I hasten to add, Katharine, that you were the second best, despite your whatever you want to call it, your lifestyle."

"You're going to play it alone, are you Katharine?" Julia's dad steered at the conversation as if at the wheel of an out-of-control semitrailer.

"There's Molly," Grandpa continued. "Does she ever live a day without a drink? Which is why she's on to husband number three and her sons have nothing to do with her. And Alma — that woman has an emotional problem with food. Never stops eating. She must be over two hundred and fifty pounds now and her heart keeps on ticking. Like a Timex. Damn, she had both the jacks and the ace." One inadequate tear dragged itself down his left cheek, then stopped in its tracks. Maybe it wasn't a tear but an eye problem related to age.

"Two points," Katharine said.

And Julia's dad interjected: "We're going to have to try harder than that, Joe," but he sounded tense. Being a Raine, he could never say what he really meant. Raines did not say what was on their minds; they sent letters two or three days later expressing their disappointment, their utter disappointment that Abraham had not managed to pay back one cent of the downpayment owed to Grandpa and Grandma Raine. This would create problems for the estate when they were gone, and they would prefer not to have any hard feelings.

"That's enough talk about the Morrisseys, Dad," Julia's mom interjected.

"I'll just keep my mouth shut then. That's what works best at the home, too," Grandpa said. But he and Julia's dad won the next two hands, which cheered them both up. After that, no further mention was made of that side of the family. Julia had hoped Grandpa Corrigan might ask about Gertie, but Gertie was not mentioned on that day or any other. Gertie remained a quiet pulse transmitted through the floorboards, from the soles of Katharine's feet to Julia's, making Julia feel a little wobbly now and again.

~ ~ ~ ~

"**My friend Jannette** said she might drop by," said Julia to Katharine. Jannette had only recently got her licence, so to speak of dropping by seemed affected. "I guess she wants to meet you," Julia embellished. Then, a little closer to the truth, "I've probably talked about you quite a bit."

Katharine was in her room. Evenings and weekend afternoons, she tended to retreat there, the role of guest being oppressive with time. She escaped behind four solid walls and a closed door. No one minded particularly. Julia knocked and entered frequently because this was her room, really, but she had niggling worries that some part of her appearance was unacceptable — her hair parted crookedly or her elbows dirty. Was it possible for Katharine not to see her as the high-school student she was, a constant reminder of hundreds of biology labs and physics lessons taught on freezing cold days when she would rather have stayed in bed? Not likely.

"Do you mind if I bring my record player over? I'll just bring a couple of records."

"You mean we're going to have a party? Does this mean I'm going to have to share my gin?"

"Only if it's lemon. That's what Jannette drinks. She has a bottle in her locker. Mostly for show."

"Well, if it's going to be a party would you be a good girl and get me some ice? And don't let your mother see. I've gone to great pains to drink in privacy up here and if she found out now, I'd have to go back to Calgary with her thinking I have a booze problem, which I don't. Two a day — three on Fridays — and it's none of your mother's business, but if a woman spends time alone in a room and drinks, people draw the wrong conclusion. Another example of bad science."

Julia returned promptly with a measuring cup of ice cubes. "You didn't need to be precise about quantity," said Katharine.

"It was the first container I could lay my hands on. Anyway … the record player?"

"Oh, certainly." Katharine was splashing gin and tonic over ice in a tumbler she kept by the bed. Her movements were large and convivial, no doubt practised for years with Gertie and their friends. Julia plugged in the white box, lifted the lid, checked the needle for dust, then leaned a couple of records against the wall at a partyish angle.

"Did I tell you I spent a week at my friend Rose's cottage in Parry Sound this summer? It was the best week of my life. The best. I'd never stayed with people who own a cottage before. It was very educational to see how people with cottages live. One thing is they visit with each other all the time. There's no set time for lunch or supper so nobody makes a fuss.

"Have a drink," Julia said in Rose's mother's voice, picking up the gin bottle. "Did you see the Johannsons' new catamaran?" Turning to her great-aunt, Julia asked, "Do you know what that is?"

"I have a general idea."

"I learned a lot about nervousness and hospitality. Here, if somebody drops in, it's an immediate fuss, and if you don't have some squares in the freezer, you're in trouble. Maybe it's because Rose's parents are the richest ones, so they're less nervous about people showing up unannounced. They're more relaxed about everything. Rose's mom spends hours in the sun getting a deep, dark tan. And she says things like 'You two girls look terrific.' Or 'You've got a great pair of legs, Julia.' My mother would never in a million years say that kind of thing. I kept trying to imagine my mom there at Rose's cottage, and what she'd be doing. She'd probably decide they needed some sod or something like that."

Julia decided not to play a record yet. She hoped she'd made the right selections: Eric Burden and the Animals, because Jannette loved "House of the Rising Sun." And the Supremes album cover, for display only — the record was in two pieces.

"Rose's family is like a TV family. You could put a television camera in every room of their cottage and on the beach and it wouldn't capture anything embarrassing on film. That's Rose's family. All of my friends' families are less embarrassing and less nervous about people dropping in than mine."

"Julia! Jannette's here."

"Do you want me to see if there are any squares in the freezer?" asked Katharine from the bed, her eraser-bun of hair appearing brighter than usual. Maybe, secretly, she had given it a fresh dye job.

Jannette was already at the top of the stairs, a home economist's vision of good taste in her skirt and sweater set. "I cannot *believe* how far out of town you live," she said. "I swear it gets farther every time I visit. No wonder we hardly ever see you in Mesmer."

"Jannette, this is my great-aunt on my mother's side, Katharine Morrissey. She moved to Calgary all by herself after World War I and taught high school. Don't you think that was adventuresome?"

"Pleased to meet you," Jannette said, blinking, as if adventuresomeness in this old body were a good joke. "Yes, travel is adventuresome," Jannette continued, seating herself in one of the two chairs Julia had positioned on either side of the so-called occasional table. She was clearly searching for words. She hadn't anticipated an old woman sitting up on a bed, like a hospital visit. "Everyone should travel, especially Julia Raine. She should travel more to Mesmer. Then she'd have more fun."

Before Julia could introduce a new topic, Jannette jumped in again. "Did you tell your aunt about the casket factory?"

"No, I wasn't there. Remember?"

"But you heard." And Jannette aimed her face in the general direction of Katharine's bed, talking to the footboard and the blankets. "Rose's dad owns a casket factory. Currah Casket, it's called. Alliteration for emphasis, I guess. Did you teach English, Mrs. Morrissey?"

"Miss."

"Oh, excuse me."

"And no. I taught sciences."

"Oh. Well, anyway, on the night of the last day of school last summer, Rose snuck the key to the factory and we went inside and the four of us — because Julia lives out here and didn't have her licence yet — the four of us tried out every casket. After a while it was hardly even creepy, unless you thought about the lid coming down. We took turns pretending to view the body. We couldn't turn the lights on, but we had brought candles. It was fabulous. Annie actually started to cry, looking at me in this gorgeous casket with velvet lining. I was a bit worried it might be hard on Patty because of her brother, but in the end I think it brought us all closer."

Silence again. Julia could not think of a single word to say.

"I guess it's an example of the advantages of travel," Jannette summarized, trying to extract a lesson for Katharine's benefit. "Julia misses a lot living out here, but I suppose there are advantages to being out in the boonies."

"Julia, maybe you should offer your guest a drink."

"I was just thinking of playing some music." She had to get to the music first; that was her plan. The spontaneity of the cottage people did not come easily to her.

Oh no. "Stephen, I told you not to come in here."

"But he has a magic eight ball, Julia. Let's ask it some questions." Jannette already had the damn thing in her hand.

"What does it say?" Stephen asked.

"It says … *Yes, definitely.*"

"Good. Then I'm going to name it King."

"Name what?" asked Katharine.

"The dog I'm going to get for my birthday."

"Can we play with it for a while, Stephen?" Jannette wanted to know. He was already gone from the room. Then with a dramatic intake of breath she said, "Oh my god, I just thought of something."

With Eric Burden complaining mournfully in the background, Julia now knew the Supremes would have been a better choice. She had to be more careful with her records.

"This happened in the summer," Jannette said, "at my cousins' in Owen Sound. Their hamster was sick and my cousin, actually second cousin, Doris, asked their eight ball if the hamster would live to see another day and the eight ball's reply was *My sources say no.* The hamster was dead in the morning. Doesn't that give you the shivers? My mom thinks one of the kids killed the hamster in the night, but how would you kill a hamster? You'd have to drown it, and I asked Doris if its fur looked tampered with in any way and she said no, it looked very natural in death."

Now Jannette was leaning as if pulled by a string from her

forehead, leaning toward Julia and turning in her chair in an attitude of exclusion. She occasionally did that at school, leaning across the aisle to Rose, whispering and intentionally cutting others out. Having Jannette over to meet Katharine had obviously been a mistake.

"OK, I'm going to ask that thing a question about the future," Katharine said. "How much longer have I got here?"

"But you know the answer to that," Julia said. "You leave tomorrow. Sunday."

"And anyway," Jannette added, "it has to be a yes/no question. The magic eight ball doesn't provide short essay answers."

"I wasn't talking about here in this house. I meant above ground. So ask it this then: Will my old Morrissey heart give out tonight? Give it a shake. What's it saying?"

Jannette glanced at Julia. Was that a face of enthusiastic dread? She read, *You can depend on it.*

"Oh give me that thing," Julia said, annoyed. "That's not the kind of question you ask. You ask, 'Will there be questions about the Seven Years' War?' Or even about the past like, 'Did I have bad breath yesterday?'"

"It seemed to have a good understanding of the hamster's prognosis," Katharine said.

"Oh come on, Julia," Jannette said. "Don't freak out on me. It's just a toy. OK, watch. Will a meteorite crash into my room tonight, killing me instantly? *Yes, definitely.* And here's another: 'Will Julia Raine ever offer her guest a drink or a snack?' *Outlook not so good.* I knew it."

After which the eight ball provided the entertainment, and Julia felt that, at the very least, Jannette wouldn't show up at school on Monday morning complaining about the incredibly boring time she'd endured at Julia's. Even though the visit was not what she had hoped for and imagined, but what was that exactly anyway?

Later that evening, Julia stood at an upstairs window, watching her parents in one of the greenhouses, two figures moving in a spaceship of light. Their togetherness, usually hidden from sight, was easily visible, might even show up on a photograph if you had the right camera, one with such a high-powered flash that it could catch the foggy images of ghosts on film. Had she owned such a camera, Julia would have wanted a picture taken of herself, Jannette and Katharine. Maybe something unexpected would have shown up when the photos came back from the developer, an inexplicable sketch of a fourth person, unseen but present. Gertie, perhaps.

~ ~ ~ ~

The glow-in-the-dark alarm clock said 1:15. Everyone was in bed, asleep. But were they breathing? This was Julia's question. Should she get up and check on everyone? Checking would keep them breathing. Should she ask the eight ball? No, that thing had been the cause of all the trouble in the first place. She'd had to ask it numerous questions before bed to verify its unreliability. Do I have yellow hair? *As I see it, yes.* Am I living in Brazil? *Yes, definitely.* Does Stephen have two heads? *It is certain.* Would Jannette like to rule the world? *My reply is no.*

And just when she was feeling better, Julia had asked Katharine, "Why do you always refer to your heart as a Morrissey heart?"

"Because it's a bad kind of heart to have. Sickly, I mean. Prone to stopping. But I know I don't have it; I would never have seen eighty if I had the genuine Morrissey heart. But you know how it is; you don't want to get overly confident about questions of fate. Your grandma, my youngest sister Elizabeth, she had the Morrissey heart, which is why she died at fifty-three, and why your mother should stop smoking. My dad died when he was forty-six years old. I can't remember how old his brother Albert was, but not very. It goes back generations. Certain Morrissey hearts are like cheap wristwatches."

This was news to Julia. She had been led to believe her grandmother's weak heart was from rheumatic fever, not a genetic predisposition. That her very own mother might contain the gene for premature heart failure enveloped Julia with a hot and worrying sensation, as if a layer of blanket material had formed between her clothing and her skin.

"Don't be alarmed. Not everyone gets it. Look at my sister Molly, in Wisconsin. Her heart's fine, but unfortunately she has a case of the Morrissey liver."

"What's that?" Julia asked, now truly horrified at the prospect of another familial curse.

"She likes her booze, I mean. That's all. You worry too much, my girl."

"So it's not some genetic flaw?"

"Not as far as I know. Anyway, relax. Most of us turned out quite well. Some even perfect. Look at me, for example," Katharine said, winking. Julia disliked winking. It was a gesture used with children, to put them in their place. Katharine could be very provoking at times. Even so, she might have to check on her. It was possible that Julia would come along at precisely the right moment, the second Katharine's heart had managed only a half-beat, or a quarter-beat, some misfiring where all that would be required was a little touch from Julia, and Katharine would be saved.

Now it was 1:20. Earlier in the day she had taken out the atlas to get a measure of the distance to Calgary, since Katharine was returning there. Three hundred miles to the inch and five-and-a-half inches as the crow flies made it about two thousand miles away. Having to drive all the way around the Great Lakes, whether she went through the forests of northern Ontario or the conges-tion of Detroit and Chicago, she'd never make it in time to save Katharine. And she'd have to steal her parents' truck and would inevitably end up being imprisoned in small-town Minnesota or Saskatchewan, the prospect of which had caused a welling up of tears two or three times during the day.

She wished she had never heard about this Morrissey heart

problem. What if her mother had it? What if she had it? They both had the Morrissey black hair and brown eyes, but there would surely be more subtle signs. Julia would have to consult the family photographs more carefully, take note of any similarities among her grandmother, great-grandfather and his brother Albert. That was how genetics worked, groups of DNA travelled together to give you black hair, dark eyes, maybe a certain problem with wisdom teeth coming in sideways, like her mother's had.

She probably should check on everyone. She got out of bed and stood in her summer pyjamas, the seersucker kind, since the weather had not yet turned even cool. Stephen was fine, she knew that already from his loud breathing, which was probably what woke her in the first place. But she leaned over him nonetheless, pyjama legs jammed up to his knees, his blankets on the floor. He was a Raine — that was obvious from his curly, fair hair — his heart would no doubt keep beating well into his nineties.

The floorboards creaked, but this was not cause for concern. They all slept like logs, or like a variety of plant, since they spent so much time in those greenhouses. She could have turned a sprinkler on her parents and caused only a slight stir, a tightening of the blankets around them. There were the cigarettes and ashtray on the bedside table, her mother's Morrissey hair against the pillow. Her heart beat valiantly to support the flow of blood dirtied with tar, sticky like a rooftop. She had recently switched brands because of the superior filter, claiming to have done some research. But where? Julia certainly hadn't seen any medical journals around the house.

Katharine kept her door ajar and it creaked like crazy. Embarrassing if Julia were to be caught like this, sneaking into her room. Katharine was on her side, facing the window, her hair tied back with a large barrette. No sound of breathing whatsoever, no motion from the narrow body beneath the covers. Dear god. What if the eight ball had been correct? What if Katharine's heart had stopped and Julia were the one to make that discovery? She would have to call Jannette, who would for certain call her cousins in Owen Sound. And then there would be Margaret to think of back in Calgary, and arrangements to make. Julia would insist that Katharine's body be sent back to Calgary for burial next to Gertie. She might even need to fly out to Calgary to attend the funeral and support Margaret in her grief. "Who is that brave young thing?" people would ask. "Who is that lovely young woman with Margaret?"

Standing at the foot of Katharine's bed, Julia could make out soft breathing. No need to touch her; people around Flax didn't go through life grabbing one another for no reason. Everyone in the house was alive and breathing regularly, thanks to Julia's rounds. Back in bed, she thought she would definitely like to become a nurse. Since Katharine's arrival, Julia had put herself to sleep with a series of luxurious fantasies involving slightly younger versions of Gertie and Katharine, and a somewhat older Julia, who lived with them, attended university or nursing school, prepared unforgettable meals and was always available when acts of heroism were required. Julia closed her eyes and opened them again to the light of day and the smell of chopped egg and onion. Her mother was making sandwiches for the trip to the airport.

As part of her application to the University of Guelph, Julia had been asked to complete a computer-scored dormitory compatibility form. The pages of questions and their specificity — Do you ever dream in black-and-white? Are you optimistic about the prospect of peaceful co-existence? — had generated hopes of being assigned to accommodation with such like-minded students that tele-pathic exchange of ideas from one understanding forehead to the next would replace the anachronism of talk. Impres-sions of Bob Dylan, Leonard Cohen and the gloomier

Russian novelists would form molecular clouds of correspondence in the hallways. Goodbye Flax. Hello Guelph. What did it matter that all her friends had chosen to go elsewhere? Julia was thrilled to be here at last. She adored the fat course catalogue and the idea of general studies.

"Just pull up there, Dad. The sign says student drop-off."

Two old suitcases, the record player and Julia's collection of almost thirty albums had to be carried through the halls of the new and cavernous residence to which Julia had been computer matched. Above the sound of Stephen hooting like an owl to enjoy the echo, Julia reassured her parents, "I could tell from the brochure it was architecturally innovative. I'll just ask here for directions."

"So innovative I wouldn't be surprised if the occasional skeleton showed up in a stairwell. How are we ever going to find our way out of here?" her mom asked as they descended and circled their way to Julia's room.

After several goodbyes, and Stephen having to be pried from her waist, they were gone. Julia was on her own. On her own, in her new room, listening to a small voice that believed there might still be time to run after the Chevrolet, cling to its roof for the eighty-odd miles back to Flax. Who would have to know? But there was already a girl in the doorway.

"Hi, I'm Jocelyn. As soon as all the parents are gone, we're going to have a couple of joints in the lounge."

Complex A, the architecturally innovative dormitory, was an enormous concrete honeycomb divided into houses with soothing, astrological names. Rising Moon House, Julia's new home, was a cluster of eight single rooms opening into a shared lounge and kitchen. With irresistible and centrifugal force, social events were conceived and convened in this communal living area, events Julia would not miss in her search for compatibility. She liked the Vulcan ears and was happy enough to sit in silence with the others at five o'clock for "Star Trek." And look at the way that roll of toilet paper — thrown from Myles Ritter's window into the courtyard — had pinballed its way among the branches of a young maple tree.

"No thanks, smoking only makes me nervous," she said whenever a joint was passed around. And everyone in Rising Moon House was OK with that. "Hey, don't hassle her," Jocelyn had said to Normy, a second-year student in biological science. The guys loved the way she kept the fridge organized — last year it was a cornucopia of moulds in there, Normy said — and she was more than welcome to clean the sinks. She's straight but a good head, was Jocelyn's assessment. And Myles wanted to marry her, but not for another ten years at least.

Two weeks after her arrival, Julia considered telephoning her parents to tell them to buy some proper HB pencils. The inferior quality lead she had used to complete the dormitory questionnaire must have caused her form to be discarded, her name added to the random placement list. There had to be some explanation. Thank god for introductory sociology with its definitions of roles and norms and social groups and change: some alienation was to be expected in these circumstances.

But why another offer of marriage? This was the second proposal Julia had received in less than three months. Along with the Morrissey heart and the Morrissey liver, did she have a genetic condition resulting in premature aging? Was she old and wifely before her time?

Clint Jardine, Julia's date for the Mesmer High graduation dance, had been the first to ask for her hand. "Why don't we run away to the southern U.S. and get married? Someplace like Louisiana, where you can get married when you're sixteen. Seems kind of sexy, don't you think?" he had said, placing her hand on his erection. This was on their third date, the third date of Julia's life. The root-like sensation of an erect penis was emphatically unfamiliar. From listening in on conversations between Jannette and Patty — the only two in

their group who claimed experience — Julia had acquired a dense
and buzzing layer of sexual anxiety that rose up now, swarming and
aphid-like, rendering her speechless. Her blinking eyes watched,
hoping these insects might spell out a word of instruction, but they
didn't. More kissing. Julia's hand rested on Clint's hardness. Exactly
how big could it get? "I'm afraid I'm going to university in the fall."
Could it actually tear open his pants the way a tree root will burst
through the earth, appearing in the grass?

She did not want to be "straight but a good head." And she was-
n't. Of all her friends from high school, she was the only one capa-
ble of uttering the words vagina and penis and sexual intercourse.
"That's called coitus interruptus," she had explained in health class.
"Julia has been a tremendous asset to the class," Miss Crombie
wrote in her final report. And even though she was inexperienced,
she wasn't far enough off the norms to be considered statistically
deviant. In sociology class, Dr. Gottlieb's pie graphs on teenage sexual activity grouped Julia, thanks to Clint Jardine, with the 15 percent of eighteen-year-olds who had at least once participated in
heavy petting. So there really was no problem. The night when the
four girls of Rising Moon House — Jocelyn, Beth, Audrey and Julia
— stayed up in Beth's room talking about boyfriends, Clint Jardine's proposal of marriage actually elicited some approval from
Audrey.

"He's right. It is sexy. Kind of a beat thing. But you're lucky you
didn't go. Likely would have accidentally shot you in the head,"
Audrey said, laughing a phlegmy laugh. And Julia made a mental
note to read up on things beat.

Jocelyn was old-fashioned; she got too emotionally involved.
Audrey volunteered no information about her intimate life other
than what her status as a published poet conveyed. And Beth
described herself as a cock enthusiast. Julia repeated the phrase
to herself innumerable times, alone in her cinder-block room
and between classes, sipping coffee from a Styrofoam cup: a cock

enthusiast. In the entire annals of sociology, there could be no graph of psychosexual development elastic enough to accommodate both Beth and Julia. Beth, along with the other .001 percent of the populace known to be cock enthusiasts, would require her own graph. Although Julia supposed the numbers might be a little higher, but realistically, how many might there be in all of Complex A? Or in Rising Moon House? Surely it wasn't possible the girls of Rising Moon House could be represented by an undivided pie, a homogeneous sample of cock enthusiasts, except for the smaller pie known as Julia Raine, budding from its side. She didn't think so.

In the early afternoons, when life was at its quietest in Complex A, Julia did some exploring of the other houses. Being modelled on a honeycomb, somewhere there was certain to be a queen bee, a winged Mama Cass assigned to the room in the very centre of the place. That was how she met Pam.

Julia had seen Pam before, in her introductory psychology tutorial, a class that met once a week with a graduate student named Gisela to discuss, or so it seemed, applications of the text to their relatives' experience. "I have a cousin who lost an arm in an accident and she swears she can still feel her hand, especially in the cold. She finds herself looking for another glove."

"Hmmm. Any more comments on phantom limb?"

Pam didn't say much, but everyone noticed her because of her heavy makeup, Cleopatra hairstyle and long dresses. Julia half expected Pam to arrive at class one day in a cobra headband, but despite her eccentric appearance, there was something familiar and small-town about this woman. And now here she stood in the kitchen of Aries Sun, whirring a beige liquid in a blender.

"You're in my psych tutorial," Julia said.

"What a coincidence. You're in mine too. You looking for someone?"

"Not in particular."

"Well, sit down. You can be my taste tester. I'm making a

Brewer's yeast frappé for Marcia. If it's not good, I'll throw it out and then hide in my room until she's gone. If it's good, you can stay and have some too. Meet Marcia. She's very important."

Pam poured the frothy liquid into a heavy ceramic mug. "Well?"

"It's a little bit chalky."

"Yes, chalky is good. It's supposed to be chalky. Can you taste the pineapple?"

"Yes."

"Faintly or distinctly?"

"Mmm, distinctly."

"Then it's good. Excellent. Marcia's chemistry class just ended. She should be here in five minutes."

~ ~ ~ ~

Marcia was in second year, general science. She lived off campus but had trained Pam, as if she were a sort of wife, to prepare drinks and snacks for her in the afternoon when her energy levels were low. Pam thought nothing of missing a class in order to experiment with combinations of soy flour, yeast and marmite, saying (was it with a hint of irony?) that heavy and indigestible foods had important lessons to teach about earlier times when, as a consequence of whole grain diets, people were less aggressive and materialistic. According to Marcia, one look at Pam's irises could tell you she had been eating quantities of the most incorrect foods for years, not to mention the additives and chemicals in her cigarettes. Julia's irises told a similar story, but in hers could be seen the moderating influence of consistently good produce from the greenhouses.

"That is so far out," said Marcia. "Your parents have twelve greenhouses? That's what I want to do. Own and operate an organic market garden. I can't believe this. I have to meet them."

Julia glowed. If only her friends from Mesmer could see her with the important Marcia. Why had they all gone to Western, except for Rose, who was in Toronto? Marcia would have been a striking sight anywhere, with her long dark hair woven into a single braid, her bushy eyebrows and her wholesomely dirty hands, like a car mechanic's. Men were attracted to her. According to Pam, who wanted to major in astronomy, Marcia's sex life had created a separate solar system on campus, blue and hospitable neighbouring planets full of guys Julia would meet. And Marcia genuinely liked her women friends, collected as they were for varying purposes.

"She likes me because I wear these rayon dresses," said Pam. "She thinks because I wear these dresses I'm a specific type of person. Calm and loving with a heart of granola. But I'm not. I like making snacks for her though. That's genuine. What do you suppose that means, psychologically speaking?"

Julia didn't know. "Maybe you could ask Gisela." What she did know was that Pam had performed an important sociological function for her by reducing her alienation. Julia liked Pam's incongruity. Beneath her rayon dresses was a person who would have been at ease in the Flax curling rink, drinking a rye and coke and shouting "Sweep!" Like it or not, this was a comfort to Julia. Pam was simply in the wrong get-up, a condition Julia's mother often diagnosed and Julia herself could easily appreciate, although she could safely say she was never in the wrong get-up.

~ ~ ~ ~

One Saturday in October, Marcia picked Julia up in the old Volvo her parents had given her. They were going to drive to Flax. Julia hadn't been back since the day her parents dropped her off, and she wondered how the collapse of the barn had progressed during that time. Had any of the sides crashed inward? If the entire structure would just implode, the overall appearance of the place would be improved significantly. What would Marcia think of the worn linoleum? Her parents lived in Burlington. They gave away old Volvos and encouraged their daughter in whatever she might want to do.

"But their marriage is a sham," Marcia said. "Seriously. Dad's been getting it on with the neighbour's wife for years. Such a cliché. It's a burden to me — such a clichéd family life. Mom turns a blind eye."

"How do you know he's having an affair?"

"Dad told me. I'm his confidante, his only daughter. He tells me something major, then gives me a big material object as compensation for having to know. Hence the car. But I'm not complaining. I use it to good purpose, and for every ion of fossil fuel this burns up, I'll save the planet tenfold with my organic market garden. It's kind of an investment that will reap future savings. Like today. This is research."

"You do know my parents use herbicides and pesticides and all manner of fertilizers."

"I know. That's cool. I don't expect miracles. Just to learn a little, study at the feet of practitioners."

Already they were in Mesmer, a town that now felt as if a natural disaster had forced all her friends to evacuate with only a suitcase of belongings. They'd be back at Thanksgiving, the very next weekend, and so would she. All the talk would be of dorms and classes and guys, and are you still wearing those desert boots, Julia? Desert boots seem so ... Mesmer High.

"What are your parents like?" Marcia asked.

"They're both interested in plants — that's their number one interest. After that, my dad likes food and my mom likes saving time and money. But they're friendly and they'll like you because you like greenhouses. It's a given. And I have a brother, Stephen, who's six. I brought him these Vulcan ears." Audrey had never condescended to wear them, so why should Julia? And now she usually only watched "Star Trek" once a week, if at all.

"Well, well, well," said Mrs. Raine at the first sight of Julia.

"This is Marcia, who's interested in greenhouses."

"Well, you're just in time to eat." Lunch offered a reason to avoid sitting on the broken couch, for which Julia was grateful. And she had every good intention of going to the greenhouses with the three of them after, contributing what she could to the discussion of roots and heat units, but she was unable to resist when Stephen begged her to stay and play with his Meccano set. He missed her in a frantic and energetic way, jumping onto her, hanging and clinging like a monkey or a bear cub. If their parents were killed in a car accident tomorrow, Julia would have to quit school and raise Stephen. Or take him with her to Rising Moon House. He liked that echo chamber place.

Her room remained unchanged, the furniture purchased for Katharine's visit looking brand new and still somehow occupied by her. Julia would have to mention this in her Sunday letter.

"How's grade two?"

"I don't want fat pencils anymore."

"That'll all change soon enough. What do you want to do?"

"Nothing," he said, leaping onto her where she sat on the bed, growling and fighting until she had him in a headlock, his sweaty-smelling head on her chest. As usual, he pretended to faint. Are you all right? she was supposed to ask. No answer, which meant he wanted to be held like that for a moment.

~ ~ ~ ~

Pam couldn't sleep; she had insomnia, exacerbated by Aries Sun House and its disregard for the rights of serious students. Rising Moon, on the other hand, with midterms imminent, was policing itself well. Partying was allowed Friday nights only — Julia's idea — and as a result, Pam was apt to invite herself to sleep on Julia's floor any other night of the week. That Saturday night, the day of the trip to Flax, Pam made her appearance at eleven o'clock, the latest she was allowed to appear (another of Julia's rules).

Pam was unfurling her sleeping bag when the lounge phone rang.

"Julia, it's for you."

Her parents, calling to say how much they had enjoyed meeting Marcia and when did Julia think she might bring her again.

"She's so skilled at making people like her," Julia said, back in her room. "How does she do that?"

"I think it's that she's so remarkably free of anxiety, other people feel the same in her presence," said Pam.

"Not me. She increases my anxiety. As do my parents by calling at this time of night. Each time they do that, I'm convinced it's Dad calling to say Mom is dead of a heart attack. Maybe I have the opposite effect of Marcia; my worry increases theirs. I mean, my parents didn't seem particularly happy to see me. But then, I spent most of the time in the house while Marcia was dazzling them with her views on monocots and dicots. And it's not that I'm jealous, because I'm not. They should just be a little more considerate of me and my worrying, and at least not call after eleven."

"Do they know you worry?"

"No, of course not."

"You don't tell them?"

"No."

"Then you should. If you went to Ruth Ann, the resident advisor, that's what she'd say. Open and direct communication. So I told my mother I was going on the pill and could I charge that to her benefits plan at work? And she said most certainly not, but the next day she called back and said to send her the receipts. So Ruth Ann was right. I kind of like to promote her now."

What was Pam talking about? Julia had been distracted by the image of open and direct communication, Ruth Ann training a firehose of words on her.

"Anyway," Pam continued, "I can give you another reason why people like Marcia Klinck — they like her because she's bossy. She

tells people what to do and they like that, even if they don't necessarily obey. People mistake bossiness for interest. It's a bit like the
church. I grew up in the church and you didn't, so you don't know
how many people are out there in search of some kind of proctor
to hand their free will over to."

"Wait a minute. You're going on the pill?"

"Yes. I'm on it already, and you're not allowed to tell Marcia.
She's adamantly opposed to birth control pills and their contami-
nating effect on the female body. I kind of agree, but not strongly
enough to get myself pregnant. I love Marcia, but I wouldn't put it
past her to be on the pill herself. How can she sleep with all those
guys and not ever get pregnant? Unless she's got some kind of condition or it's another of her miracles at work."

Despite Pam's alleged deep affection for Marcia, she took pleasure in telling bedtime stories about her, derived from the New
Testament. The organic conception of Marcia Klinck, for example.
From the dark of Julia's floor, late one night, Pam's story began: "Mr.
and Mrs. Klinck are really very ordinary, much like Mary and
Joseph. What was exceptional about them at the time of Marcia's
conception is that on the entire planet, including the continent of
Antarctica, Mr. and Mrs. Klinck were the only human beings never
to have absorbed even one part per million of DDT. Through no
fault of their own — pure happenstance. They'd be thinking of taking a walk through a freshly sprayed park when Mrs. Klinck would
turn her ankle, forcing a change in plans. Or Mr. Klinck would be
reeling in a large and toxic Lake Ontario trout when his line would
snap. Damn. This sort of luck prevailed until the conception and
birth of Marcia, immediately after which Mr. Klinck called the
Green Drop people, saying he'd been meaning to for years."

And, there were the miracles. "In the first grade, Marcia's
teacher ran out of paste during an important arts and crafts
activity. Marcia, having brought a single serving of millet casserole
with her for lunch, volunteered to divide this into twenty-four

equal paste pots. The lesson continued, leaving Marcia with enough casserole for a nourishing lunch." Pam sat up, struggling in her sleeping bag. "Do you think I'm mean?"

"A little." That was before she knew Pam was taking the pill. Now she might say more than a little.

"Well, you're right. I guess I am. But like Gisela says, it's not good to repress. It will just come out on your skin as a symptom like that Blake guy's brother who got hair all over his back when he forced himself to stop being a kleptomaniac."

Pam walked to Rising Moon House in polo pyjamas — a dramatic change from the long, loose dresses — carrying her bundled sleeping bag. Julia said she could leave it, but the rooms were so small, Pam hated to occupy valuable floor space. Other girls most likely would have worn a bathrobe over their polo pyjamas, but not Pam. Under that thin cotton, her breasts were rather compelling to the eye, as the art history professor would say. Suddenly there she would be, with the faint smell of wood smoke and canvas on her sleeping bag, and Julia never seemed to have changed in time, which posed a problem. With Pam lying there on the floor, she wasn't about to stand on her bed to undress, or hide in the closet, which was the sort of thing Barbara and Lesley from Flax Elementary would do. The only solution was to slide beneath the covers, secure them between chin and throat, remove her clothing and ease into her pyjamas much the way one would in a tent. Folding her underwear and bra between her pants and shirt, she hoped Pam wouldn't think she intended to wear the same underwear two days in a row. After that they talked for hours.

When Pam wasn't there, Julia sometimes slept in nothing. She liked to push the blankets back, billow up the sheet and let it parachute down, conforming to her shape, imagining she was hospitalized, surrounded by worried and efficient nurses. Why did everyone but her seem to know what to do with their body parts? Julia wanted to ask, her final dying question. How many of her acquaintances were involved in secret and complicated sex lives while she, Julia Raine, walked from class to class imprisoned in the naive emotional life of a pre-adolescent? Maybe her genetic condition was actually one of arrested psychological development, an eleven-year-old trapped inside her skin, curious and demanding: Who exactly is having sex and why? Beth, obviously, and Marcia too, but she was in second year, which made things a little different. And Audrey was a poet and had to have sexual experiences in order to complete her "Trilogy of Decay." But Pam? Why did Pam have to go on the pill? She didn't even have a boyfriend.

Once recently Julia had been in Normy's room, asking about a biology lab she had to finish. She was distracted by seeing a used condom clinging to the side of his garbage can, couldn't stop looking at it, even though she knew it was rude.

"Sorry," Normy said, "I should've got rid of that thing. I gotta have safes in the room because I get to a point where I know I won't be able to stop."

Maybe she could ask Ruth Ann, the advisor, this: When do you get to the point where you can't stop? And how do you know you're there? Or how do you avoid getting there, since the idea didn't appeal to her, especially as embodied in Normy. Would her vagina, like a hypnotist, one day compel her to perform entirely unexpected acts? This seemed doubtful, but then everything about Rising Moon House, Pam, Marcia, sociology, art history and the psych tutorial had been unexpected. Who could imagine the next link in Julia Raine's great chain of unpreparedness? Such was the cost of growing up two miles west of Flax, she concluded.

Wrapped in a sheet was a good place for her then, surrounded above and below and on both sides by others who might not be so securely girdled into place. They couldn't stop and they were all a little horrifying, like Normy. Which didn't worry her at that moment, because she had been offered a job. Very part time, starting in mid-November. Marcia had been made manager of the

Grain Exchange, a whole foods store. She was dropping a couple of courses in order to take this on and was offering part-time jobs to Pam and Julia. Pam was going to have to ease up on the eye makeup. And Julia, without being told, knew she might have to borrow one or two of Pam's long rayon dresses.

~ ~ ~ ~

Julia was no longer a virgin. Three hours ago, she and Lucas Reef — or the man who called himself Lucas Reef — had had sex. Name changes were the fad among affiliates of the Grain Exchange: Donna Thompson had recently become Ariadne Solstice; Linda Barker was now Phoebe Ringstone. That Lucas, a marine biology major, had been born into the family name "Reef" seemed unlikely to Julia. But with earth, wind, fire and sun providing inspiration for many of the chosen names, Lucas may have had his suspicions about Raine as well. Once the new names were adopted, questions of genealogy seemed tasteless or invasive, although fascinating, anthropologically speaking. What effect would the self-selection of surnames have on the study of lineage? Julia pictured future generations of anthropology students puzzling over inexplicable breaks in patrilineal family trees — and here Dodd begat Reef, and we have no idea why, none.

Whatever. Julia had had sex with the man now lying asleep next to her in the attic apartment of an ailing red brick house somewhere on Arthur Street. He had been asleep for at least two and three-quarter hours now, during which time, from a quick check of the prescriptions in the bathroom, Julia had deduced Lucas's real name to be Lance Dodd. There was something in a tube for Harold Minifee, Lucas's roommate, a little container of green pills to combat occasional sleeplessness for Lance Dodd, but nothing at all for the fictional Lucas Reef. Also mouthwash, Pepto-Bismol, organic toothpaste and deodorant, along with shampoo made of tar. No antibiotics. Nothing quite as worrisome as the reflection of Julia Raine in the mirror of the fluorescent and institutionally white

87

bathroom. How had her skin managed to wrap itself around some-one else? Someone rolled in egg white and dipped in flour — she looked so pasty and undercooked. Maybe this was a state of shock. Decreased blood volume caused shock, her high-school biology teacher had said. Contrary to what you may have learned from Dr. Kildare, you don't go into shock from a scare or bad news or unex-pected sexual activity. So maybe she had lost quantities of blood, more than usual from the inaugural sexual act, enough to cause circulatory shock. She'd better go back and check.

Nothing. No blood at all on the flannelette sheets for Lucas to show his neighbours. That was a surprise, and yet not. How like her body to co-operate with the program no matter how unready. It really was in league with her vocal chords, talking, explaining, opening up its legs and being penetrated with relative ease when the rest of her, whatever remained, watched in speechless disbelief. Or at best, protested with some vigour: I didn't even know for sure we were on a date. And whose fault was that? Hers, she supposed. Like a fieldworker in an unfamiliar social group, she had spent the evening taking mental notes and still missing the most significant details, the most auspicious warnings. Lucas placing his hand on the back of her neck while clearing away the dishes; Lucas sitting very close to show her photographs from his visit to the Gaspé, their shoulders touching. Julia might as well have been examining an inkblot for content: Hmmm, looks a little like two crushed bears, or maybe it's a winged alligator.

Julia met Lucas at the Grain Exchange one of the evenings she was wearing Pam's blue rayon dress. The blue dress, unlike the green dress with its modest Nehru collar, was cut low, and its shirred bodice displayed her breasts in a manner that had a stir-ring effect on Julia's thinking. Her whole body seemed to undergo a transformation when she wore the blue dress, becoming alert to its breasts and nipples, the swish-swish of its legs. Beneath that mute and draping fabric, loud parts of Julia conducted workshops with other, quieter parts, saying now just let yourself enjoy that man's admiring glance and yes, you are allowed to push the hair back from your forehead in that manner; there's no law against it; it's quite all right to have that Lucas man stay and talk. She knew if he were ever going to ask her out, it would be on a day when she was wearing the blue dress, and she was right. But she couldn't make it to dinner that night because she had two papers overdue.

She didn't think he would ask again. He had since been into the store twice and been cool and almost dismissive. Until today, when he had said, "Dinner's going to be on at eight-thirty. What do you think?" And because Julia was in jeans and a sweater, she interpreted this invitation as a gesture of friendliness, having nothing to do with sexual interest. "OK, sure, that would be great."

"It's Friday, after all," Lucas said. "You can't tell me you're working on papers tonight."

"No, you're right, I'm not that statistically deviant," Julia said.

Dinner was baked onions, baked squash and baked potatoes. Yellow and white, with cream sauce and butter, and occasional flashbacks to Clint Jardine. Cheap wine had facilitated their relationship, but Lucas and Harold didn't drink. Clint had liked to talk about running away from Mesmer, getting a job in Mexico and which of the cheerleaders was stuck-up. Lucas gently prodded Julia to reveal her zeal for the social sciences, and just as gently relayed his contempt. "Who really is normal? It's all about social control anyway. Haven't you read Goffman?" Harold ate in less than five minutes and disappeared into the living room to play old and scratchy jazz recordings. Sometimes he moaned to himself, or maybe it was the recording. Surely he wasn't masturbating in there; surely this wasn't a house of serial sex killers.

When Lucas invited Julia upstairs to his room, she understood that the teasing about the social sciences had been flirtatious and a clear signal to expect further stages of courtship. Would she take her clothing off for him? he wondered. And yes, she answered unambiguously, as if her body had been chafing for some time at the ridiculous and needless custom of being clothed. Off came everything, with a little staggering over the socks. Then it was Lucas's turn. With the light on, the bedroom door open and the blind up, Lucas walked about the room with the first adult erection Julia had ever seen. Apparently there were some books to shelve and papers to arrange while she sat on the bed watching with a fixed and frozen smile.

Then Lucas approached, hovering and unfamiliar as a flying saucer, and began kissing and touching her. It would seem they were not planning to get under the blankets, and apparently the door to the hallway would remain open. Where was Harold? The records continued to play, but that meant nothing; he could have a stack of three or four on the turntable. Then Lucas was on top of her, making arrangements with his right hand for what Julia knew would be sexual intercourse heading in for a landing. Pain, then a progressive and suffocating sting, and Lucas's face moved far away from hers as he listened to telegraphic orders from the galaxy he called home. After a few mechanical jerks, Lucas collapsed, rolled off and asked if Julia would like a drink of water.

The bathroom door didn't close easily, requiring three pushes from Lucas before the latch caught. Julia heard water running, pipes clanging off, then more running water. He was thirsty, she guessed, as he appeared erectionless but with a glass of water and asked if she would like to stay the night. Sure.

Lucas wasn't suffering from occasional sleeplessness tonight. Within five minutes he was asleep. Julia had imagined there might be some further conversation, had pictured them scaling a ladder of intimacy. She was good at asking questions. Were his parents happy? How long had he and Harold been friends? What about condoms? And if they were going to have sexual intercourse, could they please at least make time for their separate skins to stand up and look out the window for a minute or two afterward?

The only other time she had slept next to a stranger was the night of the big ice storm in eleventh grade, when all the bussed students had had to spend the night in the gyms, girls in one, boys in the other. Julia slept on a mat between the wall and Evelyn Jardine, Clint's younger sister. Even though she was in grade nine, Evelyn had never before been away from home overnight. By early evening she was so hysterical that various storm-stayed members of the staff asked if there was anyone she particularly wanted to sleep next to. Yes, Julia Raine. Because on Evelyn's third day of high school, when she had fainted in the girls' washroom, incurring a nosebleed, Julia had found her. A bit like imprinting, Julia concluded later. She'd been the first older student who'd come along, and now Evelyn wanted to sleep next to her. In fact she knew much more about Evelyn Jardine, having then gone out with Clint, so there was no basis whatsoever for comparing her with Lucas. It was just that she hadn't expected to be on such intimate terms with anyone tonight.

Well it was all over now — almost. The next time Pam slept on the floor, Julia would need to allude to this experience and let it be known that yes, no big deal, she had gone to bed with Lucas Reef. You mean that guy with the curly hair who buys so many acorn squash? One and the same. And Pam would make approving noises. *Then* it would all be over with.

Julia believed she was recovering from the shock now, but made another trip to the bathroom to check. Some colour had returned to her face, but there were still unnatural goings-on beneath the skin. And what was that good memory caught somewhere beneath her ribcage? Oh yes. Pam in the biology building. Julia was taking a biology elective and had run into Pam in the biology building yesterday. This had happened before, but this time Pam was wearing a lab coat, which thrilled Julia to the astonished roots of her teeth. Thrilled her in an uncontrolled way, much like jumping from a cliff into the cold water of Georgian Bay the week she had spent with Rose. Immediate giddiness followed by a leaden sinking into a heavy medium where your thoughts came louder and a little panicky, but not necessarily clearer.

Julia adored Pam, which was a good thing, according to Marcia. Marcia adored lots of women. She said women shouldn't be so invested in the patriarchy, which had historically pitted women against one another in a battle for goods and protection. It was time to break free from mediaeval habits. So that was lucky.

Julia thought she might get up and go home now. It was after two, and Harold had gone to bed. The house had no wish to keep her there, silent except for the far-off roar of the furnace, breathing through its vents. Everyone was sleeping, and she was reminded again of the gym the night of the ice storm, when she stayed awake most of the night worrying that Evelyn would need to hold her hand. Dressed and in the kitchen, Julia sat for a while. What was that Russian advice? Always sit for a couple of minutes before you embark on a journey. She used to do that in high school: before getting on the bus or driving to Flax for the groceries, she'd stop herself in her room and marvel at the interruption. That pause had the same pleasing melancholy as a photograph. Stop action and wonder at what had come before, what would that person do next.

She was going to leave now. Outside in the December night was a surprise: first snowfall of the season and everything was beautiful, snowflakes beneath the street lights resembling millions of trained moths, fluttering downward in perfect symmetry. Goodbye Lucas Reef. Goodbye Harold. She wondered if Clint Jardine had made his way to Louisiana, and if so, was he missing the snow.

~ ~ ~ ~

"So it is possible to become pregnant the first time you have sex?" Julia asked the doctor when he gave her the positive results of the pregnancy test.

"First, last and any time in between. What do you want to do?"

"I want to think for a while," she told him, robotically serene in Pam's green dress. And she had every intention of thinking, but for the first time in her life, she couldn't seem to do that.

"How does thinking happen anyway?" she asked Gisela. "How do we make sounds, an auditory experience, inside a slushy grey organ. The liver can't do that, or the kidneys. What kick-starts it? What gets a thought going?"

Julia was hoping Gisela would tell her what to think about being pregnant, but the teaching assistant smiled the way she did when she no longer wished to pursue a particular line of questioning. I'm only a master's degree student, after all. I don't know everything.

The words were there in Julia's mind, but they fluttered about, unaware they might group together with others of their kind to organize a thought or idea. Baby. Cells. Mitosis. Fat. Most likely her body wouldn't change shape for several months, but Julia began to wear Pam's dresses every day. She even bought one for herself, a brown and loosely woven garment that might have been suitable attire for a party thrown by one of the Apostles. "Is that sackcloth?" Pam asked. "Interesting weave."

The brown dress, like the blue dress, had an important effect on thought. In the brown dress, Julia was from another century when you might be killed for pregnancy out of wedlock; or perhaps the bubonic plague was at its zenith, and no one would notice one single female pregnant at the wrong time. Either way, circumstances would resolve the situation. The brown dress had a way of lifting Julia safely into the arms of determinism.

And there was still a remote chance that Lucas was from another galaxy, and Julia an agent for alien insemination. This made a certain amount of sense in view of her cortical inactivity. The moment conception occurred, there had been a slowing down of all bodily responses, perhaps due to the release of a morphine-derivative that was harmless to the developing fetus and sedating to the host. Only special spawners sent to the earth carried this neurotransmitter. Look at Lucas Reef. Everyone talked about how laid-back he was.

He had been friendly since their date, clearly wanting to see more of her, inviting her to visit the Lake Huron shoreline to observe the intense freeze-up. Lucas wanted to be a limnologist, which struck Julia as a romantic ambition. But unexpected responses issued from her mouth: "I have so many assignments due before the end of January. And I'm actually seeing someone else now, Lucas. Sorry."

Pam still had no boyfriend and still stayed in Julia's room at least two nights per week. And there was no reason to panic over this. The baby wasn't due until mid-September. She wouldn't start to show (what a silly word) until March, the doctor had assured her. But Pam was terrifyingly attentive, and Julia had been sick now three different mornings. If that happened even once when Pam was there, she'd surmise the truth; it was as if she had extra glands in her nose for sniffing out that sort of information. Or special ears that could detect any unusual cell division.

Julia knew she was more talkative, nervously so, but Pam made no comment. She dreaded the moment when they both fell silent and sleep was imminent, because it was then Julia felt the ghostly and unspeakable presence of the third life in the room. What if it were to fall out of her and begin flapping around on the floor like a frantic goldfish out of water? What if it made a noise? She knew this was impossible, but she dreamed regularly of this and other phantom events. Remembered when her mother had told her she was pregnant with Stephen and lay flattened by the imagined weight of all the Raine and Corrigan females before her who had contributed to this hopelessly organic moment. Why hadn't they exercised more restraint? Not that she wished she had never been born. No, what she wished was to be indivisible.

February became March, and Julia Raine, who had always been careful with her money and an exemplary student, discovered the movies. Movies seemed more important than grades or books or food or doctor's appointments. Sitting in a sociology class, she would find herself longing for the dark and blissful detachment of the movie theatre. Where had she been all her life? She saw *Carnal Knowledge* three times. "There's a real cunt," repeated itself in her anxious mind. How could Jack Nicholson be so horrible? Would Lucas say that about her to Harold? Would Harold become uncomfortably silent like Art Garfunkel? She liked *Klute* better, but only saw it twice.

She was showing now, there was no doubt. Only a slight thickening in the waist, completely imperceptible in the dresses. Julia began to spend more time in one of the two Rising Moon bathtubs, observing her stomach. She enjoyed her stomach's progress, loved it in a perverse way, as if she had a crush on herself, and this took her by surprise. She supposed there was no explaining any of it, being under the control of chemical commands released by the developing fetus from the loins of the alien Lucas Reef. Of course he suffered from occasional sleeplessness; he was likely from a planet with fifty-six-hour days.

The fluttering sensation scared her so much she called the doctor. What if she had a miscarriage and out came a little half-baked human? Or a bird? What did one do in such a situation?

"It's the baby kicking," he said, Dr. Kind and Gentle.

"Kicking? It feels like someone waving a little fan, or like a bird flapping."

"That's about the size of it."

It's bird-sized? Would it get out of its cage and flap around her ribs or up her throat? This business of having another life inside her was all too strange, she told him. "I'm sure it is," he agreed. "I'm not sure how I would handle it myself."

Julia would have liked to have one eternally long conversation with this omniscient doctor. Could she please have a direct line to his bedside telephone? There were so many things to discuss.

"If you're applying to graduate school, do they look very closely at your first-year grades? Because mine seem to be slipping. I can't seem to concentrate and situations that would have worried me three months ago, such as a late paper, no longer seem significant."

"You'll be fine," he said. "Have you made any arrangements?"

"Arrangements? Oh yes. Things are falling into place."

Then out of the blue, perhaps as a consequence of lying to the doctor, Julia told Pam she was pregnant. At first Pam said nothing from the bedroom floor, which meant she understood this to be complicated and difficult.

"What are you going to do?"

"Have it, I guess."

"But then what?"

"I don't know, I honestly can't see that far into the future. It's as if the future ends three or four days ahead, like the numbers on the calendar blur and become unreadable."

She told Marcia, too, because she wanted to continue working at the store during the summer, as many hours as possible because she needed to save money. Her parents would just have to accept that she wasn't coming home. It was no big deal really. Women became pregnant every day of the year, every minute of the day.

How was it then, that as she became larger and larger, Julia saw herself as smaller and smaller, visible from the front, but seen sideways, nothing more than a paper-thin curve of light? Invisibility was rather comforting. Even on that day in August when she put her curved and lumbering self onto a Greyhound bus to the airport and purchased a one-way, stand-by ticket to Calgary, no one gave her a second look. Pregnant women could be prohibited from flying in their final months, so perhaps she wasn't pregnant after all. Tumours came in all shapes and sizes. Maybe the force of take-off would break the damn thing, pop its balloonish skin, resulting in nothing worse than a very full bladder, easily rectified. The stewardess had just pointed out the locations of the cabin lavatories.

She was leaving now. There was Toronto, Lake Ontario and the careful fields of yellow and green. The flight path could easily take them directly over Flax. Stephen might be out in the yard watching, taking a shot at the airplane with his cap gun. From inside the greenhouses, she doubted her parents would hear the jet engines. Clouds interrupted her view then, long grey slats. Julia had the impression of rising up out of a basement to another room, where of course she knew she was carrying a baby. She, Julia Raine of Flax, Ontario, was going to have a baby. And this was unfortunate because now she was going to have to cry and that was a nuisance. She hadn't cried for a long time, she couldn't recall when. She planned to call Katharine and get a taxi. Then she would cry a little in the back seat. Taxi drivers saw strange sights and emotional situations all the time; it was part of their job. By the time she arrived, she'd be perfectly composed.

But there was no answer at Katharine's, and somewhere inside her a wind picked up, gusting through one of those glands that can't help itself. She rushed to a bathroom in the Calgary airport, latched the metal door and sat and cried. Cried and cried, not even bothering to muffle the sound. "Do you need any help in there?" running shoes and then expensive leather boots asked. "I'm fine. I'll be fine," she said, pulling up her long skirt to ensure anonymity when she finally emerged.

~ ~ ~ ~

"S o m e t i m e s t h e o n l y thing an old person can do for a young person is just hold onto them," Katharine said when Julia arrived, obvious with her news. And by then, after a bracing taxi ride through the city, a ho-hum conversation with the cabby about the weather in Ontario, things seemed less desperate. Julia wasn't certain she needed a hug from this old and gaunt lesbian schoolteacher, but she suffered it. Her mind summoned up every platitude conceived for the education of the indigent: better show a little gratitude and not look a gift horse in the mouth. How did

Katharine manage to look so lovely even at eighty-three and with that bad dye job?

"Everything will be fine," Katharine said. "You're healthy. You'll have the baby and put it up for adoption and your life will return to normal in no time. Trust me, I've known my share of pregnant girls. Their lives did not come to an end. But you do understand I have to call your parents."

"You can't though. They'll want to know who the father is, and the embarrassing truth is I don't know." And Julia explained the identity problem with Lucas Reef/Lance Dodd. Her parents would think she had spent her time at university attending sociology orgies and Grain Exchange key parties. "When the irony of it is, I only had sex once. Only once."

"Well, it makes no difference to me if you had sex once or thousands of times, and as far as this Lance/Lucas thing goes, you'll have to sort that out with the social workers, not your parents. Just say it's too painful to talk about. I've always found that works."

"What do I have to sort out with the social workers?"

"The details surrounding the adoption. I think they have to know something about the father to tell the adoptive parents."

"But how will they even know I'm here?"

"I don't really know how it works, but the hospital will. Believe me, everything will be fine. You're welcome to stay here as long as you need. I could use the company."

Everything will be fine, Julia told herself again and again. If you took the broad ecological perspective, everything probably was. She had adapted, following some atavistic map: she'd flown in, found shelter and explored her surroundings in a wordless and bird-eyed fashion. The baby wasn't due for another ten days at least, so she had time to become familiar with the territory.

Each morning, after a dutiful breakfast of oatmeal, while Katharine listened to the radio and read her two newspapers, Julia went for a walk. The weather was cool, so she wore Katharine's overcoat, which was too long and full and angled out over Julia's belly like a tent. When she stopped to rest, Julia tried to think of herself as a tent pole, supporting a poorly balanced and lopsided structure, rather than a very pregnant, unmarried and friendless out-of-towner. She found a hat of Katharine's and began to wear that as well, now resembling an apiarist without her veil, in search of a hive. That was fine. People could think what they thought.

Katharine's house was on an older, shady street of smallish lots and many bungalows squished between the river and the hospital and the architecturally difficult North Hill. A few blocks from Katharine's house, on First Avenue, stood a cluster of Italian gro-cery stores, and to the east, another hill: Tom Campbell. Why did all the hills have names? She supposed this was a western practice, hills being rare, as were trees. Everyone walked by hurriedly, faces set like compasses: must go this way, must go that. In a hurry to strike oil someplace, Julia supposed, or check their wells. Except for the woman who'd asked for directions yesterday. She took the time to check Julia's left hand for a wedding band, or diamond at the very least.

"No, I'm afraid I don't know where the nearest drugstore is," Julia had replied, thinking she might find a pair of Katharine's gloves to complete her disguise. She arrived back at Katharine's in time to overhear a conversation she was having in the backyard with Phil, her neighbour. Julia made herself invisible, standing just inside the screen door.

"She seems to be settling in all right," Katharine was saying, hold-ing the pruning shears, snipping occasionally at the Nanking cherry.

"She got family around? I mean besides you?" asked Phil. And Katharine changed position, turned her back to Julia, mumbled something.

Dear god. So she was now the subject of mumbled conversation: "How's her family taking it?" Hushed and velvety coffin-side talk. She'd go down to the basement and sit there for a while. Cool down a bit. The walk in the overcoat was a little suffocating. She would leave it on a chair and Katharine could spend a few minutes wondering where she was.

The basement was pleasant, with its smell of old and slightly damp books, its jars of preserves, Gertie's canning legacy. A good place for Julia Raine, vessel that she was, one-hundred-and-fifity-pound pod. A good place to sit and listen to the quiet music of cell division.

"Julia! Julia, where are you?"

Ha. There she was. Julia had been too absorbed in her thoughts to hear.

"Julia?"

Oh for heaven's sake. Was there no peace to be had? "I'm in the basement."

"Julia!"

She was not going to trundle up those steep stairs: wasn't that a sure-fire method of inducing labour? "I'm in the basement," she shouted.

The door opened. Light. "What are you doing?"

"I got a little overheated on my walk. And I rather like being down here with the organic matter."

A sigh from Katharine.

"And what does Phil have to say?"

"Phil? About what?"

"About me?"

"Very little. He was curious as to who you are, that's all. He lives next door. He sees you coming and going."

"And the rest of the neighbourhood? Have there been comments in the community newspaper?"

"Not that I'm aware of. There may have been some sightings of an overdressed woman in our midst, but they haven't made it into print."

No response from Julia.

"Come up here. I can't stand at the top of the stairs and shout. It reminds me too much of being back at work."

"Fine."

"If you're not happy here," Katharine said as Julia heaved herself up the stairs, "you can always go back to Ontario."

"No, I'm happy. Or something," Julia said, reaching the kitchen. "I have to sit down for a second. Oh, the coat." Katharine did not like disorder.

"Never mind the coat. On the subject of happy, you were saying?"

"I don't really know. I can't say I have any moods right now. I can think about moods, but not experience them. Like my moods have been stuck with pins to a hunk of cardboard, like an insect collection. They're being preserved for some future purpose, I'm sure. For the time being, I'm moodless. Moodless in Calgary. Which is not to say I'm unhappy."

Which was not even remotely true. Each day, upon awakening, there was a mood, waiting by her bed. Sometimes heavy and leaden, like the X-ray shields dentists thump onto patients' chests; other times, buoyant, her stomach a large life preserver, suggesting Julia might like to float down the Bow River. Or if she woke in the night, she occasionally felt an odd contentment. She was glad to be here, in this bed, blanketed by the three provinces separating her from the family she had left. She was quiet and safe while the rest of the world did what it did.

And there was the shopping. Julia loved the trips to buy baby supplies with Katharine. "Money is no object," Katharine said. "I've always loved buying things. Just haven't had much reason to lately."

"Do you think they think of us as the happy couple?" Julia asked once, feeling playful.

"Who?"

"The store clerks."

"I'm sure they've seen stranger sights."

The last item was the crib, now assembled and wedged into a corner of Julia's room. That very night, September fifth crossing into the sixth, she woke up feeling odd, as if her body were trying to say a new word. What was it? Went back to sleep. Woke up an hour later and there it was again, only louder. Oh no. The word was "birth." Fear and relief reverberated deep inside her, a kind of electrocuted purr.

Katharine was still driving, so Julia didn't have to take a sad and impersonal taxi to the hospital. For some reason, that had been one of her biggest fears. And Katharine had stayed for the first couple of hours, until Julia insisted she leave; she wanted to be alone. She would do fine in the company of the nurses and her own thinking. So think about something, she instructed her body as it dug deeper into itself, creating a tunnel. Did the baby have its own little shovels? Think about something. By now Pam and Marcia would be back at school. Pam had written first, then Marcia too, but Julia had yet to reply. They would be in their science labs, in the biology building. Pam might even be in that lab coat. If Julia were there, she'd have been in the Arts building, likely in a sociology class. The sociology of what? Religion or crime. She might die from the pain now. The baby was expanding and expanding, it was not about to stay in this confining cave another minute. Think about something. Think about the sociology of birth. What did she know about it? Not much, they hadn't covered that topic, so much time had been devoted to lineage. And sociology was the study of groups and social behaviour and birth was never performed by a group. It should by rights be added to the list of personal inevitables: death, taxes and childbirth.

Only a few nights ago Julia had realized there was no escape. This was not like a seminar presentation or a shift at the Grain Exchange where you could always call in sick. This was your body dragging you along to a two-hundred-kilowatt lit type of aloneness, with the added indignity of endless poking and measuring of the interior of her vagina. She wanted to ask how would a baby ever come out of a place Lucas Reef's penis could barely fit into, but at that precise moment she was given a shot of something, after which her head and body went their separate ways. "Just push as much as you can," the nurse said. Push? How do you push when your back and legs are made of wood? The baby was chugging along on its own. Nothing could stop babyhood from occurring. That was the number one rule of biology. Everyone was dressed in white and the lights were even brighter now, fish-tank lights. Julia felt as if she were holding her breath and diving down into her own throat, watching from the interior.

It's a baby boy. And Babyboy became Peter.

The next day her parents arrived, without Stephen, who was staying with neighbours but had sent his magic eight ball. Just the thing for a newborn with a lot of future to predict. No one mentioned social workers, although Julia examined each new nurse for a badge, some emblem of the government's interest. And no one asked "Who's the father?" although Julia could certainly hear the question as they examined the little face and body for bloodlines.

To Julia's surprise, her mom and dad seemed to accept the baby. They pronounced him Morrissey through and through, which pleased Katharine. They held him, called him a keeper, then looked anxiously at Julia and asked how she felt. They offered to stay with Katharine until things were sorted out. With her parents and the nurses in and out and Katharine excited about being back in the General, Gertie's old stomping grounds, the atmosphere was festive, almost like a reunion.

And Julia's roommate, Mary, who'd had a girl, was kind and helpful. She didn't seem interested in husbands or Lucas Reef's name, or to mind that, twenty-four hours after the birth, Julia's tear ducts had arranged for uncontrolled, unlimited bouts of crying.

"A baby is a funny-shaped thing, always melting away," she told Mary late at night.

"That won't last for long," said Mary.

"Are you sure?"

"No. No, I'm not. But I like to sound certain, which is the next best thing. To my knowledge, most women who give birth do some crying but stop eventually."

"I hope so. I can't go to school or get a job if I'm always sitting up in bed, sobbing."

"You'll work things out."

~ ~ ~ ~

Mary had the window side of the room, and Julia had to look past her to see outside. During the day Mary was always moving and arranging, taking off her glasses and putting in contacts, stabbing at her messy blondish hair with pins, or fetching them drinks from the fridge down the hall. Or feeding Kristy and changing her, so practiced, it seemed to Julia, even though this was her first child too. And at night, when they happened to be awake together for feedings, there was something consoling about her profile against the glass and the lights of the neighbourhood. Julia felt as if they were sharing an apartment, had been computer-matched for postpartum living.

"How old are you?" Julia asked, her third night there. Mary would be leaving tomorrow.

"Twenty-eight. And you?"

"Nineteen."

No comment.

"So what do you think?" Julia asked. "Do you think I should keep him?"

"That's one question that's entirely up to you to answer."

"I know, I know."

Silence from the window side. Three in the morning and they were both dead tired. Mary could fall asleep in a minute. The clatter and light from the hallway didn't disturb her in the least, whereas Julia was awakened by the slightest noise or activity. Nurses lived in a world of brilliant yellow hallways and extra-strength bulbs, while in the rooms, it was lights on or lights off — no reading lamps. Reading at night had to be done by the halo of the door, which was the one advantage to having the hall-side bed. Julia reached for the eight ball, shook it, flipped it over and leaned into the dim light. *Yes, definitely.* She shook again. *As I see it, yes.*

She had known that was the answer anyway.

chapter

4

The name of the course was Learning Theory 244. Scheduled topics of discussion for the past two weeks included fixed and variable schedules of reinforcement, also known as the social manipulation of choice. More often than not, attention turned to B. F. Skinner, the man, and more importantly, the daughter in the experimental box.

"To me that just discredits the entire body of work," said Monica from her seat in the second row. Turning herself sideways to address both the class and Professor Aiello, she continued, "I know I've said this before, but where did he get off?

And if he would do that, what else would he do? It calls everything into question, ethically."

"Class? Any comment? Do we throw the experimental bath water out with the baby, as it were? Richard?"

Richard had something to say about Skinner's motives and *Walden Two*, and Julia stopped listening, assuring herself that if the topic came up again, she would respond then. But she knew from the cowardice she so often felt nibbling at her shaky resolve that she wouldn't. What was the point? She was twenty-one; they were nineteen, twenty at most. She had a child; not one of them did, she was certain. They wouldn't understand. Or worse, they would become interested and sympathetic and require background information (they were students, after all). They'd encourage her to take the podium, where she'd begin talking, withholding key bits of information, diverting the facts, forcing U-turns in her throat, until deep within her lungs would be a gridlock. Like the recurring dream in which she found herself at the front of the class, explaining with pointers and charts and sweaty armpits why her son had been kept in an experimental box. Bad methodology, they always said, donning coats and hats, their never-pregnant bodies swarming toward the door. But wait, wait everyone, there's one thing I forgot to tell you: the unknown variable is Lucas Reef. Oh, they all said in unison, as if everything now made perfect sense. Now we'll come back and listen; now we understand.

No, you don't, Julia wanted to argue. *I* understand. I understand B.F. Skinner and his relationship with his daughter. I feel much the same way with my own son. Although I've never placed him in an experimental box per se, I observe him with the same scientific rigour and take innumerable mental notes. Instead of the normal baby book, I've developed a set of Mendelian inferences, chi squares in answer to the questions: Who is Peter Raine? And who is Lucas Reef? Who are the other Reefs? And who is the maternal side of his family? The Sandbars? The Quagmires? The Sinkholes?

What genetic secrets lay spiralled in their chromosomes? Were they all predisposed to the study of shorelines? At age ten, would Peter build a raft and disappear down the Bow River? Would he change his name? Eat only squash?

Julia had even run experiments, made mashed squash, for example, and mashed carrots (her favourite), keeping all variables constant and comparing Peter's reactions to both. He showed a definite preference for the carrots, so that was one point for the Raines and Corrigans. Although perhaps some experimenter bias had crept in. Had she smiled more while presenting the carrots? Communicated approval through the angle of her neck?

The continuing investigation was hampered by Julia's limited knowledge of Lucas. Was it really true she could scarcely recall one distinguishing feature of the man who had fathered her son? Yes. Colour of eyes? No idea. Nose? Unremarkable. Mouth? Rather large and friendly but inexpressive. Build? Surprisingly muscular, as if he'd done a stint of manual labour or exercised daily, following a strict callisthenic routine. She could see him doing that. To be honest, her vividest memory was of the calmly erect penis, shifting this way and that while Lucas Reef organized texts on his bookshelf. Very little to extrapolate from that image to a twenty-month-old boy. Would Peter, in later years, be compelled to complete small domestic duties prior to sex? Or was Lucas Reef simply a compulsive tidier? That house of his had had a military neatness to it, now that Julia forced herself to remember: boots, shoes, containers of rice and grains, potted plants — all lined up, single file, ready to march.

Peter had not yet, to Julia's knowledge, lined up a single thing. His specialty seemed to be backhanded hurling, performed while leaning into the toy box. He also liked jumping from chairs, steps and any ledge he could access. Then there was his lack of recognizable words. Where had this come from? Lucas was not a big talker, but Julia knew this much: his speech was clear as a bell. What if, however, he had been avoiding using certain sounds because he couldn't actually form them? *Th* or *ch* or *sh?* Thinking back, all she could clearly remember him saying was, "Would you like a drink of water?" Nothing too challenging there. In a couple of months, Peter would be as articulate, if not more so.

"Maybe you should take him to a specialist," Katharine had suggested not long ago.

"But he's not even two, for heaven's sake. He's fine. He says lots of things like 'Mommy' and 'moo' and 'mik.'"

"All *m* words though. He should be expanding his repertoire; you can't get by in life on words that begin with *m*. The Morrisseys talked early; my sisters and I were all talking a blue streak by two."

"Katharine, he'll be fine. He makes *b* sounds and all the vowels, too, as far as I can tell. It's just the Reef/Quagmire influence," she said in an attempt at humour.

Katharine rarely laughed at Julia's efforts to create an extended family for Peter of bogs and wetlands. Nor did she laugh when Peter hurled his toys, or even smile when, after three glasses of wine, Julia told Katharine about the lining up business, then moved seamlessly on to the subject of the books and the erect penis. No response from Katharine, which seemed unfair, as she occasionally made unapologetically sexual comments about women who were walking by or on the bus. "My my, look at her" or "Isn't she something else?" Or "Hubba hubba," as if to suggest a level of confidential exchange — until it was Julia's turn.

Maybe from time to time Katharine mistook Julia for Gertie, then snapped back to the present in her little tweed time capsule, filled with teacherly observations: "Maybe you shouldn't speak so fast to him." Or "I never skip over pages when I'm reading to him; I think he knows." Fear and dread of Katharine's judgement were like two big hands on Julia's shoulders, steering her one way, then the other, occasionally shaking her until her teeth hurt. Daily she found herself looking deeply into Katharine's eyes for some sign. Did Katharine think, despite the year — 1974 — and despite her own sexual pro-clivities, that Julia was an embarrassment? The bad seed growing and reproducing under her very own roof? Julia wished she could attach a meter reader to Katharine's skin, a device wired to measure shock or disapproval. She would have happily gone to bed each night with a handful of graph paper displaying peaks and valleys against co-ordi-nates of time and place. Oh, so that's when I told Katharine I wasn't planning to return to the parents' group.

The parents' group, no, the single mothers' group, had been Katharine's idea. She'd found the notice in the paper, clipped it out and said, "This might be helpful. Gertie always said young mothers needed support. She worked in maternity for quite some time, you know." So Julia went, because certainly Katharine was doing her an inestimable favour by allowing her and Peter to live rent-free, sometimes not even paying for groceries.

At the first meeting there were introductions while Paul Simon's "Mother and Child Reunion" played on the tape deck. Mag-dalena, the facilitator, took them through a series of relaxation exercises, then lectured a little on current feminist principles. Infants cried while toddlers ran around the room. "It's OK, they can't hurt themselves. Just let them be," counselled Magdalena. "They're young mammals; they need to be left to socialize. And they need to know mom needs her own space once in a while."

The lack of structure, the noise, Magdalena's tendency to lower her voice to an inaudible and all-knowing whisper, the pressure to claim one's space, along with worries that Peter might be choking or bleeding in the nether regions of the mammals' play area, all these distractions made Julia frantic. It was as if her attention had grown several sets of little feet that were running in fifteen direc-tions. And there was Pauline's son, Roger, to be concerned about. Roger was one of the older children, close to three, Julia guessed. He enjoyed ramming Peter in the chest or back with his little bul-let head, appearing to be very entertained by the sight of Peter crashing into the Fisher Price kitchen or the cardboard box of dress-up clothes. After the fourth incident, Julia felt confident Pauline would intervene, but she seemed to have an advanced case of Roger-blindness and did not. So maternal rage was added to the group dynamic. Julia thought she might like to give Pauline a shove, see how she liked that. Thought of suggesting Roger needed a parole officer.

The second meeting was worse. Participants were expected to share details — "whatever you're comfortable with" — of their relationship with the child's father. "Get in touch with any anger you have. Feelings of betrayal," Magdalena urged while the young-sters pitched and hammered brightly coloured plastic objects. Roger had clearly established himself as leader of the pack, a situation Peter could not seem to grasp or retain for even five minutes. While Julia prepared her story (first long-term relationship, knew he wasn't right for me, left on an airplane), Peter managed to climb onto an overturned box. Roger, seeing this as a challenge — Julia tried to think of wolf pups at play, or bear cubs by a salmon-filled stream — torpedoed across the room and shoved, sending Peter face-first into a fire truck.

Oh no. Blood. Julia scooped up Peter, returned to the group, had had enough. "Your son is more than a little aggressive," she shouted to Pauline above the din. Peter's lip was bleeding onto his shirt and dripping to the dirt-coloured carpet. But instead of being defensive or hostile, Pauline was apologetic, almost abject.

"I know, I know. I don't know what it's all about. I'm awfully sorry. Roger. ROGER! Come and sit with Mommy."

"I think I'd better go," Julia told the group. "He's got some teeth coming in and he's just not been very happy the past week."

"Oh no no no. Don't go. I'll feel terrible." Pauline was near tears.

Two infants began to cry in perfect synchrony, and Peter turned up the volume. All eyes were on Pauline and Julia. Not critical eyes or better-you-than-me eyes but eyes that might like to have replaced the proceedings with an agenda requiring less intensity, a let's-all-call-it-quits type of roster.

"I really must go," Julia said with finality, giving Pauline a hug to staunch the flow of terribly sorrys. "It's OK. These things happen. They're nothing but little ids on two feet."

Julia made it to Katharine's Oldsmobile and drove off, her foot and the accelerator enjoying a passionate reunion, long-lost friends, let's get out of here.

But they couldn't go home yet: there would be too many questions from Katharine. Julia would tell her next Tuesday that she wasn't planning to go back. "It's not for me," she'd say, using Katharine's all-purpose excuse. In the meantime, she decided to go for a drive. Julia's driving experience was limited to routes to the university, Mary Nordstrom's house and the Co-op grocery store. Where to go? West on Eleventh Avenue, then north on Fourteenth Street toward Nose Hill Park. Julia turned the car onto a rutted gravel road and up a steep incline to the parking lot. Peter was asleep, blood on his lip, a very fly-weight boxer confined to a ratty second-hand car seat. The problem with children, Julia had learned, was determining whether they had sustained a closed head injury or merely a superficial scrape. How could you know? No doubt he would be fine.

Julia turned to the view of downtown. It was early spring, but finding the promise of warmth and lengthening days suddenly oppressive, she rested her head on the steering wheel and studied the contours of the floor mat. Now she wished Pauline were there with her, provided Roger were confined to a separate vehicle. No doubt Pauline was as confounded as she was. And her story had been interesting. She'd just begun describing her affair with a married man — "Quite prominent, really, some of you might know him" — sounding jolly in a desperate bid for respectability. How pathetic. But hadn't Julia herself been busy revising her own story? It was all such a mess, a big, bleeding, open-heart surgery on the motherhood experience. But it took one to know one, which was why Pauline would have been a welcome companion. Julia might try to get her number from Magdalena and give her a call. She might. Most likely she wouldn't.

Instead, in the middle of that night, while Katharine snored and Peter slept with his miraculously unscabbed lip, Julia called directory assistance.

"For what city?"

"Guelph."

"No, I'm sorry we have no listing for a Lucas Reef," came the smooth ribbon of voice, the sentence pronounced as one long musical word.

"Well are you familiar with any Reefs there at all?"

"I'm in Toronto, miss."

"Oh right, of course you are. Thanks anyway," Julia said, returning the receiver to its cradle. In the bright porcelain white of Katharine's bathroom, she sat for a while after making this furtive call. Then she returned the phone and its long cord to the street-lit shadows of the living room.

~ ~ ~ ~

Mary and Julia were going camping, just for one night, with the kids, of course. Peter and Kristy were old enough, almost two, and it was high time Julia got out into the environment like an Albertan should, the environment meaning the mountains. Julia liked the mountains but preferred them at a distance and piled up on the horizon like a snowy train wreck, not up close, not being on or between their perilous slopes. Mary had tried to take Julia skiing before but had met with resistance.

"Don't you think it's a bit soon after giving birth?" Julia had said the first winter. And the following winter, "I find it all a little excessively bourgeois." But the truth was Julia was afraid of mountains. They were slippery, hard and cold, big broken backs, the result of some tectonic plates' failure to yield to the geological right-of-way.

In Julia's opinion, mountains didn't seem to like people, so often killing them with their avalanches and falling rocks. She imagined them in possession of big, slow brains, triangular in shape, generating big, slow thoughts: Stay off me. I don't like the look of you. Where are my bears?

Now, Julia concluded, perhaps she should have gone skiing. At least skiing was public, social and a group activity. Whereas camping, there you were living together, spending the night. Camping was an outdoor form of marriage, sociologically speaking. What had she got herself into?

Julia had devoted considerable time to examining her relationship with Mary, and Mary's relationship with her, because they were not reciprocal, not even parallel. If anything, the two were misaligned, one section being hammered into place by one oblivious carpenter and the next by another. This certainly wasn't a typical friendship. At first, immediately after their children were born, Julia had suspected Mary of being an undercover social worker. Mary offered lots of advice and instruction: get yourself a credit card, put Peter on the waiting list of the university day care, come skiing with me. But a social worker wouldn't get so many speeding tickets and she would certainly pay them on time, wouldn't she? Julia didn't know. She didn't know what constituted a typical social worker, or a typical friendship, for that matter. What were the laws of normal friendship, anyway? According to B.F. Skinner, any exchange that is mutually rewarding. And what were the rewards of this exchange? For Julia, being in the presence of an individual she found visually pleasing. Apparently this was the cardinal rule of friendship for her. There had been Pam, and before her, Jannette, and before her, Lois. As if her social instincts had been crossbred with Clint "Let's Talk About Which Cheerleaders Are the Sexiest" Jardine. As if there were a short in her sociological wiring, a poor connection.

But Julia had a good male friend, Harvey Gill, whom she'd gotten to know near the end of Learning Theory 244. While working together on a project, Julia had disclosed her views on the experimental baby box debate, told Harvey about her recurring dream and concluded with the complete Lucas Reef saga. This was followed by a thirty-second interlude of sobbing and an out-of-body experience. Wedged against the classroom ceiling, she told herself everyone else is gone, it doesn't matter.

"Knowing where you come from genetically doesn't really make that much difference, predictability-wise, I mean," Harvey had said. "Take me, for instance. I have bipolar manic-depressive tendencies and no one in my family on either side is even remotely extreme. In fact, they have no poles. They're the flat earth people. You know what they say in statistics about regression toward the mean. But if everyone's at the mean, one or two of the offspring will head for the standard deviations. Don't cry. What can I say to make you feel better? If my wife hadn't taken my credit cards, I could buy you something. A car for instance."

This was a friendship. This was statistically average. Harvey told Julia he worked for the city planning department and they were paying for him to take a couple of courses. "You should think about it. Urban planning. Read a bit." And he gave her some books, which Julia read, calling him later to discuss the realities of urban blight. This was a model of friendly human exchange.

Already the mountains were closer, looming and glowering and organizing bleak thoughts, disapproving and rudimentary grunts. Signs suggested drivers should watch for falling rock. Julia and Mary had talked little since leaving Calgary, having encountered rain, then a cloudburst from Kristy, who claimed to be scared, followed by sudden braking and fishtailing for a mule deer.

Perhaps now was the time for Julia to hew for herself a healthy friendship. Magdalena would say share, talk, emote. Arrange your face as if covered in a new type of cosmetic, Deep Yet Ordinary Friendship, by Max Factor. She could do it.

"Let me tell you about Peter's dad," Julia said. This had worked with Harvey, and it was OK for Peter to hear from his back-seat chair. He understood next to nothing. Kristy, two days his senior and speaking in full sentences, could be counted on to respond with a penetrating question or two. So Julia told the story and didn't feel any urge to cry. She embellished a bit though.

"When I was in my first year at the University of Guelph, the introductory sociology professor showed us a pie chart with percentages and proportions of people who'd had different experiences and at what age. And I remember thinking I was in the 15 percent who had done something — not much, but something. Now I picture myself in the narrowest little thread of pie chart, among the group who had sex once, got pregnant, then threw in the towel. That would be me and maybe two or three others on the planet."

Why was she telling Mary this now? It was similar to telling Katharine the erect penis story: inadvisable and yet irresistible. Had childbirth caused a widening of certain talk canals? Or was lactation the cause? Was there a type of letdown reflex of the confessional hormones? She had weaned Peter completely four months ago, but there was still milk, as wild loopings of hormones endeavoured to sustain the species. The sensation was almost similar — a stretching and tingling, could be in the nipples, someplace pleasurable. Mary gave little response. Maybe she hadn't heard; maybe the entire thing had been an auditory hallucination, wind arranged by mountains, the Wild Chinook Reel.

Good. Julia hoped she hadn't said it anyway.

"Kristy, would you please not kick the back of my seat please? It's really annoying. Could you take her shoes off, Julia?"

"Kristy, your mom says I have to take your shoes off."

"No," Kristy said, pulling her feet away, bending her legs up into the car seat. "No you don't."

She was right. Julia hadn't anticipated a semantic argument. Here was Kristy, ready for the toddlers' debating club, while Peter,

wearing a cowboy sunhat, clenched the nipple of a bottle between his teeth, swinging it pendulum-like with each motion of his head. This is Peter Raine's idea of time well-spent.

"Maybe I should take Peter to a pediatrician."

"What for?" Mary asked. Then, "Did I bring those cigarettes? Damn. What good is camping without smoking? Could you look in my purse and see if they're in there?"

"Sure." Excellent, the subject had been changed. "It just seems to me he's a little slow, that's all. I mean, compared to Kristy, for example. Yeah, the cigarettes are in here."

"Don't go to a doctor. That's the way boys are; they're on a different schedule. He's probably solving spatial puzzles in his mind. Don't worry. Anyway, back to the pie chart. I'm wondering which wedge I'd be in. What were the choices again?"

"I don't remember the choices. They were sociological. You know how sociology has a way of making all human activity seem tragic. So it was serially monogamous, celibate, that kind of thing. You'd be in the happily married to a veterinarian wedge of the pie, I expect."

"And which wedge would my veterinarian husband be in, I wonder?"

"That I can't say. Isn't this the road? It says Kananaskis."

"Oh yes, god, sorry. Don't get me thinking about pie charts while I'm driving. Now we just go south and look for a sign that says Galatea, and go past that until we see another little sign with just an arrow and a tent, and that's our road. It's pretty basic. Primitive is the word they use, but it's not really. There's an outhouse and a pump. With any luck we'll be the only ones there."

The only ones there. One of the more advanced and complex of the mountains was likely thinking the very same thought, loosening its rocks, ungirdling a mud slide. They were travelling downward to the valley floor, out of the sunshine, this being late afternoon, between dense stands of conifers, crowded and shoved back from the narrow road as if watching. Not much comes by this way. Then they all vanished and there was grass and a huge blue and green expanse of valley. From the colours you would think the ocean had just retreated, leaving behind a skin of itself. It was a relief because Julia didn't like that hemmed-in feeling, that treed skylessness. She'd lived in Alberta long enough to develop a preference for western light and prairie sky.

"This is it." Mary slowed the car at the entrance to a campground, surrounded by trees again until they had found a spot facing the valley. The light on the eastern slopes looked very new, almost biblical. Perhaps they had stumbled upon Genesis, chapter one.

"How do you know about this place?" Julia asked.

"It's not a secret. It's in all the books."

"Yes, but you don't really seem like the type to read those books."

"You're right. I'm not. Someone brought me here once. Anyway, let's get set up. This is the plan. Assemble the tents. Make dinner. Go for a little walk along the creek, dragging and carrying the kids — that will be the quality time. Put them to bed. Light a fire. Drink wine and have a few smokes."

Julia was euphoric that they would be in separate tents with their respective offspring. There was something about Mary that was occasionally ... what? Julia wondered while organizing tent poles with Peter and his bottle proboscis. Too much? Overrun? Perhaps that was it. Mary was overrun with herself. Making the list of plans just like that — first we'll do this, then we'll do that, then talk. "Let's talk about Katharine and Gertie," she would no doubt say. This had been a topic of considerable interest since Julia had asked Mary to check in on Katharine last summer during her trip to Ontario. Katharine had not been feeling well, and Julia had insisted on having someone check on her. In the end, Katharine and Mary had been compatible, even spent a couple of evenings playing cards. Mary had known all along that Katharine was a lesbian, but spending time with Katharine heightened her curiosity. What was Gertie like? How did they meet? Do you think people knew? Do you suppose one was more on the "butch" side and the other "femme" (finger quotation marks around "butch" and "femme")?

"I don't know," Julia had answered, repeatedly. The laws of social learning theory didn't seem to apply to Mary's questioning, so little reward ensued.

"Here Peter. Hold these pegs. I have to find a stone to pound them in."

Mary could plan the agenda of activities, but Julia would introduce and deflect the conversational topics if need be. She wanted nothing very personal. The mountains, for instance: what are their names and why? Or bears: should they have brought a gun? Or Kristy: isn't she smart? And Peter: why does he speak only in single words beginning with the letter *m*?

As it turned out, there was no need for such tactics. The night was warm and clear, and who could believe so many stars would appear, layers of infinity all lit up like a funhouse for the mind of the mountain camper? So much for Julia's tantrum of worries. Under these conditions, what topic could induce anxiety? She couldn't think of any, could only be grateful to be here with Mary beneath that twinkling and measureless dome of light and dark.

Then it was bedtime, teeth-brushing at the pump in the dark, two women grafted to the earth by the soles of their feet and nothing more, surrounded by carnivores, unstable and malevolent rocks, and a heart-stoppingly indifferent sky full of the imponderable. Oh well. Everything would be fine, everything was fine, Julia assured the sleeping Peter inside the tent. There he lay, the mystery child, breathing in and out of his pink and uncorroded lungs, lungs such as a little dolphin would have, constantly washed clean. Too bad they couldn't take up permanent residence here, it was so lovely. And Julia realized that for the first time since Peter was conceived, she was a free man in Paris, to use Joni Mitchell's words.

She felt unfettered and alive. As if that night with Lucas Reef she'd boarded an empty boxcar and been driven blindly here and there along thousands of miles of track until tonight, when she'd been deposited here. "There you go, lady. Here's your kid. Have a nice night." No wonder she was longing to stay forever in the Kananaskis Valley.

Well you can't, and you don't really want to anyway, came the voice of sense, the voice of the most senior counsellor at Camp Reality by the Rockies. What was it she was remembering? Julia wondered, watching the roof of the nylon tent huff and fall in again. Oh yes. Camp. Camp Saugeen-upon-the-Huron, where she'd gone for one week when she was ten or maybe eleven. She had fallen in love with one of the counsellors, spent the final two or three days feeling as if her insides were a big water balloon, precarious, spongy and breakable, and possibly embarrassing. At any moment she might pee out a thousand buckets of stored-up love. The day of departure, sunny and hearty and final, she waved goodbye to Jan (yes, that was her name) from her parents' car, waved goodbye and wondered in a primordial, mountain-brained way: What was that?

"Mary," Julia whispered, wanting to say goodnight. Her tent was close enough, no more than twenty feet away.

"Mary," she said again, now above a whisper. "Mary," audible now to any low-flying bats. "Mary," just loud enough to wake up Peter if she wasn't careful. "Mary," as if calling through a bathroom door to someone in the next room.

Must be asleep already. Just as well. Mary — a one-word sentence beginning with the letter *m*. Peter could have said it.

~ ~ ~ ~

Late in October, Julia was at the dining-room table late, reading the classifieds, wondering what work in telemarketing might be like, when Katharine hauled out four big albums and asked, "Do you want to look at some photographs?" Page after page of black-and-white snapshots: Gertie at home, in the yard, with Margaret and Laura in Banff, in Jasper, in San Francisco and Seattle.

So why not ask? Julia thought. Then I can tell Mary. "Where did you two meet anyway?"

"In the hospital," Katharine answered with no hesitation. "I had to be admitted. Got pneumonia one winter and my lungs were a mess and there was Gertie, a very young nurse. There was something right from the start, but of course you don't act on it, don't even know what it is. I just thought I was in a good mood every time I saw that Gertie. But of course I had to be discharged when I got better, much to my disappointment. Then I ran into her again. That was the best day of my life, I think. I was on the hill there, up on Crescent Heights, which was just a field in 1918. I was wanting to see Katharine Stinson fly in. She was a famous woman pilot and she was flying in and taking the mail to Edmonton. It was a big deal back then, an airplane and a female pilot. And that's where I ran into Gertie. I saw her, and I remember thinking: I like that nurse. No amount of rules or regulations could stop me from thinking that, even though I knew it wasn't exactly how I was supposed to think. There it was.

"So I waved and ran over to her. 'Hi Gertie, hi.' I must have looked absurd, really, just being so happy to see her — as if I'd been looking for her for ten years. I thought everyone would notice my ... excessive happiness. But they were all looking at the sky. It was a bright sunny day in July and the airplane came, but Gertie and I were more worked up about seeing one another. I asked her where she was living and she said at the nurses' residence, but she wasn't happy there. And I said, well I'm rooming but I'd like an apartment, so we should think of looking for a place together. It being summer, I wasn't teaching, and within a week I'd found us a place for the beginning of August, an apartment on Twelfth Avenue. The Lorraine. It's still there."

"And then what?" Julia asked.

"You mean how did we become lovers?"

"Yes, I suppose that's what I mean," Julia said, unsure of the suitability of the topic, thinking Lucas, bookshelf, hubba hubba.

"Do you know, no one has ever asked me that question. And as a result, I've never told the story," Katharine said, blushing a little and causing Julia to blush as well. "We moved in together in August and by the beginning of October, people were dying like flies from the big influenza epidemic. You can't imagine what it was like. It seemed one day everyone was fine and the next everyone knew someone who had just died. I was at school and one of the teachers went home sick and never came back. And another one of my colleagues was a pallbearer for him, and the next week he was dead. It hit young people in their twenties, like Gertie and me. Nobody knew why."

"That's terrible. I didn't know that," Julia said, recognizing suddenly and possibly for the first time the density of the time separating them.

"Well that's how it was. At first she was brave, you know. The papers were still full of the war, of course, but there would be bits about the nurses and the hospitals full of dying people, how courageous the nurses were. Then, just like that, the city shut down. Everything was closed. And I think that's what really changed it for Gertie. I had to stay home — the schools were all closed — but she had to struggle off to work with her mask on her face, and you know, she really wasn't made of stern stuff. And apparently I'm not either," Katharine said, looking perplexed, then annoyed at her own untrustworthy body. "I feel as if I'm going to start blubbering."

"I'm not bothered by blubbering," Julia lied, as a strangled voice in her throat begged, "Don't cry, don't cry, I really have no advice for the crying."

"So that first night," Katharine continued, having found a tissue and blown her nose, "after the big quarantine was announced, she came home and I remember she was quiet and we ate dinner and read the paper. Later I was in bed, not sleeping, and I looked up and there was Gertie in the bedroom door. And she said, 'I don't want to die just now.' And I said, 'I don't either.' And she said, 'But chances are I'll get the influenza and I'll die and you'll find another nurse to live with.'

"'No, I won't,' I said. And then I said, just like that, 'I like this nurse.'" Katharine had fully recovered now, was nowhere near tears anymore. "I said, 'And anyway, you're going to get into bed with me now, so whatever you get, I'll get.' That's the kind of thing that comforted her, knowing she wouldn't be the only one. And she got into bed with me, wearing a cotton nightgown I'd seen her in so many times as she was preparing for bed. And the same voice that said 'You're going to get into bed with me,' told me to hold onto Gertie, it was OK. You're in a city that's shut down and everyone's wearing gauze masks and falling into caskets regardless, so why does it matter that you're holding this woman? And that moment, when we put our arms around one another, there just are no words to describe the sweetness of that moment. Like someone lit a hundred candles in the room. And then we were lovers," Katharine concluded, her eyes on Julia's. So there.

"What did your families think?"

"They didn't know until they figured it out through a process of elimination. Then there were some awkward times, for sure, especially from her family. She was the only girl, whereas I had three sisters, so the pressure wasn't on me to marry. But we were here and they were all back East, and that helped. And it wasn't like you think it was. It wasn't so repressive. There were lots of women doing what they wanted. They didn't just invent feminism in the last ten years. And there were lesbians around too. You only knew through talk, naturally, and even the talk was, well, innuendo. People were discreet. They respected your privacy. This was later, of course, but take Amelia Earhart, for example, she was a lesbian. Did you know that?"

"No, I didn't."

"Well, see, there's a lot you don't know."

~ ~ ~ ~

Julia's days were entirely eaten up by the inexhaustible appetites of school and Peter. When she was in class, he was at the day care. When she wasn't, he was with her, in Katharine's house, creating trouble and situations Julia attempted to contain through worry and fuss and continuous motion. First and foremost, there was the untidiness. Peter was at the ninety-eighth percentile rank for messiness, whereas Katharine was not even on the scale. She kept the house tidy, the garage, the yard and even the alley behind the house. Just this summer she wondered if Julia could buy her a scythe for her birthday so she could cut the weeds behind a neighbour's house.

Any clutter or disarray caused an electrical discharge from Katharine's eyes, an uncomfortable crackling and zapping until the offending sight was returned to order. Like a city crew in the wake of an unexpected weather disaster, Julia followed Peter, mopping up. "We certainly didn't see that one coming, folks; we certainly thought gas pipelines could withstand a little more wear-and-tear than that; ditto the electrical poles."

All of which led to the second problem, that of the push-and-pull of imposing upon Katharine, for however brief a time, the care and maintenance of a two-year-old. Julia routinely entertained fantasies of leaving Peter alone with Katharine while she ran out to buy milk or juice, returning to find her great-aunt clutching her chest, gasping for air, incoherent as a result of a stroke. Or simply dead, killed by the demands of living with an unappreciative great-niece and her illegitimate son.

Furthermore, Julia thought she should be getting out more, but there was the problem of babysitting. Thirteen-year-old girls wanted to babysit so as to spend time unobserved in a house with a fridge and television, not so as to sit companionably with an octo-genarian ex-schoolteacher who discussed the failings of the current science curriculum. Eloise, the girl from three houses down, had said she would watch Peter if Julia brought him over. But the one time Julia had taken her up on the offer, Peter had returned with a brilliant bruise on his forehead.

"Sorry, that's where my little sister accidentally hit him with her miniature ironing board. It was accidental. She was swinging it around and thunk, he got hit in the head."

What kind of household allowed the swinging of small ironing boards? Julia wondered. Then she upbraided herself for being too protective; such things happen. And what was Peter's problem any-way, that he never seemed to get out of the way? Did he need to be enrolled in a self-defense program? She didn't take Peter back to Eloise, even though this caused moments of anxiety when she ran into her: "Hi, Mrs. Raine. How's Peter?" I'm not Mrs. Raine, Julia suppressed saying.

In the late fall, Julia hit upon what she thought was the ideal compromise. "You don't mind if I go for a little run, do you?" she'd ask after Peter was in bed. By going running she was also doing Katharine a favour, emancipating her from the duty of domestic exchange — "What shall we watch on TV? Maybe I'll make some tea" — everything announced and jovially public.

Julia always took the same route, into Crescent Heights and along the top of the hill, then down and across the footbridge to Prince's Island, past the boarded-up paddle-boat rental shack. Past the swings and teeter-totters, which caused her to feel bottomless sorrow over all the childhood moments she was not providing for Peter, as if she were embezzling time from a fund not rightly hers. Back up the hill to stop for a moment and consider the urban future she and Harvey envisioned — no more single-use suburbs, nothing but older, established, mixed neighbourhoods, everything old before it was new, somehow or other.

Until one night in early December. Running past Christmas lights in a little snow, the river frozen only at the edges, not like the massive and collided ice chunks of January and February, Julia was particularly happy. She had done well in her course work, had decided to use her charge card to go to Ontario for a short visit. As she finished running and opened the door, she thought she might buy Katharine a good bottle of Scotch. Then there was Katharine in the living room, bun askew and face furious above the wailing, tantruming body of Peter. All recent pleasure scattered and smashed like so many unnecessary glass ornaments.

"I don't know what to do with him," Katharine said, as if delivering Peter to the principal's office. "He woke up. He won't be held. Throws himself on the floor and asks for you."

Peter was on his feet and charging toward Julia, "Mommy Mommy," thirty pounds of human desperation, need and obligation.

"How long has he been up?"

"Oh at least fifteen minutes. Of this. I don't know what woke him up but he sure as hell didn't want to see me. All he would say was, 'Where Mommy? Where Mommy?' I tried to explain but he wouldn't listen."

"I'm sorry, Katharine. Really. I won't go running again. It's not fair to you."

"No, that's silly. You mustn't stop because of one incident. However, and this may not be the most opportune moment to bring this up, but I feel we need to talk about finding you another place to live."

"Peter, it's OK, I'm here. It's OK. Yes, I know, Katharine, I know. Never mind that it's winter and we'll both likely freeze to death in a bus shelter."

"Oh don't be ridiculous."

And this is something new, Julia mumbled to a detached part of her mind. We're having a fight. Might as well fuel the flames a little; she was in the mood for it suddenly. "I'll be ridiculous if I want. It's my human right."

"Oh for god's sake, put him back to bed and we'll talk, but in between give your head a shake. And I'll get myself a drink."

In the bedroom, Julia lay down with the now-hiccuping child, whispering reassurances. "It's OK, I'm here, go to sleep. I don't blame you for not wanting to be held by Katharine. That would be like being held by a burnt umber pencil crayon or a piece of unupholstered wooden furniture. I don't blame you one bit." And he was asleep. She lowered him, crane-like, into his crib — a skill she had developed, along with lower back muscles. Still asleep. Good.

Wait a minute. "Katharine," Julia said, finding her in the kitchen refilling an ice-cube tray, "did he really say 'Where's Mommy?'"

"Oh yes. Repeatedly. Although I think it was 'Where Mommy?' The contracted verb was missing."

"Wow. He's finally asking questions. I guess he just has to be provoked into hysteria in order to fulfill his potential."

"Well he's going to have to be provoked into hysteria with someone else because I'm too old for this. Anyway, cheers. Here's to your son's full potential," Katharine said, handing Julia a tumbler of Scotch.

And that was the moment of change for Katharine. Something seemed to break, not in the damaged, fractured sense of the word, but in the relieving, palliative sense, like a decades-old fever or a prolonged hush. Julia and Peter went to Ontario as planned, saw Grandpa Corrigan (who asked at least twenty-five times if Katharine was pressuring Julia to adopt her lifestyle, calling her the last of the great swingers), saw Marcia, who dropped by twice (fulfilling the practical requirements of a course she was taking on herb growth), and returned to find that Mary, through her vast network of connections, had found them a place to live.

"It's a fourplex," Julia told Katharine. "Close to the university.

Good school. I'll want a good school, Mary says. Pay the deposit, sign some papers and I can move in March first. Isn't that great?"

"Yes. Yes it is."

~ ~ ~ ~

Julia had been a good roommate, Katharine admitted to herself. She shovelled the walk and introduced Katharine to new domestic practices such as ordering in pizza. She bought flowers when she could afford them and was willing to drive in any weather. As for Peter, at worst he was tolerable in the way Phil's loud renovation project was, or the likelihood of water in the basement each spring. At best, he was fleetingly lovable. The problem did not lie with them or their qualities and character traits or their comings and goings and wet towels in the bathroom; the problem was they weren't and never would be Gertie Vogel. And anyone other than Gertie in these rooms, walking these floors, opening these cupboard doors was a bad fit, an enormous overcoat dragging in the mud or a too-small woolen sweater scratching at your wrists and neck, a sensation the body wished to change.

Katharine and Gertie bought their house in 1939, when Katharine's salary had finally returned to its pre-Depression level and the General Hospital had announced firm plans to build a maternity wing. They bought in an area called Bridgeland, north of the river and close to the hospital, because Gertie didn't drive and could easily walk the six blocks in any weather. And Katharine was more than happy to have to buy a car and drive it daily across the Centre Street Bridge and south to Western Canada High School. As she parked, she admired her vehicle next to those of the (primarily) men with whom she worked. Then, on the way home, she usually had enough time to stop off at the grocer's or, preferably, the Bay or the Bon Marché. Having grown up in the country, Katharine's pleasure in department stores was a little like a child's delight at finding herself on the same bus route as Santa's workshop.

That's what she told Gertie by way of explaining her extrava-
gance. Sheets, towels, linen tablecloths, dishes, little things for
Gertie — all were necessary because Gertie didn't like shopping
and didn't know what suited her anyway, and because Katharine
loved her so much, with such secrecy or such understatedness, she
was never sure which. She simply had to make these domestic pur-
chases to counteract the ubiquitous flattening of their pleasure in
one another. "It's like it gets inflated and then pancaked down
again, don't you see? These towels make us real," Katharine would
say, laughing at the ludicrousness of her reasoning.

Gertie never seemed bothered in the same way, didn't really care
if no one knew the story of her love life. "Just as long as I'm happy
and we have our friends and our jobs, what does it matter? Why
make yourself miserable because your colleagues think you're a
spinster? Look at how much better off we are than most people,"
she would lecture.

"I don't know why I care. Sometimes I wish I could just show you
off. I want Mr. Barrow and Mr. Muntz and Mr. Ogilvie to know I have
a wife who's more beautiful and accomplished than any of their plain
little mice. The three plain mice, that's what I think of whenever
their wives are trotted out for the Christmas dinner or the spring
concert. I think, my Gertie would shine by comparison — not that
you need to be compared to plain mice to shine by comparison,
you understand."

"So it's your vanity that's really at stake?"

All right, yes, Katharine Morrissey would agree. She was vain
and competitive, at times a show-off, but what was the point of
showing off if there was no actual show? No show place? Do you
see what I mean?

Not really. But their friend Margaret did, or at least said she did,
once when the three of them (Margaret and her girlfriend, Laura, and
Gertie) had listened to a tirade of Katharine's on the subject of the
announcements in the newspaper: "Births, deaths, engagements,

marriages and the homosexual void," she'd said, "written entirely in invisible ink."

"Yes, it's true," Margaret agreed. "Although you have to admit, it's a little difficult to know when a homosexual's been born."

Margaret could be counted on, still, to summon up that granite-hard Canadian shield of anger and spite, which was why she and Katharine continued to get along in an occasionally hostile way. Just don't use the actual word lesbian around her, Katharine reminded herself; she seems to go into a trance whenever she hears the word, or a full stop, as if it's a telegram she simply won't acknowledge. Oh well. Nobody's perfect.

Births and deaths. Katharine wondered now how many there had been since her arrival in this city some sixty years ago. She read the Announcements, as they were called, every day, got into the habit of being interested in births when Gertie was in maternity and read the deaths because it was a small city really, until after the Second World War. And with the Morrissey heart being what it was, cardiac arrest might be just around the corner. For years Katharine had derived pleasure from mentally scripting her own obituary, changing it daily like a comic strip: Left to mourn, she used to say, seething with repressed rage, is her principal, Mr. Harold Penny, the man who would never, under any circumstances, no matter how much seniority she had, allow Katharine Morrissey to have the large new science room on the second storey, with its view over Seventeenth Avenue.

Katharine never imagined she would be the one to write Gertie's obituary, with her being the close friend left to mourn. But seeing it in the paper, reading it four days in a row — my god, was it really six years ago now? — Katharine had either gone soft or grown to like the euphemism, the euphemistic lifestyle, as she now thought of it. Close friend: what better relationship to claim? What more could there be? Yes, perhaps she was going soft, but the more the culture moved toward frankness and talk and sexual revolution, the more she wanted to keep her story private. Or did she? The problem was she wasn't sure. The problem was fits of melancholia. Because all this new public display of emotion made her not angry but melancholy, made her wish, once in a while, they'd both been born seventy years later. And that made it worse. Wishing you'd been born at a different time was no good.

Perhaps she had always needed something to wish for, and with Gertie around she'd had both the wish and the wishing. She supposed that's what was missing now — wishful thinking, apparently an essential lubricant for her particular mind, needed to keep all parts in good working order. Seemed like for the longest time she'd been stuck in a place she could liken only to a shift change at a factory, that time in between when all the machinery sits still, awaiting a new set of hands, new instructions, another start.

Just as well Julia Raine had come along with her pregnant body. Although the truth was, at first Katharine had hoped the child would be given up, forced into adoption like so many of her students' babies were for so many years. Apparently Katharine Morrissey wanted a certain set of punishing rules to prevail, no matter what she might have said to the contrary. I was lying when I told Julia everything would work out, when I played the kindly old aunt, Katharine thought to herself now. I wanted a price to be paid.

Now that Julia and Peter were moving, Katharine knew she had this to wish for: getting on with it, whatever It might be. The big move, the unknown vestibule, the one last slide along the earth's dimming hallways. Alone again, she could taxi herself out onto the architectural runway of her own living room, watch the lights, check the time, wonder if it was too late now to get her pilot's licence.

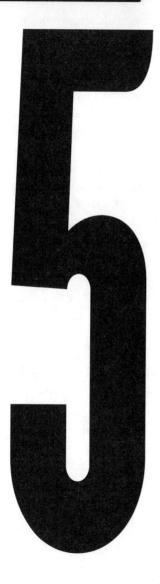

chapter

Traffic was the

uncontrolled variable. Every day
at noon, Julia rushed home from
the university, praying for an
absence of snarls, stalled vehicles and fender-benders in the
westbound lanes of Thirty-
second Avenue. She had to be
there to open the door for Peter
when he arrived home from
school, greeting him in oven
mitts and apron or whatever
domestic costume the principal
at Senator Samuel Higgin-
botham Elementary felt best
befit motherhood. At grade one
orientation, when Julia was told
that students at this school
either went home for lunch or
to one of the approved day
homes in the area, she could

scarcely believe her ears. No lunchroom? No lunch kits? No un-wrapping of sandwiches lovingly prepared by moms who needed to be someplace else when the clock struck twelve? Thought bubbles of incredulous and outraged question marks formed above her attentive skull.

Miss Deluca continued: "We encourage all our students to spend some time at home over the lunch hour with mom — or dad (indulgent smile) — having a good hot lunch before returning to school ready for a busy afternoon. We think families benefit from this opportunity to connect at midday."

Wha-at? Wha-at? More thought bubbles crowded against one another like cells in rapid and mismanaged growth. In search of an eyebrow raised or a cheek sucked in in surprise, Julia cast a beseech-ing eye up and down the row of parents. Nothing but placid expres-sions of nurturing and businesslike concern atop gently inclined necks. That would teach her to move to the perimeter of an area known for its good schools. What had she expected? Good schools were situated in the midst of solid, older, single-family, two-parent dwellings, flanked only on the perimeter of their catchment areas by new and flimsy fourplexes. Had she taken the time to opera-tionalize the adjective "good" as it applied to schools, she would have been better prepared for this startling announcement. But she had not taken that time, and now she was confronted with the dif-ficult reality of no lunch program and a principal with an extra chromosome for conventional family practices.

And why, Julia wondered for some days after the grade one par-ents' night, had Heather Pringle introduced herself and asked her to join that committee? There were the usual social reasons, natu-rally: Julia was relatively new to the area and Heather had lived there for years. But how had she deduced Julia was in desperate need of an in-school lunch program? What had she meant by cred-ibility? Had she seen Julia slip two chocolate chip cookies into her pocket? They were for Peter, she wanted to tell Heather, not for her.

Peter needed something because he hadn't wanted to stay with the neighbour, Bonnie. Again. Julia really didn't appreciate Peter's use of that word and told him so. If she could, Julia told Peter, she would arrange to have him babysat by Santa Claus or Curious George or Raffi, anyone other than Bonnie, who wouldn't allow him to ride his bike because something might happen. She's cautious, that's all: better safe than sorry. Were all conversations with children crammed with platitudes and warnings and simple truths, like an encyclopedia of last words? It seemed that way.

As a parent, Julia made herself tired. She was muttering self-recriminations, resolutions, plans for a thorough mother-son overhaul when Heather approached her. Might her lips possibly have been moving as she stood rather vacantly, rather custodially next to the refreshments? If Heather had noticed, she hadn't been put off and that was a point in her favour. Heather was nice; it was as simple as that. She had extended both hands warmly, taken Julia's hand and said, "I don't think we've met."

"Oh no, we haven't met. I'm Julia Raine. I live in one of those fourplexes on Avalon Drive. Moved in about three years ago." Might as well lay the cards on the table.

"Did you? I've always wondered what those places are like." Heather's interest projected on the screen of Julia's imagination as mild horror seeded with shag carpet, dirt, anthills beneath bare feet.

"Maybe I can show you through mine sometime."

"That would be great. Anyway, I've just been making the rounds here, making a few inquiries, and I'm wondering if you'd be interested in sitting on a committee with me and another gal, Annette Wetherup — that's Annette over there with the shoulder-length blonde hair — to pressure the principal to change this antediluvian lunch business. I swear it's the only school in the city clinging so desperately to the glorious past," said Heather with a roll of her eyes.

"Yes, definitely," Julia agreed, the two words fairly grabbing onto Heather. "I really don't see how I can be home at lunchtime every day. I'm going to school and — " Heather was no longer listening. "Hi Rita. How was Radium?" Oh well. Women like Heather were effusive; that's all Julia would allow herself to think. She had made a resolution not to make judgements pertaining to class or social standing. No, that wasn't entirely it: she could be a participant observer, a social scientist studying social status, but all feelings on the subject were to be drowned at birth. She might comment to herself or write to Pam that Heather resembled the women who drove to the Grain Exchange in their BMWs to buy saffron and dried mushrooms. She might speak those words, but nothing more. Words themselves, without italics and innuendo, were mere bleats and puffs of sound. Let the listener, Pam, be responsible for her own judgements about social stratification and prestige.

"Let's meet at my house on Saturday. Does two o'clock work for you, Julia? Here, I have a card." The magnetized card was now on Julia's refrigerator: "Heather Pringle, BA, 1455 Avalon Crescent, Calgary. Freelance Decorating and Design. By Appointment." Julia wondered whether there was some method other than appointment by which one would engage the services of a freelance decorator/designer.

That was then — late August — and this was now — October 31 — and the committee had been an unqualified failure. Which meant Julia had to get home before Peter to feed him lunch and help him into his Spiderman costume, the outfit he'd changed into every day after school for the past two weeks. Julia might be an unbiased observer of human behaviour, but others were not, and she wished to avoid condemnation by the volunteer mothers at Sam Higginbotham for sending her son to the Halloween party in a cheap plastic outfit from a chain store, ripped at the elbows and knees before the proceedings had even begun. In September she had purchased the fabric and sewn up the costume with all its finicky black trim on Gertie's old machine (now on permanent loan to Julia), fully conscious of motives that Marcia Klinck would have scorned with every cubic centimetre of her irreproachable body. Well, Julia explained limply to Marcia's memory, bad enough that Peter has to live in this ugly fourplex with no real patrilineage. The very least I can do is make him a decent costume. And then came the ringing silence of her room, and she experienced an inarticulate and dog-like longing to crawl on all fours into Peter's room, into his single bed, next to a warm flannel pod of six-year-old skin, and stay there.

Please start, Julia said to the steering wheel of the Oldsmobile as she did every day, please, please start. The Oldsmobile — also now on long-term loan — was getting old but had been 100 percent reliable until the night Julia left the lights on, draining the battery. And Heather Pringle had stopped in the morning to give her a boost, impressing Julia with her knowledge of positive, negative, red and black. "Where did you learn that?" "I have brothers." Julia was grateful, as she was scheduled to make a presentation to Principal Deluca on behalf of the Committee to Change the School Lunch Policy at Senator Samuel Higginbotham Elementary. "Good luck," said Heather. "You have way more credibility than I do."

"Heather Pringle and Annette Wetherup are the other members of your committee?" asked Miss Deluca, no more than twenty minutes later.

"Yes, in fact they are."

"Well, it seems to me, or at least it has in the past, that those two are more concerned with the availability of tee times than the social justice of the school lunch program, and you can tell them I said that."

"So your answer is no."

"My answer is no."

Had Miss Deluca ever experienced the stress of potential ignition problems (the Olds seemed fundamentally weaker since the battery incident) and probable traffic congestion? Did her heart have occasion to race every single working day? Had Miss Deluca even once in her life been required to hurry and rush and worry on account of a vulnerable, dependent body making its way in a separate and unfeeling institution several kilometres away? And if not Miss Deluca, what about Miss Deluca's mother? Had Mrs. Deluca ever stepped out for cigarettes or a dozen eggs while the very young Miss Deluca slept? Not very likely. Mrs. Deluca had been at Miss Deluca's side every minute of the day, every day of the year until she strode off to first grade, a tiny principal without a lunch kit because she would be coming home for lunch, home where Mrs. Deluca waited with a steaming casserole and no experience of car panic.

Varooom. The Oldsmobile Delta Eighty-eight turned over in a burst of eight-valved confidence. Ah, Julia had come to love this car, considered it half living, a distant relative that occupied a spot on the evolutionary chain between dinosaurs and fossil fuels. And she adored the way its white hood and trunk stretched out behind and in front of her, boat-like yes, but more like a float in a parade, regal, if only it were covered in Kleenex flowers. When the Oldsmobile started, it was a dreammobile. She supposed she was her father's daughter after all. The only moment he'd shown much interest during their last phone call was when she told him Katharine had given her the Olds.

"Now that was a car."

"Well it still is, Dad. I mean, I'm driving it right now in the present. I'm not just waxing nostalgic about it."

"You know what I mean. Did Mom tell you we've traded? Got a Thunderbird now."

"Wow. Business must be good."

"Passable. Marcia's given me some ideas. I think she's right on several counts when it comes to this organic stuff. It's what people want right now. There's been a bit of a sea change."

Marcia visited often and had even spoken of moving to Flax with her boyfriend, Sven, a situation that Julia was unsure how to evaluate. She had discussed it in letters with Pam, who felt Marcia's love for Mr. Raine was "intuitively obvious." Having completed a personality sorter at the university counselling services two or three years ago, Pam was now both an intuitive and an extrovert. "The last time I saw Marcia she mentioned your dad three times."

"Don't you think it's time you found some new friends?" Julia asked when she wrote back. "Marcia isn't allowed to be in love with my dad. Any further shame brought upon the family name is unthinkable at this time. Undoubtedly my legacy in Flax is to be remembered as that Raine girl who got herself in the family way, then ran away to Calgary. Nobody's seen her since. And she was friendly with some really nice girls in Mesmer, they'll be saying as they shake their heads in happy dismay."

Pam didn't understand. She might be doing graduate work in chemistry, but she didn't understand that everything changed once you had a child — especially the judgment of social relationships. Which was why she couldn't form an opinion of Heather Pringle or Miss Deluca. Authority figures in particular had changed for Julia soon after Peter's birth. She assumed it was a biological response to any real or perceived threat to her child — which made evolutionary sense. One day when she was driving Katharine around in the Olds — Peter was crying and struggling in his ugly vinyl car seat, Katharine barking directions — and a cop pulled her over for failing to signal a lane change, she had surprised herself with her disrespect. "Oh and you always signal lane changes, do you Officer Milne? You always let people know your intentions? Call your wife when you're going to be ten minutes late?" To which he answered, "That'll cost you seventy-two dollars."

She would never have done that before Peter. Or felt such hostility toward a school principal, suddenly swinging back to smiling approbation in response to Principal Deluca's assessment of

Heather Pringle and Annette Wetherup. She was right: they were a pair of upper-middle-class women of leisure. And yet, Heather had stopped to give her a boost. Would Marcia have done that? Pam, in her simplistic, intuitive, cause-effect universe, knew nothing. Marcia Klinck was not in love with Mr. Raine: this was patently obvious.

Oh no. There was a flashing yellow traffic light at Shaganappi Drive, indicating electrical failure and erratic, backed-up traffic. Now the flow was contingent upon the mood and politeness of drivers travelling in all four directions. Julia could pull over, park and run to her fourplex from here, but this was a no-parking zone. Oh no. Oh no. She had rehearsed with Peter a dozen times what to do if she happened not to be there: go around to the back where the secret key was hidden, unlock the door, come inside and rest assured Mom would arrive soon. But children didn't believe this. They were born with a cynical fear of abandonment.

Jesus. Come on cars. Pam certainly didn't know the meaning of a mother's worry. Worry produced its own DNA, strands of remembrance and anticipation that knit themselves around the vital organs, inhabiting the stomach and constricting the lungs with their woolly grasp. Julia could taste it in her throat as she sat waiting her turn at the four-way stop. Wet laundry, best-before dates, domestic dissonance — so many banal details and objects that might leap up to utter a criticism or two, adding to her worries. "Having a child can certainly increase your anxiety," she had written to Pam. "Very interesting from a biological point of view. My vigilance is likely not much different from that of a black bear."

Which was not entirely true. Did a black bear worry what the neighbours would think or concern itself that Heather Pringle might be driving by just as Peter was unlocking the front door, a latchkey kid? No, a black bear did not entertain such worries. Or wonder why the homes in Avalon Estates and Avalon Village all seemed to have protected doorways, concealed by trellises and caragana hedges, while her doorstep stood concrete and white, visible to all motorists who might comment to themselves on the tragic condition of today's family. Here we have a six-year-old boy letting himself into his own home on Halloween. I'm half tempted to call CKLW's Phone-in-a-Sorry-Sight program and let my views be known on the subject.

What's this? The traffic had begun to move in an orderly fashion. And by 12:07 Julia was home and there was Peter less than a block away. The school was so close, another reason for living in the fourplex, and a volunteer crossing guard made certain the children safely traversed the main thoroughfares. One less worry to purl its bumpy way across Julia's heart.

Peter's cheeks were red with the anticipation of his first real Halloween party and the bliss of his Spiderman costume. Back in kindergarten, the teacher had allowed only nutritious snacks and masks made in class. Together they unlocked the door, Julia a little weak and sick with the happiness invested in her by this boy and the enormity of his possible disappointment. Had she not been there to meet him, two big plugs would have been pulled from the soles of his feet, draining him away. Julia couldn't bear to think of that.

~ ~ ~ ~

Julia was waiting for Mary Nordstrom to show up in exactly the same way she used to wait in her dormitory room for Pam to arrive. An unordinary kind of waiting, too eager, like someone scraping ice from windows, melting peepholes with her breath and enjoying the cold frost beneath her nails. Thursday nights Mary had her real estate class, which was held not far from Stirrups, the enormous Western-style bar where Julia waitressed part time, mainly for the tips. She was following Harvey's advice, studying urban sociology, but with only student loan money and one teaching assistantship, she had to supplement her income — either that or share accommodation, which she would consider only as a last resort. At twenty-five years, independence was her most valued possession, and she protected it as if it were tangible, as if the fourplex were a small plot of land. She and Peter even called it "the ranch." She was not about to subdivide it.

Bonnie preferred to babysit for cash rather than trade on nights when Julia worked. Her husband David was at home with their daughter, so she could stay late and fall asleep on Julia's couch if she wanted, though she never did. Bonnie liked getting out of the house, she said. And she liked snooping through Julia's possessions, Julia knew, having set traps for her — tiny scraps of paper or threads atop stacks of bills or underwear. The following day, the bait was always missing or moved. In fact, Julia enjoyed Bonnie's snooping. The fact that Bonnie wouldn't turn up anything salacious or questionable — a pornographic movie or magazine, even a tube of KY lubricant or a battery-operated device — made Julia feel clean all over, like being rushed to the hospital in her newest underwear. Bonnie could look and look, she could rearrange furniture, lift floorboards, disassemble the bed, but she would find nothing, because a good and appropriate parent lived in that fourplex. If the city vice squad or sanitation departments were doing their jobs, they would give plaques of recognition to people like Julia Raine, she told herself one day, only half jokingly.

Stirrups offered only one point of entry for the public, a door opening onto Eleventh Avenue. Julia watched it with furtive pleasure, a pleasure that, in a moment of drunkenness, she had described to her two best friends at school as one of the greatest pleasures in her life. Then she had asked Harvey, who remembered more about learning theory than she ever would, to please explain this phenomenon.

"Well," he said, "it's all about random schedules of reinforcement, the most powerful of the rewarding consequences — what we see in gambling addictions and the belief in rabbits' feet. I think the pleasure of anticipating your pleasure builds and builds, and then when the desired event happens, you're rewarded for waiting for a reward. Do you see what I mean?"

"But aren't we missing the main point here?" a woman named Celeste interrupted. "Which is, what is so pleasurable about Mary Nordstrom?"

"I don't exactly know," Julia said, knowing exactly, but also not. Her interest in Mary was a road sign, readable by its shape rather than its message, blurred by rain.

"Well, it's fairly obvious. You have a crush on this Mary Nord-strom. You're not looking for her to show up after her real estate class because you want to borrow her notes."

Celeste, largish and six feet two, seemed able to function as a transmission tower for the patently evident. Pronouncements were broadcast.

"I might be," Julia said. "The psyche works in mysterious ways. Ask Harvey."

They were at Julia's house and had drunk enough so that Celeste's girlfriend had to pick her up, communicating her annoyance and sizing up Julia as if she were possibly radioactive. And Harvey had to leave his car, returning for it the next day, pale and hung over, his hair sticking to one side of his head. Julia had hoped they'd both forget the entire discussion, but that was unlikely, they were both such colossal gossips. Celeste now asked occasional but darkly important questions about Mary, raising her eyebrows above her glasses. Julia raised her eyebrows even higher. Declining to answer, Julia raised her eyebrows even higher. "Harvey keeps asking what's going on," was Celeste's rejoinder.

Mary's class was over at ten and it was now ten-fifteen. The very latest she had ever come was ten forty-five, when she had stayed behind to ask the instructor a few questions. What were the complexities of retailing houses? Julia wondered. Were realtors tested on the durability of various furnace brands or roofing materials? Were they required to write short essay answers on the benefits of berber carpet? Julia wished she could invoke a rule similar to the one she had set for Pam: if you can't be here by eleven, don't bother showing up at all.

Good thing she had this job to keep her busy and smiling, as if she were having a fabulous time carrying trays of beer and sweet mixed drinks. Always smile: this was the first law of waitressing. If you were serving a group of women, smile in a circular motion at each and every one of them before starting with the order at twelve o'clock and moving clockwise with deft and unerring efficiency. With couples, smile at the women first, then be businesslike with the men. Never be overly friendly unless serving a group of men, in which case you might venture some sisterly camaraderie, locate that narrow seam where a sister might be understood as someone with sexual leanings. Anything overt and they'd call you a slut, and sluts don't deserve good tips because sluts perform services for free. This seemed to be the logic, as Julia had divined it. Laugh at all jokes. Mary might walk in at that moment and notice Julia and suggest lunch, or a ride in her Oldsmobile or a weekend in Banff. Hard to say what.

What was it about Mary Nordstrom anyway? She was a friend, nothing more. Helpful, but so was Bonnie. Mary knew more about child rearing because she was nine years older and her sister was a nurse and her husband a veterinarian. And she was kind, right from when they first met in the hospital. During those first lonely months when Julia felt as if she'd been let out of a warm elevator at the top of a mountain and left to slide and tumble her way down with nothing but frozen roots to grab onto, Mary had offered a shoulder to cry on. Katharine didn't know anything about babies, and her mother's advice over the phone was disembodied, miles and lakes and grasslands away from Peter and his topography. So when Peter was younger, Mary had been a surrogate mother, almost, or a sister.

Now Julia thought of her more as a husband, calling on Mary

when appliances refused to work or the smoke detector wouldn't stop screaming. Mary always had a useful suggestion and once even arrived with a toolbox and fixed a light switch for her. That had the same swooping effect as the sight of Pam in a lab coat. Julia had said, "It's too bad you and Lenny can't qualify for a federal or provincial stipend for your interventions on my behalf," which offended Mary and she said so, meaning Julia had to apologize. The next time there was a problem, Mary was too busy to even think about coming over: maybe Julia should consider calling Fortress Appliance. But now everything was back to normal, with Peter and Julia invited for dinner once in a while and Julia reciprocating when she could afford it. If she had anything to drink, she felt an irrepressible urge to disclose Mary's virtues to Lenny, urging him to appreciate her charm and beauty and versatility. Julia made strict rules for herself: only one lavish tribute to Mary per evening.

Ten forty-five. Might as well accept Mary was not about to show up. She was likely at home already, climbing into bed with Lenny. Julia couldn't remember if her last order was for a rum and orange juice or a rum and coke. As far as she was concerned, all mixed drinks were a ridiculous and syrupy waste of time. As was this job. She was nothing more than a purveyor of poisons, legal opiates to numb the masses into accepting their miserable and meaningless existences. She should be at home with Peter; really, she should. Nothing caused her quite as much anxiety, not even the race home at noon, as leaving him on Thursday and Friday nights when he seemed to want her the most. The force and fury of maternal anxiety was amazing. It might even cause insulators to explode on electrical equipment outside Stirrups, or bring on tornadoes and lightning, so that the manager, Gus, would have to close the bar and send everyone home.

Or this, dear god. Julia had never once imagined Heather Pringle dropping in some night. Yet there she was with Annette Wetherup and both their husbands, out for a post-hockey drink perhaps. Julia wasn't sure how she ended up in the back explaining to Gus that she was suddenly so sick she had to leave. Here was her float, she was so sorry but she didn't want to vomit on any of the clients. "Yeah, yeah, go home," Gus said, but he wasn't happy. Well tough. Julia wasn't going to serve Heather and Annette while enduring their ironic observations on Stirrups and their questions about Peter. As if he were out in the car with his nose pressed to the freezing window, which is what they would think.

Julia was going home. The Oldsmobile started and she was going home. See, it could happen. Maternal stress could collect electrostatically or meteorologically and shape the course of events — rattle the synapses in Heather Pringle's mind until she said, "Let's go to Stirrups after the game. I hear it's a real blast," — hurling Julia out the back employees' door and home to Peter where she wanted to be.

It was the middle of November and the streets were empty already, as if the earth had tipped a little too far from the sun and everyone had slipped off its icy surface. No, just Thursday night and all sensible people were in bed. Bonnie would still be up. Like every night when Julia got home, she'd ask, "When are you going to get cable?"

~ ~ ~ ~

Julia was considering writing her thesis on "Cultural Responses to the Celibate in Late-Twentieth-Century North America." Subjects willing to volunteer their opinions were plentiful, and with the trend to qualitative statistical analysis, she could submit video-taped interviews with many of her acquaintances as data. This would also formalize the process of Katharine's, Mary's, Celeste's and even Harvey's tyrannical interest in and concern for Julia's missing sex life. As Christmas approached, they seemed increasingly determined to corral her into some construct of romantic love.

Thus far, she wanted to tell them, occurrences of muscle weakness in both legs had been the only outcome. When the phone rang, sometimes her legs wouldn't carry her to it. Other times, her voice told Peter not to answer, it was likely someone canvassing.

"What's that?"

"People asking for donations for organizations that need money."

"Like the Humane Society?" They had a week ago made the mistake of visiting, just to look, and had come home with Popeye, the one-eyed mutt they couldn't afford.

"Yes."

"But if we don't give them any money, all the dogs will have to be killed."

She shouldn't have taken him there, or told him that. She could actually watch his small head swell with imagined horrors when he learned the animals that weren't adopted would be put to sleep. But she didn't like to lie to him, and he had asked. What was she supposed to do? So now he insisted on answering the phone. Luckily it was only Katharine.

"What are you doing this weekend?"

"I'm not sure really."

"Well do you want me to keep Peter for you?" This was her way of saying you must get out and find a sexual partner; I will not rest until you have performed this duty.

"Actually," Julia said, "I thought I might take Peter to Heritage Park this weekend. Do you want to come along?"

"No thank you. I lived heritage before it became a park. You don't see people my age at Heritage Park, do you? That's because we'd rather forget about freezing in our sod huts and dropping dead with bacterial infections."

Now she was crabby because Julia was not making the appropriate effort. "You should get out more. You're only twenty-five. My god, when I was your age we were going off to Banff for the weekend and staying at the hotel. Have you ever even been to the Cave and Basin?"

"Yes, I have."

"Oh fine, I'll come to Heritage Park with you."

And Celeste was worse. Her attention was like a psychology experiment from the late nineteenth century, something electro-convulsive involving a snug-fitting cap and wires that conveyed the subliminal instruction "Become a lesbian now." She wanted to have a dinner party for Julia, a kind of coming-out celebration.

"But I'm not coming out."

"Well, you will be soon."

"Then can it be an I-might-be-coming-out-later-in-this-decade dinner party?"

"I don't think that would work."

"Oh, Celeste," Julia whined, "can't I just not be interested in either sex for a while? I've told you, I had sex once and the result was Peter. Not a bad consequence, but traumatizing in its own way. I talked to Harvey about it and he said it was the opposite of antic-ipating Mary at Stirrups, it created a constant schedule of punish-ment." Julia kept her voice down because Peter was in the next room watching television. "He said an analogy would be flying in an airplane the first time and crash landing. Or eating sushi for the first time and getting food poisoning. Anyway, I know what I have to do. Harvey says I have to have a sexual experience with birth control and screening for sexually transmitted disease in order to establish a pleasurable association with sex and eliminate the pun-ishment schedule."

"Well, you won't eliminate it, sweetheart. That'll never happen."

"What do you mean?"

"Never mind. How about a mixed dinner party then? I'll invite my straight friends Kim and Morgan, and it won't have any ritual importance."

"Which is which of Kim and Morgan?"

"What do you mean?"

"Remind me again: Is Kim the man or the woman?"

"What does it matter?"

Julia was actually avoiding Celeste at school, staying away from the graduate student offices and reading at home. Christmas was just six weeks away, and now even Mary was trying to match Julia up. Sean, Mary's eldest sister's son, was at loose ends. Mary thought Julia would like him; they had things in common.

At loose ends. What did that mean? To be at loose ends most certainly meant romantically unattached, but not all single people were at loose ends. Could it mean unemployed? Ill? Who in Julia's experience might be considered at loose ends? She thought instantly of a teacher at Sam Higginbotham who had recently gone on stress leave and was last seen sitting in her car in the school parking lot, wearing sunglasses on a gloomy November afternoon. Her pained expression suggested that white light was pulling her apart like a giant seam ripper. At loose ends meant unravelling in your Ford Gremlin.

It turned out Sean wasn't on stress leave. He was an artist and at the university, so he decided to drop by and introduce himself to Julia. Lucky to find her in, no doubt. She was likely pretty busy.

Sean was thin as a rail and stooped in the manner of a self-conscious adolescent who is a foot taller than everyone else. His long hair was pushed behind his ears, and round, thick glasses magnified his eyes. Did he want to grab a coffee somewhere? No, he had heard from Mary that Julia had contacts with the city. "You're into all this neighbourhoods for people stuff and the urban landscape, she told me. That kind of thing?"

"I know people who know people in the planning department, not much else. I can introduce you to my friend Harvey. He's on an educational leave from the city and he seems to know everyone."

"Well here's my situation," Sean said. "Now don't make any

laughing sounds or change your facial expression in any way when
I say this, because I'll notice. I'm an artist and I have an idea for
some stumps down by the zoo. They've just been left there by the
city crews — maybe you've seen them near the west entrance? OK,
now get ready, here's the second part: I'm not only an artist, I'm a
chainsaw artist. I bet my aunt didn't tell you that. Anyway, I want
to chainsaw those stumps into sculptures."

Julia searched for some resemblance to Mary in this nephew,
found none. "Let's see if Harvey's in," she said. And he was.

Within days Sean had met the city arborists and obtained con-
sent from them to do whatever he wanted with the stumps, on the
understanding that they might disappear at any time because
there were a lot of crews and sometimes the right hand didn't
know what the left hand was doing. Sean called to thank Julia and
asked how he could possibly make it up to her. Would she go out
for dinner with him? Of course.

The next day, Julia, Harvey and Celeste drove past the stumps to
have a look. "He's really sweet," Julia said, feeling that she was now
the antithesis of "at loose ends." The afternoon sun was warming
even those parts of her covered by clothing, causing a shedding of
all loose ends. She's a really together person — that's what they
would say of her now.

For their dinner date, Julia and Sean went to a Mexican restaurant and talked about travel, of which Julia had done very little.
One minute her eyelids were heavy, the next they were raised in
attentive concentration. Was she the round-eyed girl with the
pageboy hairdo from the grade seven health text? The one thinking in her thought bubble: I'd better read up on the football game
before Russ picks me up? Possibly.

A walk to the stumps was planned for their second date, followed by a return walk to Sean's apartment for a bottle of wine and
enthusiastic talk of a living, breathing city of the future. Julia pro-
fessed her undying love for Jane Jacobs. Two condoms were used in

vigorous acts of grateful sex. If Julia hadn't introduced Sean to Harvey Gill, his career would be at a standstill; now people would begin to pay attention.

The following day, Julia felt over-thanked and sore, but untraumatized. The condoms had not broken; pregnancy was unlikely. She was a little hung over, her nipples felt tender, but other than that, she was unsure of what she felt. She wished she could raise an antenna from the crown of her skull to receive a radio wave instruction on the correct emotional response to this situation. She even positioned herself near the kitchen radio for a while and then lingered by the Oldsmobile's aerial, but reception was poor.

Answers to very concrete questions would have been appreciated, but the magic eight ball was no help. Should she call Sean? *Better not tell you now.* Would he call her? *Ask again later.* Were they dating? *My sources say no.* Why had she told Celeste, Harvey and Mary she was "seeing" Sean? She had no idea if she was seeing Sean or not, or what that might imply. Was she that desperate to participate in a Sears-catalogue-cover Christmas scene, the two of them in bathrobes, with Sean assembling a bicycle?

Well, she liked Sean and his ideas. She had even dreamed about a tree stump sculpture of Mary Nordstrom as a large-limbed Picasso woman with a towel over her shoulder, walking to the pool. This was frankly haywire, dreaming of Sean's aunt rather than him, having a crush on Mary while no amount of wistful languishing at her desk could effect even the tiniest crush on Sean. Julia liked Sean; he was the person she imagined her brother might become. That was a stumbling block. And Sean's relationship to Mary made the entire affair a little off-colour, a little hard on the stomach.

Should she call him? Not to call would be rude. Four rings and a feeble voice answered. He had the flu; he might die. Had she heard about the virulent new strain called Moscow-B? Yes, she had, so she would make him some soup. That was how someone who loved someone might behave: take time off school, buy a few chicken necks to make stock, add barley, vegetables and ultimately a bouillon cube, be at home in a vapour cloud of soup smells when son arrived for lunch. Julia felt as though she were being appliquéd onto the fabric of Canadian domestic experience by a smoothly whirring sewing machine. Christmas was coming.

After lunch, Julia poured the soup into a Mason jar and drove to Sean's apartment. "Come in." His voice sounded as if he were auditioning for the part of a dying swan. She called out that she'd made him soup. "Just leave it on the counter." Julia followed the voice into Sean's bedroom, where he lay in a confusion of dark plaid blankets brightened by feverish eyes. He looked terrible. "I know," he said. "I can't really talk. When I'm sick I can't talk, but you can stay a while if you want. Be advised the place is crawling with Moscow-B."

"I should probably just go," Julia said, staying for a moment to examine the bed, the site of her detraumatization. She felt nothing. No indication of how this room might later show up on a satellite image of her mind. "Yes, I should probably just go."

Everyone was making social offers. When Julia arrived home she found two invitations in the mail and had to rush to the phone in her snowy boots and exclaim, "That would be great." Katharine had called wondering if she wanted to bring her friend along when she and Peter came for dinner next weekend.

Celeste's invitation read: "I'm having a dinner party on the eighteenth. Mixed. You can bring Sean if you want, but not Mary, like you did last year." And Harvey's said: "Joan and I are having a little get-together on the twentieth. Please bring the chainsaw artist; we have a rather unsightly poplar in the back."

Why had she been so eager to tell everyone about Sean and insist they drive past the stumps? How adolescent of her — broadcasting the news as if she were the first human on the planet to be asked out on a date. This was all Mary Nordstrom's fault. She'd better call her and obtain some clarification as to what exactly Sean's intentions might be. "Hi Mary." A few preliminaries and then, "What has Sean told you about me?"

"Sean told me? Sean tells me next to nothing. About ten years ago he told me he won a public speaking contest, but since that disclosure, the news has dried up. Twenty-four-year-old nephews don't usually confide in their elderly aunts. Is there something he should have told me?"

"No, of course not. I don't know what I'm talking about. He's very nice. I'm glad to have met him."

"Good then. You two might want to attend the Nordstrom Christmas affair. It'll be here on the twenty-third. The tradition is drinks, food, and then, usually beginning around eleven, verbal abuse from Donalda's husband, Richard. This forces everyone to leave by midnight."

"OK, I'll ask."

You two? When had she become "you two"? Julia was suddenly aware of a low-grade headache that might signal the beginning of a serious bout of Moscow-B. Actually it wasn't so much an ache as a crowded sensation in her head accompanied by a dull anxiety surrounding sexual performance. Why hadn't Sean called? This was compelling proof she was a dud in bed.

As Julia skimmed over her memories of that night, certain moments appeared in boldface — eye-catching, ominous and shuddery. Her surprise at the absence of pain had inspired grateful moans of simulated passion, followed by a half-orgasm, or maybe it was a pre-orgasm. Without a doubt, Sean had noticed. Shouldn't her rhythmic and powerful contractions have been heightening his pleasure too? But she had spent far too much time worrying. Worrying that Sean might suggest impossible positions or insist she participate in a dialogue of dirty talk. Maybe she should have said something sexy like "Ride me hard, you stallion." In the end she concluded it had been a serviceable act of coupling. He had wanted to thank her, and she had wanted to have a sexual experience unconnected to pregnancy. With any luck she had had that. While still in his bed, she had begun to visualize the scene as a science movie narrated by a white-coated man. Here the male enters the female, followed by illustrations of capillary action in the penis, seminiferous tubules and an arrow indicating the position of the ovum. She used to like the darkened science room at Mesmer High when films were part of the lesson plan, was reminiscing fondly about the gas taps and the long black desks when she found herself on the road to an orgasm. "Aaah," said Sean, collapsing. Oh well.

Prior to Sean, Julia hadn't been bothered by so many psycho/social/sexual issues, to use Harvey's word. She had been content with her Spartan life consisting of graduate school, Peter and thinking about Mary Nordstrom at Stirrups. She hadn't thought of buying *Cosmopolitan* to read articles titled "Why She'll Say Yes to Everything this Month" or "X-rated Xmas Surprises." Then the phone rang.

It was Sean. He had managed to drag himself out of bed to eat some of her fabulous soup and wanted to let her know how much better he felt as a result. Oh no, more gratitude. And he wanted her to know he'd like to see her again, soon. Which would be great, but Julia thought she might be coming down with the Moscow-B herself, and Peter had looked a little flushed this morning. But she was glad the soup was good and she would call as soon as she felt better.

The phone book was right there in the drawer. Travel agencies — there were plenty. "We have several charters," said the voice of Colleen. "Can I quote you some prices?" And Julia's credit card had enough space for two return flights to Toronto. She'd pay it off over the next year somehow.

~ ~ ~ ~

Nerves were frayed all round. By December twenty-fourth the Raine house, that is, the structure itself, the bricks and mortar, might have asked for a drink or a pill had it a voice to do so. Julia pictured the snapping and short-circuiting of wires behind plaster, pipes disassembling and clattering to floorboards, floods, possible electrocution and then nothing but smithereens. If Harvey were here she would ask him how much emotional pressure was required to explode the average North American home. At least now, with Marcia and Sven gone, a valve had opened and some of the load was released, only to be replenished by the worrisome calls to Katharine. Why couldn't she just stay in the house like a normal eighty-nine-year-old? Each time she didn't answer, another of Julia's larger nerves aged and weakened.

The arrangement was that Julia was to call every other day to check on Katharine — "check on" being a euphemism for "was she still breathing?"

"To check will make very little difference if I'm dead," Katharine had once said. "And if I happen to have broken my hip and feel obliged to drag myself to the phone, then what? Irreversible bone damage. Canes, walkers, extended care. I know the sequence."

"Oh you know what I'm saying, and I'm not going to get drawn into this discussion," Julia had said with finality. "If there's no answer, I'll call someone to come and check on you."

"There it is again. That verb 'to check.' Seems it can't be avoided. And who might you have in mind as this … checker?"

"Obviously your neighbour would be the logical choice."

"Phil? Not him. No thank you. And how did you get his phone number? You've been making arrangements behind my back, haven't you? I can see we should have discussed these details long ago because I don't want Phil checking on me. If I happened to be dead, he'd take my camera. He's wanted it for years. He'd probably take it even if I were lying there conscious but immobilized, following him around the room with my eyes. He'd dangle it over my head and make taunting sounds. Don't send anyone. I'm happy to wait for you; I don't care if you're in Australia. Promise me you won't send anyone."

Julia had learned to agree to all of Katharine's demands; there was no use arguing. "All right, all right. I promise." And then there'd been a silence. They were on the phone; the wires transmitted nothing but Katharine's breathing, which spooked Julia. She viewed breathing as an account on which Katharine could only make so many more withdrawals. Breathe in, breathe out. Don't waste your breath, she wanted to say, but that was absurd; you couldn't save it, really.

"Does it worry you, having to check on me, as you put it?"

"A little. I've never had to deal with any situations involving emergencies."

"Just do me a favour and don't go all dramatic and be sick in the toilet," Katharine answered. "Don't imagine you're on a stage. Don't press the back of your hand to your mouth like an actress in a silent movie. When you find me dead, think of it as just an abandoned bag of bones, my bag of bones. No, better yet, think of it as luggage."

"But most likely you'll be in a hospital anyway ..."

"No, I don't think so."

The luggage conversation had taken place more than a year ago, when Julia and Peter had gone to Vancouver with Celeste. Since then, frequent reference had been made to it. "When you find my luggage, stay with it for a while. Don't be afraid to touch it. It would be nice, actually, if you made yourself some tea and sat for a while before you started calling all the men in lab coats, and so on."

"Yes, I'll do whatever you ask," Julia always said, and didn't say, I'm not a trained health care worker you know. And on the actual subject of death, I don't do well.

The night of December twenty-second she had made her usual call at ten o'clock eastern, eight o'clock mountain time, and there was no answer. The way her knees and ankles reacted — softening into a substance that might be spreadable with a putty knife — she knew she couldn't be trusted to behave professionally or believe any stories about luggage.

But the next morning Katharine answered on the second ring. She'd gone out to a movie by herself, wanted to see *California Suite*.

"Why do you do that sort of thing when I'm out of town?" Julia asked. "You never go to movies when I'm in Calgary. It's to scare me, isn't it?"

"Oh don't be ridiculous."

"But you never do that sort of thing unless I'm someplace else calling you. And you shouldn't walk that far."

"I took a cab."

"I don't care; it's dangerous."

"Dangerous? The mean streets of Calgary, Alberta? Cabs?"

"You know what I mean."

"No, I don't, in actual fact. Anyway, how's your mother?" And they'd managed a decent conversation. With the only telephone in the kitchen, unreserved conversation was generally difficult, but today everyone except Peter and Stephen was out.

Julia's mom had gone to see Eugenia Wilde. The Wildes had moved back to Flax, though not Lois, who was living in Ottawa and working as a feminist mechanic. Marcia and Sven had been practically living at the Raines' for the past few days, with Julia's dad cooking and her mom refusing to have anything to do with the kitchen. Marcia and Sven and now Abraham Raine had philosophical objections to ornamentals and their assembly-line production, so Franny had to do all the work with the poinsettias and amaryllis. She was worn-out and had constructed a den for herself in the basement, using an old floor lamp, a stained paisley print armchair and an ashtray on a stand. Julia wasn't sure, but her mother seemed to be smoking more. And in order to interact equitably with all camps and have some time to herself, Julia constantly had to move between all three levels of the house. She felt as if she were in a department store without escalators or merchandise.

Her only solace was that Sven seemed a little torn as well. Or maybe he simply liked companionship while smoking, because he was spending more than a little time in the basement den while Marcia and Julia's dad were in the greenhouses. Sven had knee problems and could only stand for so long, physician's orders, and this seemed to be creating tension. Maybe his knees would be a little more robust if he didn't subject them to nicotine poisoning, Marcia had said. It deposits in the joints, she was pretty sure. Thank god they'd all be leaving; then maybe things would return to normal.

Which they had not, but there'd been no opportunity yet to discuss this with Katharine. The morning of the twenty-fourth, Julia's mom was up out of the basement, hoping for TNT and a detonator in her stocking so she could blow up the unsold stock of poinsettias. She'd never had this problem before that new operation opened in Sussex County; everyone knew there wasn't enough business in the area to support so much industry. And then to everyone's horror she cried a few reluctant tears. "Let's all have a rum and eggnog," said Julia's dad. Julia watched and wondered how many years those tears had been stashed in their ducts. Hard to put an age on salt water.

"It's not easy for your mom," her dad said when they drove to Mesmer for a couple of last-minute items. "This is the first Christmas Grandpa Corrigan won't be here. He's too far gone to come out of the home, doesn't know where he is or who anybody is. He thinks your mother is Aunt Katharine and bellows at her to stop dressing like a man. And with the greenhouse business changing, that's been hard too. Your mother likes things to stay the same, but that's simply not possible in this day and age."

"She and Sven seemed to hit it off."

"Poor Sven. I don't know if you've noticed, but he doesn't have a whole lot of oomph."

Julia half expected to find cavernous holes in place of the greenhouses when she and her dad returned from Mesmer, every bit of glass TNT-ed from the earth's old mouth. But the buildings stood as always in years past, except for the barn, which at last lay in neat collapse beneath a loaf of snow. Inside, Peter and Stephen were helping her mom make shortbread, all three of them appearing almost joyful. Christmas at last. "Deck the halls," Julia said. She had made her mother a grandmother, precipitously and illegitimately, and introduced Marcia Klinck to Flax and her father, thus destroying her parents' business partnership and maybe their marriage. This combination of guilts, along with Katharine's lonely frailty and unpredictable telephone habits, had kneaded themselves and risen against the interior of Julia's skin with such rubbery strength that she was surprised not to find herself covered in balloonish eruptions when she looked in the mirror. The very least she could do was sing a carol or two. "Fa la-la-la-la. Should we call Katharine tonight?"

~ ~ ~ ~

Boxing Day night Katharine hadn't answered. There was no way she would go to two movies in one week, unless she was playing a mind game with Julia, which wasn't beyond the realm of the possible. In Julia's relations with Katharine she had learned there was no age limit to that sort of chicanery. Julia had gone away over Christmas without warning, so some punishment from Katharine was to be expected sooner or later, most likely sooner. And Julia had been so much looking forward to saying "See you tomorrow, I can't wait to be back, I'll have you over for dinner on the weekend" — but there had been that terrible ringing sound again. Ring, ring, ring, ring, ring. Answer for god's sake. Should she call Phil? No, she had promised not to. Oh she was likely in the tub, or maybe even just next door. Even though she claimed to detest Phil, occasionally he had her in for a drink. He really didn't want Katharine's camera. Dammit, how long was Julia expected to let this thing ring? She'd call in the morning.

But the next morning had been such a rush, with her mother

making turkey sandwiches, and what if there was no answer? What if? She wouldn't say anything because she didn't want to leave in a geyser of anxiety just when peace had been established and Sven and Marcia weren't expected back until after New Year's. She'd call Katharine from the airport. But they'd missed the exit and been late for the plane, said goodbyes at the departures drop-off in freezing weather and diesel fumes. A bus drove by just as her mother said something from the far side of the car — she was driving home — but Julia couldn't catch it. Maybe I'll come out west one of these days? Maybe it would be best if you stayed? She didn't know. They had to get going. Had to get going.

"Doesn't the lake look cold, Mom?" Peter said as the plane roared skyward, circling the water, heading west. At last. "What's that lake called?"

"Ontario."

"Seems like everything's called Ontario here."

"Not quite everything."

"I wish we could stay. I could help out in the greenhouses and go to school on the bus. Oh look, there's a boat. It looks like in 'Battleship.' I liked playing that with Stephen," Peter said, looking out the window at the bug-sized boats and buildings until the airplane pierced the shell-blue sky above the clouds. Then he read comics, old *Spiderman* and *Batman* issues culled from the Raine collection. Perfectly happy, replete with turkey, much like the bald head occupying the seat ahead of her, Julia surmised. All these heads travelling together and not one could possibly be as sick with worry as she was. Could we please speed it up a little? She would have liked to grab the public address system from the stewardess and order them all to worry along with her. Get this crate into fifth gear, why don't you, Captain Beliveau?

What was she going to do? She couldn't possibly ask Bonnie to keep Peter while she went to check on Katharine, not after seven days with Popeye. No, she'd call Mary and hope she could drive over. She wanted to see Mary anyway. What about the Oldsmobile? Katharine had said they'd had warm weather, one long chinook, so it would likely start. But what would she do if Katharine were dead? What would she do? She didn't know. The thought seemed to open a trapdoor in her stomach through which her whole self hurtled, as if from this very aircraft. She didn't know. Surely some deeply stored biological response would provide direction. Do this, call there, touch that. She had never touched a dead person, only seen both Raine grandparents in their velvety coffins, one after the other, six months apart. No amount of hoping they might blink, sit up and say it was just a joke had made a difference. You could flood every synapse in your brain with hope, allow the neurotransmitters to leak from your eyes and drench your clothing, but death wouldn't even twitch. OK, let's not overreact. Chances are Katharine was out or not answering just to be contrary. Chances are …

Ding-dong. Ding-dong. Ding-dong. No answer. Ding-dong. Ding-dong. Was the deeply stored biological response about to identify itself? Was it shifting in its chair like a contestant on "To Tell the Truth"? No, Julia wasn't ready for this. She had wanted a hospital scene, not this. Now the key was in the lock and the door was open and she knew, right away she knew, because the place didn't smell alive. Not that it smelled bad exactly, but her nose had relayed the message to some deeply articulate place where preparations were already underway, where the news was old and read and faded before it had even gone to print. Come in, come in, a voice was saying from the mechanics of necessity housed someplace behind her nose, beneath her eyes. Look, she's not on the floor. She wouldn't have gone away without saying; she couldn't have taken the bus to Banff. Impossible. She's not in the kitchen or the bathroom and that leaves the bedroom. That leaves the bedroom.

The door was ajar and needed only to be pushed open. There. No resistance, not even a creak, because Katharine was the sort of person who oiled hinges annually, every March. Yes, she was that sort of person. Was would be the appropriate tense from now on.

She was on her side, beneath the blankets, facing away from Julia, toward the window. Motionless in the same way Grandpa and Grandma Raine had been, motionless like objects invested with some terrible incongruity, objects that had vanished but remained visible. How could that be? Made you want to shake your head hard, slap your own forehead, push inward on those sockets until you said waah, waah, like a baby. But there were to be no dramatics. That was the instruction.

Take the little mirror from the dresser and hold it to her nose; check for breathing. She may have had a stroke, may be unconscious. No, apparently not. She was dead and that was that. With a very deep breath, Julia cleared a passage to that bulb of human knowledge that understood death is part of life. Here's the luggage metaphor, now get on with it.

The shopping Katharine had done over the past couple of years had paid off: as planned, the pale blue pyjamas looked good against the yellow sheets. She never wore anything to bed that clashed with the sheets; the aesthetics should be pleasing for those who had to find her. She wanted people to say she looked lovely, really, just as lovely as in life. Same with the brown tweed suit she had recently purchased. "Were I to crumple onto the floor, this would look good against it, don't you think?" she had said, laughing.

Should Julia perform CPR? No, that would destroy the look, and also it was too late, ridiculously late to go hammering on such an old sternum. The way the living go at things. Katharine would already think like the dearly departed; as a rule she wasted no time in adapting to circumstances beyond her control. Had she been dead when the phone rang Boxing Day night? Or had she heard and not answered, not wanting her death to be interrupted?

What Julia had been told to do was to make some tea and stay a while before making any calls. She hoped her obedience could be observed from where Katharine was now. Luggage or no luggage, whichever metaphor you chose, the place was now haunted — or totemized might be a better word for it. The interior of the fridge, for example, jumping to light like that, the one litre of milk, the teapot upside down in the draining rack. Last will — there was a phrase Julia had never before considered, but here it was all around her. And testament.

Katharine had never bought an electric kettle, insisting they gave the water a wiry taste. All water should be boiled over a flame, she'd come down the hall any minute to explain again. Food should be cooked over a flame also. People with electric stoves have an anemic look to them; I could pick them out of a crowd. Bet you'd be right nine times out of ten.

Maybe Julia should call Mary. No, make tea first. Now her hands were in an odd state. She had reached for the cups with unreliable joints, as if they were being held together with small bits of Chiclets. Don't get two cups, for heaven's sake. If there was one thing Katharine couldn't bear, it was that sort of maudlin, sentimental behaviour. When Margaret's friend Laura died, she persisted in setting an extra plate for her and sobbing into her table napkin until Katharine told her, "Laura is not the unseen guest at every meal; she is not. She has bigger fish to fry now, and you have to get on with your own smaller ones."

Did Katharine have bigger fish to fry already? Where would she be by now? One had to think these thoughts because gone was not a readily understood term in the mind's glossary. She'd be out tidying alleys by now, that's where she'd be, swooping down on the messiest because she could not bear a mess. Although she disliked the cold with equal intensity. Maybe she'd be on her way to the Bay downtown. Katharine had applied for a job in the linen department a few years ago and been turned down, politely. "I suppose I am too old," she'd said, but she had been disappointed. That would be her first destination: folding, arranging and displaying, and possibly seeking some small revenge.

This cup of tea was not going to taste very good. Julia thumped her forehead onto the kitchen table in a too-vigorous display of disappointment. Ouch. What was she supposed to do without Katharine bossing her around and delivering judgements? And what on earth was that? Oh, the telephone. The telephone shouldn't ring in the houses of the deceased. You would think out of respect the utilities would be disconnected automatically at the moment of death, but apparently not.

"Hello. Oh hi Mary. I'm sorry I didn't call." She couldn't bring herself to say the four-letter word meaning the opposite of alive, so Mary would have to ask her twenty questions. Well, only two. "Yes. No. No, I'm having some tea before I call the ambulance; that's what Katharine wanted. What do you mean, the coroner? The coroner will have to come? Well, will it look suspicious, me sitting here drinking tea? I have to follow her wishes in this. After all, she was my best … I don't know what … not friend exactly, but my best relative, my closest living DNA. You don't think the coroner will consider this irregular? OK. OK. I'll call in less than ten minutes."

The kettle was boiling, but who was it who wanted tea? She had promised to make tea, not necessarily drink it. Now she was worried. She'd better call and get the lab-coated people moving. But who should she call? The response from dialling 911 would be too prompt. She'd call Gertie's hospital, the General. Katharine would prefer to go there. The woman was brisk and helpful, but did she sound a little suspicious? Was it possible she thought Julia might have done it? I didn't kill her, she wanted to say. I rushed all the way back from Ontario because she wouldn't allow Phil into her house, because I was responsible for all the last wishes.

Get on with it now, because there's very little time. She'll be stiff and cold but never mind. But what if the blankets look all funny and disturbed when the ambulance arrives? So what. She'd get under them and not be freaked out. Lie behind her aunt and put an arm around her. They had never touched much, so what Katharine felt like in life as compared to death who could say, but surely not this cold. Julia's forehead found the space between Katharine's hard shoulder blades and wedged itself there. All she was prepared to see was the solid blue of pyjama top. All she was prepared to think was, this is it then, irreversibility. Solid blue. And then Julia had a full-body memory of a reversible jacket she had received for her birthday when she was maybe nine or ten. She'd been thrilled by the technology of reversibility. The jacket was pale blue on one side and had a small red-and-navy check on the inside. The real pleasure was in the zipper, the hidden seams, the absence of loose threads and the clever utility of two garments in one. Julia had wanted all her clothing to be reversible, no more seam bindings or facings or dangling thread. Katharine would have understood this perfectly. She would agree: that which is irreversible is a sad and sorry sight.

chapter

6

As Mary Nordstrom had predicted more than once, Katharine left Julia an extremely helpful sum of money, sufficient to make a reasonable down payment on a bungalow and repair the Oldsmobile's transmission. Accustomed to the neighbourhood of Avalon and Senator Higginbotham school, Julia bought on the fringes, closer in than the fourplexes but nowhere near the Village, the Acres or the Ridge. It was February 1980 by the time the estate was all settled, and Mary had just earned her realtor's license. Julia's house was her first sale; the entire transaction had seemed candidly sexual. Never mind. To buy a house was very prudent, and Julia couldn't help feeling more than a little satisfied: I've worked hard for this, I deserve it; god knows I've had no help whatsoever from Lucas Reef.

After the house, taxes, a few items of furniture and a bike for Peter, there were eighty-five hundred dollars left in the account. Julia insisted on taking Mary and her daughter to Hawaii for a week in March; she *insisted*. Mary had saved her life when Peter was born; if she was any sort of friend she would allow herself to be repaid. The week of her return, Julia bought an expensive water-cooled vacuum cleaner from a door-to-door saleswoman; the dust-free guarantee alone seemed worth the money. Next, a new television and VCR. Then a trumpet for Peter, so that he could take lessons and be prepared for band in junior high three years hence. When there was fifteen hundred dollars remaining, Heather Pringle came canvassing for the Heart and Stroke Foundation and Julia wrote a cheque for one thousand dollars. Her mother was still smoking; she could have a heart attack any day now. This money might, in some small way, have a prophylactic effect.

"That's very generous," Heather said with a skeptical glance at the living-room furniture. "Are you certain you want to give this much?"

"Yes, that's the amount I've decided on. I could make it eleven hundred," Julia couldn't resist saying.

"Oh no, this is more than sufficient. I'll write you a receipt, and as is the custom with gifts of this size, you'll receive a letter and most likely a visit from one of the executive members."

"Oh really?" This was an unexpected bonus.

And indeed it came to pass. An intoxicatingly vibrant and confident woman named April Drury called one Saturday afternoon and asked to drop by with a little token of appreciation from the Foundation, as she called it. Withdrawing a framed certificate from a canvas bag with "Books Books Books" printed in twenty or more

different fonts, April said, "This is what we give our benefactors."
Benefactors? Julia was thrilled to be a benefactor, thrilled to the
very hair on the back of her neck. Perhaps the fan belt on her heart
or some other cooling mechanism weakened or failed at that precise moment, because she found herself admiring April's straight
skirt, her nylons, heels and crisp cotton shirt. Very nicely put
together, Julia's father would have said. A very becoming skirt and
a nice pair of leather shoes. Abraham Raine wasn't so much interested in women's bodies as the clothing covering them, and apparently Julia had inherited a gene for strong pleasurable response to
certain articles of women's clothing.

Oh my, but she was a fraud, listening to April enthuse about the
importance of ongoing support from their benefactors when she
had less than two hundred dollars in the bank. What exactly was
her problem? The substantial bank account had had the effect of a
full tank of fuel, igniting a rocket-fired compulsion to spend,
spend, spend to depletion and beyond, sputtering to a halt with
cash donations she could ill afford. Julia Raine was a fake benefactor, thrilled, in truth, by the sight of this executive member's legs.

Peter hung the certificate in his room. "If I blur my vision it
looks just like a student-of-the-month award." At eight he seemed
too old for this frankly delusional thinking, but Julia tried not to
worry. At least she had a job. Early in May, when Julia was finished
her course work, there had been another posting with the city
planning department and Celeste helped her write the letter of
application. Thank god she had taken two graduate courses in statistics. Claiming to have an instinctive understanding of central
tendency and the analysis of variance, Julia got the job and the
benefits and the pension plan and the underground parking spot
for the Oldsmobile.

She was now a Planning Co-ordinator — Community Development, one of a team representing the human element in development. Julia would construct and interpret surveys, speak to

engineers and architects, present results to community leaders and, as Harvey said, shelve those studies in their low-budget coil bindings and watch them accumulate. So what? She liked being a Planning Co-ordinator — Community Development, even if the title did elicit a blinking response from most people, as if it were nothing more than a pleasing and meaningless group of syllables. Hello, my name is Julia Raine and I am employed by the city as a Plymouth Timonium.

And to have two friends on site — Harvey was back and Celeste had been hired months ago — was so fortunate. At last Julia was the sort of person meant to sit outdoors at lunch with a group of friends, smiling and being observed by passers-by. There is a woman with a conventional love life (or even an unconventional love life) who has the capacity to sustain an intimate relationship, strangers would think. Were this not the case, she would never have been hired by the city. Between her university connections and her job, Julia was really very comfortable, warm and snug, as if her entire body were encased in a perfectly fitting bra, exerting an elastic and reassuring pressure on her chest and ribs.

So why these hyperventilation and panic attacks? Who would ever have expected her body to spring this surprise on her? The first time it happened she'd been at work, sitting at her new desk, when she felt tingling in her fingertips. That was odd, and why had her mind climbed aboard such a rapidly descending escalator? Her lungs were out of oxygen, breathing moon-air. "I think I'm dying," she said to Harvey, casually, as if going for coffee.

"It's nothing to worry about," he assured her, having read more than his share of psychology texts. "Anxiety is caused by an imag-ined future, which never arrives. It's a response to an imagined threat to the physical organism, the body. Your body thinks there's a sabre-toothed tiger somewhere in the room, but clearly there is not. Unless you want to count Lorne the engineer, there is no tiger."

Maybe not, but there were twentieth-century problems Julia

had not invented. She worried, for example, about Peter at school. Every year some new concern appeared on his report card. In grade one he had seemed too withdrawn; in grade two his reading was delayed; in grade three he lacked focus, was doing too much pencil sharpening. Each report card sent Julia scurrying to the teacher supplies store in search of skill-builders, co-operative games and confidence-boosting projects. If Lucas Reef/Dodd were in the picture, would things be different? *My reply is yes.* Would Peter's bedroom walls be papered with awards and certificates? *It is decidedly so.* The eight ball seemed to know.

And don't forget the community association: plenty of metaphorical sabre-teeth there. Heather Pringle knocked on Julia's door one day late in April to say the association's secretary was planning to move to Edmonton and would she please consider filling in for the rest of the year. It was a commitment of only three more meetings. This was apparently the sort of request one received when one had made a one-thousand-dollar donation to a charitable organization.

The very first meeting dished up her second anxiety attack, transforming the Avalon community hall into a classically conditioned source of terror. She had been at the plywood table with the other executive members, thinking about not much, wondering if anyone else in the room had given birth to a child whose patrilineal surname was unknown and whether any of the other women present had been in love with a great-aunt for several years. Then that sudden interior descent occurred, all systems yo-yo: you are about to die. She couldn't leave but she could get to the bathroom on her shaking dying legs. Breathe breathe gasp. Harvey had told her about the paper bag trick, but she wasn't about to carry a lunch sack with her everywhere she went: that would be nothing more than a carefully folded invitation to doom. She would be fine. She would bring date squares to the next meeting. She would take flawless minutes. She would be fine.

Summer was coming. A series of beautiful spring evenings was passed en worried route to sleep. Julia was surprised at her body's nocturnal capacity to occupy continents of despair, flooding them with anxiety that left no sign in the morning — a line of salt per-haps, nothing more. She had a job, a house. Get a grip.

Once again, Celeste wanted to arrange a dinner party for her. This time it would mean Julia was definitely a lesbian and there was no going back. It was her own fault, she supposed, for blabbing too much to Celeste. Since the trip to Hawaii, Julia had carried on an active and excessive inner life with Mary Nordstrom. Her body was now supporting so much emotional construction that one small cut and out would slide, in the manner of very complex origami, an entire cityscape of plans, developments, subdivisions and even the surrounding weather systems. She couldn't *not* talk to Celeste about Mary; telltale blueprints would appear on her skin if she didn't. "Do you think Mary guessed, when we were in Hawaii, that I was, whatever, infatuated, for want of a better word? She hasn't said anything to you?"

"Nothing other than that she had a good time."

"Good? That's the adjective she used?"

"She might have said great. We really don't talk that often. Only when I call to ask Lenny a question about rabies shots or some such thing."

"You can't recall which it was, good or great?" Cold stare from Celeste, which Julia chose to ignore, pruning it away from the con-versational tree as one would a very small, very dead branch. "When we were camping those three nights, together in the tent, I was sure she would detect something. I was really conscious of suppressing laughter and silly talk. No uncalled-for playfulness, I kept saying to myself. Rules, rules, rules; they're necessary, you know. Along with worry, always necessary as well. I started worry-ing if Mary lit a cigarette near me my breath would ignite like a flame thrower or an acetylene torch. Or my voice would go squeaky like with helium — not from her cigarette, but you know what I mean. Or some perverse stigmata would give me away; my body would play a confessional trick on me. Have you ever felt that way?"

Celeste wanted to ruin her fun: "I seem to recall Mary Nord-strom has a husband."

"And this is an imaginary relationship, so what difference does it make?"

"I suppose you have a point."

"Have you ever seen Mary in a bathing suit? She has swimmer's shoulders. She used to swim in high school and university."

"All right. This has gone far enough. I'm going to have a dinner party for you."

"No, please. No dinner parties."

Instead Celeste arranged a blind event, as she put it, with Ladonna, a linguistics student who also worked part time in a florist shop. "You need to forget about Mary," Celeste commanded, as if forgetting could be achieved by visiting a restaurant with a stranger who wore too many rings. Although Ladonna was, despite this point in her disfavour (Mary wore no rings), quite lovely. Regal in fact, Julia thought; someone who might be awarded the Order of Canada on the basis of poise and composure alone. Her tranquillity seemed to cause an electrical storm of misfiring neurons in Julia. She dropped her fork, knocked over her wine glass and began to compensate by affecting an overstated directness, as if all earlier blunders were intentional and in synchronicity with those yet to come.

Waiting for dessert, Julia said, "Celeste called this a blind event, but I'm afraid the sociologist in me is uneasy with social ambiguity. As a linguist, would you consider this a date or a possible date or as having nothing whatsoever to do with courtship?" She had just removed a section of onion that had probably been resting on her shirt pocket for some time, visually troubling for Ladonna, no doubt, along with the wine stain now concealed beneath a bread-

171

and-butter plate. Who was she kidding? At any moment the plate would be whisked away by a waiter, revealing the messy red blotch, a symbol of something, an injured Rorschach perhaps.

The evening was taking its toll; Julia was tired and worried too. Peter had insisted on a babysitter other than Bonnie, so she had hired a twelve-year-old girl from down the street. Natalie was no more than three inches taller than Peter and seemed immature. She had no breasts, but at the same time appeared precocious with her dark and lumpy mascara. By now the kitchen was likely in flames. Or the two of them were hitchhiking to Banff. And Heather Pringle would probably have seen them and notified the appropriate authorities. All this for an event with Ladonna.

"It's not really possible to name an event until after the fact, is it?" Ladonna was saying. "A party might actually be a dirge. You might plan a vacation, get into your RV, head out onto the highway and the outcome is entirely different, necessitating another name, like perhaps comedy of errors or mistake. Not that I'm saying this has been either of those, but you know what I'm saying."

"Yes, but you must have chosen some probationary term for what we're doing here," Julia said. She wanted to ask, "Are you looking for someone to date? Is this courtship or just a favour for a friend?" Instead she said, "Never mind. This is a bad line of talk."

Ladonna smiled peacefully, at peace with the universe, a walking Desiderata, while her linguist's mind busied itself dissecting speech sounds, cracking them apart like filberts to reveal hidden intents. There went the bread-and-butter plate; there was the stain. Hmmm. Was this the moment of dismissal? And if so, did Julia care? Did she wish to have another event with a woman whose unblemished body chemistry caused St. Vitus' dance in others? What would Ladonna be naming the evening after the fact? Late-night horror show? Endurance test? Trial? Sentence? That was a good one for a linguist.

"Why is it we have the word 'misnomer' but not 'nomer'?" Now she was trying to be clever and deferential, trying to make up for talk of blind events, not wanting an answer really, but Ladonna was happy to explain the rules of conduct governing prefixes. They were in Ladonna's truck, an unusual vehicle with a plywood box, as if Ladonna might have had a drywall business or been a gardener prior to working at the florist shop. Julia would ask, given enough time, but Ladonna was still on the subject of prefixes. "Some just negate while others are more generous," she was saying.

"Here's my driveway," Julia interrupted.

"Oh right. Sorry, I almost missed it."

They were stopped now, parking brake engaged, engine running. "Well that was fun. That's my nomer for it," Julia said. What was the protocol? Would Ladonna endeavour to kiss her?

"Yes, I had a good time. So I'll see you," Ladonna concluded politely, non-specifically, implying, Julia surmised, we will continue to inhabit the same planet.

"Yes, I'll see you." And then the door wouldn't open and Ladonna had to lean over and yank at the handle, her hair smelling of apples or kiwis in a soap suspension. And the thought of Ladonna possibly showering and shampooing and fussing for this event caused a little landslide of desire: Julia wanted to touch her but didn't.

"I have a new babysitter tonight. She says she's twelve but I have my doubts. I was thinking the place might have burned down or the police might be here, but everything looks OK on the surface, from here anyway," Julia blurted. Ladonna was smiling and poised, poised and smiling. "So I guess I should go. Thanks again."

Where was her key? My god what had she been thinking? Where was that key? She should at least have told Bonnie to look in on them. There it was and the damn lock so tricky, her hands were trembling, but of course they were both safe and sound, Peter asleep on the living-room floor, Natalie on the couch eating potato chips. Julia would quickly walk her home, leaving Peter illuminated in a landing pad of television light as if preparing to be sucked up by its silver-grey tongue, transported to Jupiter. She would be back in two minutes. And then what?

Without warning, Julia was overcome by the possibility of loss. What if he were ever taken from her? Keep the breathing under control, she commanded, keep it even. Peter gone would be much like moving to another planet, or the ruin of this one. How would it ever support life again? She supposed it was the red wine and the stress of an unnameable social outing, because now she needed to cry for a moment but she couldn't muster the tears. What she really wanted was to lie down next to Peter, but he was getting too old for that. So instead she found a channel with the late news and sat beside him in the TV light, turned down the volume and tried to read the newscaster's lips.

~ ~ ~ ~

Ladonna wanted another date. She would pick Julia up in her drywalling truck and take her to a movie. She would call it a date from the outset. "Well that's great, that would be great, I mean, but I'm afraid I'm actually seeing someone. I guess I should have mentioned it after all that prodding you to state your intentions."

"Yes, that would have been the polite thing to do." Linguistically speaking. She hung up without saying goodbye, smashed the receiver into its socket. And Julia was filled with remorse, more than she might have anticipated; beads of embarrassing sweat surfaced on her forehead.

One moment please. Confess; if you don't, you'll start breathing funny. Julia wasn't seeing anyone; she had only very recently met Robert, the school psychologist, at the school resource fair night and she *might* — anything was possible — be seeing him, should she give him a call. Rather tenuous use of the language, Julia would freely admit were she to have to answer to a panel of concerned phraseologists. Robert had given her his card; he was flirting, that's why, not because he felt she needed psychological help. She wished now she had exercised more restraint in her descriptions of Peter's annually reported afflictions, was very glad she'd held back on mentioning the pencil sharpening. For sure he would have read some sexual meaning into that. He had touched her arm twice and laughed loudly at all her attempts at humour.

But to call that seeing him was a joke. Still, Peter needed a father figure and Robert had made it clear he was single — "my ex-wife, my ex-wife, my ex-wife" — a sort of branding iron to the short-term memory. And now that she'd told Ladonna she was seeing Robert, she should at least make the effort, although that was ridiculous. But what was not? Julia dared Ladonna to come up with one idea, notion, concept, person, place or thing that wasn't in some way absurd. All right. She would call Robert. Chances are he would be out. But no, he was delighted to hear from her. (*Delighted* bobbing in her stomach like one of those red-and-white fishing floats.) Certainly he could meet her for coffee or a drink. Well, which would he prefer? How about a drink?

At first, having Robert in the house was like being in the company of a panel of Olympic judges. Being a school psychologist, he would most certainly be judging Julia's interactions with Peter, his grades, her intelligence, her behaviour management practices, her choice of foods and selection of reading material. Having secured the job with the city prior to meeting Robert was an inspired bit of planning. Julia was now a mother with a dental plan and supplementary health insurance, information she casually shared with Robert. And she was very pleased to announce one night that she couldn't go out because of her secretarial duties with the community association.

In truth, Robert had worked in his field long enough to be deadly tired of psychology and the assessment of human behaviour. More and more often he found himself wanting to say, I simply don't know. And as for what was appropriate, his experiences growing up in a fundamentalist Christian family had taught him to suspect all appearance. At thirty-eight, he still longed for the normal world he thought existed everywhere outside his parents' house, a planet populated with the uninhibited and unashamed, those who had just managed to do up their flies and straighten their skirts before the door opened.

Robert and Julia hit it off. Julia was determined to enjoy the sex and at least once make an offer of fellatio — maybe next weekend. The age difference was sexy, and she loved his stories of schools and teachers, and was flattered and grateful when he told her Peter was a great kid. Had she thought the absence of a father would act on her son like one of those genetic conditions that waits for adolescence to announce its presence, unravelling DNA and messing up the interior of hitherto tidy cells? She wound up telling Robert the entire story of Lucas Reef and about the general shortage of Reefs in Ontario telephone directories. How she worried about Peter's inevitable efforts to trace Reef genealogical records when in reality his name was Dodd, or was it? In fact, all future sadness — she was being a little melodramatic now — was tied up in the moment Peter would press her for specifics on this issue. Would she have the courage to say, "Well, his name was either Lucas Reef or Lance Dodd"? She should have found out and not been so selfishly stubborn about talking to Lucas. The Raines hadn't provided much in the way of kinship, but at least she knew who they were and could make herself a family tree, not a lopsided thing that would seem to have been struck by lightning.

"There are lots of worse situations than not knowing your biological father," Robert said, "like, for example, knowing your biological father." Robert and his father hadn't really spoken to one another for years, in the sense of exchanging meaningful information. "Not that he's a bad guy, but what do you say when your cosmologies are diametrically opposed? He has to journey to the outer fringes of his just to ask how my day was, and I have to do the same and still there seems to be a space of about five or six feet between our worlds. I don't think I could even jump it, not from a standing position.

"Peter'll be OK. He has your dad and your brother, and didn't you say your friend Harvey does things with him? It's not as if he's been totally abandoned by the male gender."

Kindly assurances, but suddenly Julia wanted to talk about Robert's family.

"All right. Did I tell you we're all Rs?" Robert asked. "The whole family — Roberta and Ralph, Ruth, Randy, Rose and Robert. The Ruperts. That was my dad's idea. I like to think of it as an alphabetic fence designed to keep out everyone who hasn't experienced full-body immersion baptism. I'd like you to meet my sister Ruth; I think you'd like her."

And oh no, Julia thought two weeks later when the door to Ruth's tiny apartment opened and she felt her body levitate forward on the supernatural wings of attraction. What was it? It was Jannette in the girls' bathroom, Pamela in her lab coat, Mary on the beach. It was the language of the immune systems, some people said, very low amplitude wave action, epidermal chirping heard only at night, but this was in broad daylight. Maybe, in reality, it was nothing more than ovulation. Had she been extending her hand to Robert at that precise moment, would the same response have occurred? Possibly.

Ruth Rupert was forty-seven years old, nine years older than Robert was and twenty years older than Julia. She painted exteriors of houses in the summer, interiors in the winter and her own watercolours year round. She had just completed a series of scenes from the city's indoor pools, all blues and pale yellows and underwater lights at night. Lockers and benches. "I love these," Julia said. "You should have a show."

"Well, I'm trying."

She had green eyes, salt-and-pepper hair to her ear lobes, and large hands. Over the course of dinner, she managed to shoo

Robert out of the small room he had begun to occupy in Julia's affections, knock out a few walls, paint, redecorate and move in.

Oh, there was Stella, Ruth's girlfriend from the art college, but this was irrelevant to the heart-sized generator working within Julia's body. Humming quietly, it created enough electricity to provide heat and light to a small town in the midst of the windy prairie. Or a panic attack, if conditions were favourable. But what did it matter? Julia had embarked on a brief and deeply humiliating career as a fool for love. After it was all over, she would consider buying fifteen minutes of the Canadian Broadcasting Corporation's time so as to explain herself, like the Prime Minister might do in times of trouble, with a fireplace in the background, framed photos on the mantel.

First, she found herself looking for reasons to bring up Ruth's name in conversation with Robert, then looking forward to those reasons much as one anticipates a favourite moment in a movie or a song on the radio. They would discuss work, the personalities there, the situation in Iran, a movie they had seen, all the while her mind nervously reading ahead to the portion of script with Ruth's name highlighted in yellow.

"What's Ruth working on now? Has she heard anything from any of the galleries?" Julia asked.

"Not that I know of."

Stella's name began to crop up in conversation too. "So, how did Ruth and Stella meet? What exactly does Stella do?"

"Completes grant application forms."

"Oh, so she doesn't have an actual job?"

Finally Robert asked, "Why do you keep bringing up Ruth's name?"

"Keep?"

"Yes, as in repeatedly."

"I hadn't realized."

Forced to stop mentioning her name, Julia predictably began

driving past Ruth's apartment. Her place was more or less on the way to work, and what harm did it do? Julia thought she might get a glimpse of the mysterious Stella. And the pleasure derived was irresistible. Julia felt as if she'd been wired up with interior Christmas lights, those narrow, bubbling, fake candles all along her bones, visible only when she was passing by the seven hundred block of Twenty-Fifth Avenue South West.

Then Julia encountered Robert. Weather and happenstance will conspire in these situations to expose the furtive. The middle of May and typically for Calgary, the temperature took an abrupt dive and they had an enormous dump of snow. For twenty-four hours, side streets were reduced to one frozen track. Recognizing Robert's car half a block away, Julia considered rapidly constructing a pirate hat from her map of Alberta or covering her face with both hands as if sneezing or sobbing.

"What are you doing here?" asked Robert, pulling up alongside her.

"My friend Mary's considering buying a house on this street" — partly true, she was thinking of leaving Lenny — "and she asked me to take a look at it. It's on the next block. See that realtor's sign down there? That's the place. What are you doing here?"

"Ruth needed my pruning shears."

"Oh." Pause. "Well. We're still on for tomorrow night?"

"I certainly hope so," Robert said. But something had given Julia away. Like acolytes of the virgin Mary who see her image in loaves of bread or find her likeness in a bowl of cereal, had Julia grown the profile of Ruth on the back of her left hand? Her throat? Robert seemed to be noticing something.

The very next day, Robert arrived with his sister's dry cleaning. Julia opened the door and there he was, holding a clear plastic bag with Ruth's things. "Can I hang this in your closet for now? I don't want it to get wrinkled in the car."

"Sure," Julia said. "Fine. I hadn't expected you until this

evening." Truth be told, she was not in the mood for Robert. She was in the mood for the opposite of Robert, the absence of Robert.

Anyway, he was going to cut to the chase. He was thinking they might go to bed together; they hadn't for some time, meaning two weeks and three days. He couldn't wait for tonight.

"No. Peter's in his room listening to music; I wouldn't feel right."

"Then let's hire a babysitter and go to my house."

"No, I don't think so ... " And then Robert kissed Julia hard and asked, like an experimental psychologist, did she like that.

"No, I can't say I did, and why are you being so weird? What are you trying to do here?"

"What am I trying to do? What am I trying to do?" he repeated. "I'm trying to figure out if you would like me better if I slipped into Ruth's skirt?"

"Oh for heaven's sake. So that's why you brought Ruth's dry cleaning here? To stage this little drama?"

Yes, he had. He knew it was ridiculous, but Julia drove him to the ridiculous because she was ridiculous. Did she think he hadn't noticed she was attracted to Ruth, was cathecting on her, clearly had some unresolved issues? Shouldn't she think long and hard about what she really wanted?

Then he grabbed the clothes in a huff and they didn't speak for a week, until he called to say he had thought things were coming together for them but now it was all on the back burner as far as he was concerned. And Julia didn't argue. She had every opportunity to tell him he was overreacting, imagining things, projecting, but she said nothing. She wanted to feel hurt, and she remembered a friend from university saying she smashed three jars in the sink when her boyfriend dumped her. So Julia found a jar, took it to the sink and rolled it around, stood it up, knocked it over — but it didn't smash. Seemed like a waste of a good Mason jar.

Then she went one step farther, one step too far. Robert had mentioned before their break-up that Ruth's birthday was approaching and perhaps they'd take her out for dinner. Julia had looked forward to this evening with glaring anticipation, as if her eyes were high-beam headlights, illuminating the days between now and June eighth. But the cancellation of the dinner didn't mean she couldn't do something. She could still buy a gift, a riotous bouquet of flowers, for example, something in the range of seventy-five dollars. She could put it on Visa.

The seventy-five-dollar bouquet fit nicely on the back seat of the Oldsmobile. The night before Ruth's birthday would be a good time to deliver it, as she'd likely be out celebrating the next day. Using a sort of social dimmer switch, Julia reasoned, I'll tell her they're from Robert and me. Ruth probably doesn't know we've split up, and even if she does, when I drop off the flowers she'll assume we're back together. Peter would rather go to his friend's and watch television, and no he didn't want to stay with Bonnie and Dave. "OK, I'll be half an hour or maybe a little longer." And away went Julia, face bright with misguided joy. Do not hesitate, she thought; drive to your destination. Hope Stella is absent so that at the very least you might have a moment alone with the world's loveliest human form. There's the house. Open car door. Shimmy the flowers out of the car. Walk. Knock knock knock. Door opens to tall woman with cascading dark hair, passing resemblance to Cher, with boyish androgynous cast.

"Well, hello!" Like a telephone solicitation service, Julia does not falter over salutations. "I'm Julia Raine, Robert's friend, and I'm dropping these off for Ruth on behalf of both of us. Tell her happy birthday and best wishes, etcetera, etcetera."

"She's just run out to buy some milk; she'll be back in ten minutes if you want to wait."

"Oh no. I'd love to, but must be going." Must be going. Waved from the car, cheery. Sensible and thoughtful too. But she could feel the strings of activity inside, teaching her a lesson, rows of lights extinguishing, could actually hear the sound of all those switches flick flick flicking off. Well, what on earth had she expected? You don't just march into someone's house with a bunch of overpriced flowers and expect ... You are not the centre of the universe ... Your feelings do not elicit a matching realignment of others' feelings. Bleat bleat bleat, honk honk honk, the sound of the adult voice from Charlie Brown cartoons completed each sentence. Then the breathing started to change and this time Julia did have a paper bag in the glove box of the car. She stopped three streets over and hoped no one was watching. Hoped Robert wouldn't drive by.

~ ~ ~ ~

And so that was then and this is now. Late August already, and Julia Raine is spending as much time as possible in the back yard, on her lounge chair, winterized in scarf and cardigan. She must take it easy; her body no longer seems familiar with its habitat. Like a grizzly airlifted into the wilderness for its own protection, she should spend some time sniffing the air, awaiting further news. Yes, the bear would like to sleep more, but first must check its pulse, monitor its breathing, concern itself with oxygen levels. Stare cataleptically at the blue Alberta sky. How on earth did you get here, it wonders behind the watchtower prisms of its eyes. Surely there's a button you can push on the wall of this mountain, pass through a sliding rock door and into a warm and insulated cave. Hibernate.

But there was always some interruption. From where she lay, Julia could hear the telephone and her new answering machine. There it was, ringing again. Peter was at a friend's; there was no one to answer it. Ring. Ring. "Hi Julia. Mary here. Guess what? I've bought a house on your street, two blocks from yours. You have to come and see it."

chapter

7

Mary Nordstrom

had indeed sold herself a house, in reality slightly more than two blocks from Julia's, up the hill and on a crescent in the general direc-tion of Heather Pringle and the ladies who golfed during the school day. And this annoyed Julia, coming out of the blue as it had, with no warning or discussion or opportunity for giving advice. Don't you think you and Lenny should try to work things out? With her sociologist's training, she could have pulled from her hat all the magical doves of logic and convention to convince Mary to stay put.

"But I told you I was looking for my own place."

"I thought that was just real estate mumbo-jumbo."

"Mumbo-jumbo? No, I was looking for my own place. Isn't that fairly straightforward?"

"Still."

"Still what?"

"Still nothing." Fine. Be that way. Move into the neighbourhood and stir the place with a stick. Julia was not imagining this: since Mary had taken possession of her house November first, there'd been a change in the weather. She could feel it on her eyes when she left for work in the morning, an increase in barometric pressure sensed by the vitreous fluids surrounding her retinas, pushing on them, exerting an equal increase in pressure on the rest of her mind, leaving insufficient room for thought. A crowded sensation and many short, smouldering fuses.

At least daily, Mary dropped in or called. "Guess who was just here? Heather Pringle. She's the Welcome Wagon person."

"Heather Pringle is the Welcome Wagoneer? I thought they only had Welcome Wagons in small towns like Mesmer. And besides, she didn't welcome me when I bought this place."

"Maybe because you were already living in the area."

"Well, she didn't welcome me when I moved into the fourplex either."

"I think she gets her list of people from realtors. I know so. I gave her the list myself with my name on it. It wasn't much of a list actually — M. Nordstrom was all it said. I wanted to make sure I got the free stuff."

"So. I see. Renters are not deserving of a welcome wagon welcome. That says a lot about this so-called community." Every time Mary phoned, Julia was aware of anger carpeting portions of her interior, tacking itself into place so that now it was just part of the decor; kind of bristly, like indoor/outdoor. "And what did Heather bring you in her wagon? A big basket of cleaning supplies? That's what Augustina Schmidt brings around in Mesmer. It's all promotional, just a bunch of free samples. Little boxes of detergent big enough to do one small load of delicates, if you happen to own delicates."

"So? And why are you so crabby? Am I annoying you too now? Along with all of Lenny's and my ex-friends? Don't tell me you're going to line yourself up with them and start flaring your nostrils every time my name comes up in conversation." Her voice went wavery like a little pool between them where a stone had dropped.

"No, no, no. Of course not. I'm sorry." What was wrong with her? It was the stress of work and the weather. "The meteorologists are saying we're under an Arctic dome that's not moving." But primarily her indoor/outdoor anger could not withstand the wear of any challenge from Mary. Explanations were offered, ample bowing and scraping, followed by introspective dithering. The least she could do was offer support to Mary while her former married friends abandoned her to comfort Lenny. The least she could do was remember what a good friend Mary had been to her over the years. Although Julia had taken her to Hawaii — in the great ledger of friendship, no one could say the accounts had not been balanced. And why had Mary just up and left Lenny like that? Weren't you at least supposed to try counselling and mediation and an open letter to *Chatelaine* detailing infidelities, open wounds and pitiable financial bungles, asking if the marriage could be saved?

"You're my friend, Mary," Julia said, but the sentence came out all wrong, uninflected and tentative as if she'd just recovered from voice box surgery.

"So if you're my friend, can I count on you to come to my Ex-mas party? I'm serious, about counting on you, I mean. I don't know how many people I can count on." Another pebble in the pond. Please don't cry, Mary. "I've invited a few realtor acquaintances and three sets of friends from my past life. Maybe the wives will come and maybe not. And Celeste, but not Miriam because she hates parties."

Realtors? A party of real estate agents? This had a spectacularly unappealing ring to it, but Julia supposed that was a learned response inculcated by her parents or Protestantism: somehow the words unscrupulous and realtor were dovetailed together, but surely she could pry them apart for one evening. As for Mary, she was at the outer edges of the normal bell curve of realtors, a realtor with a difference, a realtor with lovely breasts. And that was the other problem: cognitive dissonance, rogue thoughts, there was no stopping them. Julia was clearly on some major telepathic grid, the TransCanada of psychic movement. One day she found herself daydreaming about living with Mary, cooking meals for her, waiting for her to come home after a hard day of selling houses, while the next day the fillings of her teeth were apparently receiving signals from some testosterone-saturated man's fantasy life: Julia wanted to sink her teeth into Mary's ass or kiss her neck. Impossible images filled her mind and she swerved and lost track while on the phone or at work.

"You will come?"

"Of course I'll come. What? You think I wouldn't come to my best friend's party? That's a dim view."

This entire situation was partly the fault of those women's magazines at the supermarket, Julia was telling Celeste, having already admitted she was angry with Mary and wanted a good reason to continue to be.

"I don't understand what the women's magazine industry wants from us," Julia reasoned. "Frankly, when I look at those pictures on the cover of *Cosmo*, those shining big breasts, it doesn't make me think I have to have that designer dress or I wonder if that's available in a Butterick pattern. I have a reaction in my ribcage that seems to involve wanting to get closer to those breasts. Really, I'm being honest here."

"Yes. Go on." Celeste with the therapist voice learned from Miriam.

"I'm just saying those magazine covers make me want to touch breasts. Do you think that's their intent, or is it more just a general stimulating of desire for all things we can't have — great bodies, enormous and firm cleavages? Do you think they're making us want those things, materially but also physically, right inside our bodies? If we want them as in desire, that's considered wrong, so it gets sublimated into wanting the dress, which gets sublimated even further into wanting the magazine, which we can have for five bucks, if we want."

"You're saying without the women's magazines it would never have occurred to you to want to touch a woman's — and by that I mean Mary Nordstrom's — breasts?" Celeste was no help at all.

Of course Julia would go to Mary's Christmas party. Over the years she had attended dozens of parties and dinners at Lenny and Mary's and always had a good time. But Lenny had always been there, looking like an astronaut in his eternal brush cut. An astronaut expelled from the training program for womanizing. He'd had that affair with Lucille Demchuk and not even attempted to conceal it. He'd probably had other affairs and was certainly an inveterate flirt, always hugging Julia too hard and for longer than necessary. A hug was intended to be brief or not at all — but there she was again and again, crushed against Lenny Nordstrom's big ribcage. And there came a moment of sympathy for the sad ex-husband who merely wanted to hold women next to his ribs. Yes, Julia would go to the party, but she would go out of loyalty to both Lenny and Mary.

"Pardon me?" Celeste wanted further clarification.

"Never mind, never mind. What should I wear?"

"I don't know. Not a Christmas sweater please, or Christmas earrings — not those little bulbs made into jewellery. Wear a dress."

"OK. Sure." With Julia's distorted thinking, a clear signal was a welcome relief. She would have been an easy target for a cult or any of the fundamentalist religious groups.

"Not velvet. Not crushed velvet."

"All right, all right. I'm sorry I asked."

"Listen, I'll pick you up," Celeste said.

"But I can walk. It's five minutes from here."

"No, please. I insist. Something about arriving alone at parties ruins it for me."

A patent lie, Julia knew. Celeste needed to arrive with Julia so as not to miss one second of observation time, one tiny shred of sociological data. From the moment they arrived, Celeste's big eyes would be moving from Mary to Julia and back again like the zigzag function on a sewing machine: even though I think it's a bad idea, let's bring these two together and prove once and for all that I am right and they are l-e-s-b-i-a-n-s.

As if she hadn't already more or less agreed to this, Julia wanted to shout at Celeste when she came by to pick her up. Didn't I go out on a date with Ladonna for god's sake? Does that not prove I'm accepting of my homosexual leanings? Once inside Celeste's car, Julia thought now might be the time to bait her a little.

"What exactly are the characteristics of a lesbian anyway?" she asked. "Are there any documentaries on the topic? Or perhaps you could recommend a nature program, something narrated by Lorne Greene or Bruce Marsh, beginning with the animal kingdom and extrapolating from, say, cheetahs to people. Or maybe you have a pamphlet or two in your purse."

"People say I'm the life of the party cuz I tell a joke or two," Celeste half sang, half spoke. Every once in a while she made attempts at sermonizing through popular song. "Much has been sung on this subject you know, crying on the inside, laughing on the outside. I suppose it's banal, but life's not always a joke."

"No, it's not, I agree. But since you refer to popular song, you might be interested to know that of late I can't seem to get Neil Diamond's 'Solitary Man' out of my mind. Why do you think, Celeste? Because what difference does your sexual preference make when your emotional preference is singleness." Did she have to get on stage in a glittery jumpsuit to make her point? Now they were parked outside Mary's in the dark of December, and Julia could imagine the shadows their semi-polite selves might cast on the nearest wall: two individuals strangling one another's elongated throats, tongues extended cartoonishly, and this made her want to laugh. "All right," Julia said, "for tonight's purposes, I'll be a lesbian. Simple as that. So don't go trying to prove anything, Celeste Muehler. I'm perfectly comfortable with Mary Nordstrom. Just watch me."

But she wasn't, she didn't want things to change, she wanted the unfulfilled longing to hang in the air forever like dangerous pending weather. Eyes watching the sky, closing a circuit. Waiting.

~ ~ ~ ~

Everyone had left, even Celeste, and Julia thought she might have one more drink, just one more, then walk home. She was having a delightful time. Those hardwood floors certainly were shiny, and with each step she could swear lightning bugs rose up and sank back down. Should she sit down next to Mary on the sofa? Why not? They were both up to their necks in kissing plans.

"What a great party," Julia said, although the realtors had huddled together for much of the evening, discussing the most likely site for the Olympic Coliseum. Two of the three wives had come, but one cornered Julia and urged her to talk some sense into Mary.

"Lenny's losing weight."

"But I think he's been working out."

"No no. He is not a well man."

Did Mary actually have her arm around Julia or was that just how she liked to sit, with one arm extended, falling ever-so-slightly forward?

"Where's Kristy?"

"She's at her dad's."

"Oh, of course. Peter wanted to come but I told him no."

"He could have. That would have been fine with me."

Stop being so kind. Then Julia thought of something. "Do you know what my mother says sometimes, out of the blue? She'll be sitting, looking out the window or maybe driving and it's quiet, and she'll say, 'This is nothing like I thought it would be.' I used to get anxious when she said that, thinking she was unhappy and wanted to leave us all, that my brother and I were a big disappointment. But now I think I know what she meant. You kind of have an unarticulated picture of how you think it will be, and then what you're experiencing is maybe not even in that particular photo album. You know what I mean?"

"And ..." said Mary, her first contribution to the conversation.

And, Julia thought, this is worse than in the tent in Hawaii, which kick-started a conga-line of remembered electrical impulses, sent them reeling to the speech lobes of her mind where they could not be stopped. "And I think you should kiss me now." Which Mary did. Or one of them kissed the other. I may have kissed her, Julia later told Celeste, bragging. But didn't tell about the second kiss, which was a real kiss, Mary's hand causing Julia to swallow hard on the lozenge of desire moving warm and yellow down her throat, down her whole self, all vertigo and stop go stop go. Without opening her eyes, Julia could clearly see the street outside, hear it calling to her like an anxious parent.

"Well, I'd better go," Julia said, slapping her palms onto her knees decisively. She thought she was going to have a bit of a headache tomorrow. She was calm but she was moving. She was up and off the sofa. This was all in a day's work; sociology and alcohol were powerful allies of composure. Mary was finding her coat. "I probably should have been home a long time ago."

"Isn't Bonnie with Peter?"

"Yes, but she likes to get home before two."

"Well it's only one-thirty, so all is well."

"So it is." Julia gave Mary a hug, as if what had just occurred was a soulful exchange between women, a visit to the support group, the twelfth step finally reached. "Thanks for the evening."

"I'm really glad you came."

And the drunken sophomore within wanted then to laugh and offer up lewd conjugations of the verb "to come" — I came, you came, she came or didn't, as the case may be — picturing herself being thrown out the door and down the front steps. That would be so simple, so final — being slapped and told do not ever kiss me again and utter such ridiculous nonsense about the verb "to come."

"I'm glad too. See you soon. 'Bye."

~ ~ ~ ~

"There's something you need to know about yourself," Celeste counselled. "You make yourself a lightning rod for head games."

"Head games. Now there's a phrase I've always disliked. It's in the same league as head shops, which I don't like either. And before you bring it up, no I don't like references to giving head either. Basically, I guess it's the metaphorical use of the word 'head' I find distasteful."

"Oh. OK. Then how about this? You make yourself a lightning rod for mind games."

"That's a better sentence; still untrue, but more semantically pleasing."

"You don't have to agree; I'm merely expressing an opinion. But anyway, before we go back to the note, what happened? What's happened since the party?"

"Nothing. We're ignoring one another. Or I'm ignoring her, but politely, you know, nicely. I saw her two days later at the grocery store and I was friendly the way you are when you have an appointment to get to very soon. I didn't blush, I didn't make reference to the night of December nineteenth, just behaved as if that day was no longer on the calendar. 'Are you ready for Christmas?'

I asked, the world's most generic question. And she said no, everything was a mess with Lenny wanting Kristy, and I was hoping you
might call. Which wasn't fair because it was an indirect reference
to the hole in the calendar."

"And you said ... "

"Not much, because she took me by surprise so I had to concentrate on smiling and saying I had to get going because I had
some people coming for dinner. Which I did. Bonnie and her husband. But this didn't work because the minute I got home the
phone rang and it was Mary saying we had to talk, this was ridiculous. And I agreed; I could be more normal on the phone. I agreed,
but I didn't mean we would talk immediately. 'After New Year's,' I
said. 'Fine,' she said, 'but will you come and have a drink with me
tonight?' And I said yes, then cancelled later. I have a thousand
reasons for cancelling. It's like I keep a jar next to the phone and
just reach in and pull one out."

"So Christmas came and Christmas went and then what?"

"Then she called sometime between Christmas and New Year,
and I know this sounds like a very bad situation comedy, but I pretended I had laryngitis and I couldn't talk but would call as soon
as I was better. It just came to me in a flash because Bonnie had
been over for a minute and she had laryngitis, really bad laryngitis, and all she could do was whisper. So it was fresh in my con-
sciousness how to sound pathetic. 'I've heard there's a lot of that
going around,' Mary said, but then she called back ten minutes
later and I picked up the phone and said Hello clear as a bell."

"Oh-oh. What did she say?"

"She said, 'You sound better.' And I said, 'I know, it comes and
goes. I just gargled with salt.' She asked what I was doing for New
Year's Eve, and I said I was going to Harvey and Joan's, which was
the truth. Then she said, 'Oh to hell with it all,' and hung up. I
thought of calling back or showing up on New Year's Eve, but I was
worried she was angry. So then I thought of getting into the

Oldsmobile and driving to Las Vegas and starting a new life as a well-adjusted person with better relationships."

"In Las Vegas? And that was December thirtieth. And today the note came after a six-day hiatus."

"Correct."

"Read me the note again."

"OK, but do you really believe she's taking a play-writing course?"

"No. The very idea is absurd, but that's neither here nor there. Read me the note. So it was there in your mailbox when you got up Saturday morning? Meaning she either dropped it off early that morning or Friday night, under cover of darkness."

"I don't really think Mary does anything under cover of anything. It's typed and there's an introduction. It says, 'Julia, I'm enrolled in a play-writing course through the university, just an evening thing, nothing serious. Our first assignment was to write a hypothetical conversation, something you might overhear in a restaurant or bar. Tell me what you think.' OK, this is it; I'm reading it now.

'Mary: I don't like to name names.

'Julia: Oh, be brave.

'Mary: Well, there was the letter carrier.

'Julia: (sharp intake of breath) Gayle? The Avalon letter carrier?

'Mary: We had a brief affair not long ago, just after I moved in.

'Julia: But you only moved in two months ago.

'Mary: Well, I did say brief.

'Julia: Define brief.

'Mary: In this context, twenty minutes.

'Julia: I don't know if that's better or worse.

'Mary: Than what?

'Julia: A long-term affair.

'Mary: It was early December. I have to admit I was unsure of my motives when I asked Gayle in for a piece of Lenny's mother's fruitcake. She always sends fruitcake at Christmas and Lenny had sent me some via Kristy to prove what a nice guy he is and what a shrew I am. It was bitterly cold and I thought it would be a nice thing to do: invite the letter carrier in for hot chocolate. Gayle was in the house no longer than five minutes when she had my shirt unbuttoned. She fucked me on the living-room floor in full Canada Post uniform and left with two pieces of fruitcake.

'Julia: I don't have to listen to this filth!

'Mary: I want you to know I was very shaken by this incident. I avoided Gayle as much as possible, went into hiding in the basement if I happened to be home during her appointed rounds and got Kristy to bring in the mail. I couldn't touch the mailbox. It seemed tainted. Even the sight of Postal Station B on Varsity Drive gave me a queasy sensation. Finally, I called Canada Post and complained.

'Julia: About what? Grand theft fruitcake?

'The end.'"

Celeste was talking already. "Like I said, lightning rod. Plus, you have to admit it's pretty difficult to ignore. You're going to have to respond. Sooner or later you're going to have to talk."

"And therein lies the problem, Celeste. I don't like talking. I don't like the kind of intimate conversations you and Miriam have. I don't know how you can live with a therapist who makes you articulate your reactions and speak in I-statements. I'm much more comfortable speaking in impersonal generalizations, about others, preferably. If I have to talk to Mary about her and me and ... us, I might evaporate. I'll go from a solid directly into a vapour. I'll be the *National Enquirer's* lead story: 'Woman Evaporates.' I thought maybe a bonus part of being a lesbian would be not having to discuss feelings. Isn't that part of the territory? Being butch and distant?"

"No, because you're not butch."

"Well can't Mary be that type?"

"She's more butch than you are, but like many people, she feels a need to exchange information."

"So you think I'm weirder than most people."

"No, I did not say that. I think it's a bit obstinate not to respond to any of her overtures, to ignore the fact she kissed you and ignore a note she dropped off. So much unresponsiveness. It's like suddenly two new constellations just appeared in the sky — a reindeer and, I don't know, a pickup truck — and everyone but you is out looking at them."

"What do you mean? How many people know about this situation?"

"None. It was just an analogy. Lighten up. Anyway, I have to get going."'

"Will you tell them I'm not coming in to work? I'm taking a sick day. I need to think."

And Julia needed to see Gayle. Of course the script was a ridiculous invention, but there was something about Gayle: she was rather attractive; a little on the boyish side, but sexy. And Mary would do anything. But no, it's not possible. It's unseemly, like having sex with an appliance repairman: Gayle's gender was really irrelevant. That sort of behaviour belongs in a bad movie or a dirty novel, the page all the junior high kids have thumbed and read and passed to the kid in the desk behind. He entered her, like a knife through butter, thrusting hard and again. A quiet yelp of surprise followed by a soft moan. Oh yes baby, harder. Only in this instance, exactly what happened? She fucked me on the living-room floor in full Canada Post uniform. This could mean one of two things, Julia would explain to the junior high class where she was a guest speaker. Either she penetrated her with her fingers or stimulated her clitoris with her tongue. Or, she supposed, both at the same time.

A hand from the back of the class. Yes? Couldn't she have been wearing one of those strap-on things? Julia had not, in all honesty, considered this option. You mean a dildo? Or a dong or whatever? Yes, she supposed that was possible. Anything was possible, but now Julia was annoyed with this pupil; she had an insolent look about her and might just fail the first test of the term if she didn't smarten up. Yes, I suppose a dildo might have been used. Now class, isn't it time for math?

Mary Nordstrom did say "fucked."

Gayle usually came by around ten-thirty. Julia decided to clean the cupboards. She could watch the street, watch for the letter carrier's approach and accomplish something at the same time. Cups, bowls, all the glasses, she washed everything and scoured the shelves, moved on to the dry goods, jars of beans and rice and in the back of the cupboard, a long-forgotten fruitcake.

Here Gayle. Have some fruitcake.

Really. Mary Nordstrom had got herself in way over her head. Who knows what fruitcake on a plate might represent to a lesbian? There was the naïve Mary Nordstrom playing around with a group of people known for their highly coded behaviour. Fruitcake could very easily be one of those in-your-face Queer Nation code words. Have some fruitcake. Why yes, I'd love to lick your clitoris. Mary Nordstrom had no idea what she was doing; she was lucky she hadn't got herself beaten up by a bunch of Gayle's friends, those dykes on bikes.

The fruitcake landed in the garbage with a satisfying thud. Exactly how long had it been in the cupboard? Since two Christmases ago? Maybe longer. There it was, fixed in time, a brick of still-humid beige cake pocked with maraschino cherries and glacée fruit, surrounded by brittle cellophane. Best before the Palaeolithic era. Julia bet that if she had sliced it open she would have found some sort of larval creature in the centre. Blah. Why did she have to think such thoughts?

Then came the squeak of the mailbox lid. Damn. Gayle had come and was on her way back down the walk. Nothing but a rear view, and the next door neighbours had no mail so she was already practically out of sight. She'd be up the hill in no time and at Mary's house. The prospect of Mary being at home, baking cookies or

whirring up blender drinks for Gayle, preposterous as it was, fic-
titious as it was, caused a tension in Julia's lungs, an unpleasant
fullness that coughing couldn't relieve.

~ ~ ~ ~

Julia was rehearsing. She was on her way to Mary's house, a
formless and irresolute script in hand. I'm told we should talk. No,
that wouldn't do, she couldn't foist the responsibility onto someone else; must accept some agency, as Celeste would say. We should
talk. Or, it's time we talked. No no no. Why must all introductory
sentences orbit around the verb "to talk"? Could they not just sit
for a while? Let's sit, Mary, and watch television. Call Lenny and
ask him to come over and the kids will play outside. Let's hold
hands. Go swimming. Take the bus to Glengarry Pool and, I know,
I'll tell you about Ruth's paintings.

It was early evening. With any luck, Mary would be out selling
condominiums and convincing people to burden themselves with
debt at 17 percent interest. Weren't these the real estate hours?
Seven to nine? Peter had demanded to stay home on his own,
which was fine because Julia would be out for less than an hour.
Most likely Mary wouldn't be home, and in that case she'd just go
for a short walk.

"Why don't you call and see if she's there? I'll call for you," Peter
offered.

"No, I'd like to surprise her."

She'd really like to go for a walk. The night was beautiful and
there was a moon. Why didn't she go for walks more often?
Because of Peter, naturally. Even though he wanted to be indepen-
dent, let himself in after school (and was thus now officially a
latchkey kid, symbol of the decline of Western society), Julia could-
n't leave him except maybe to dash to the corner store for milk.
Had she stopped worrying since he was born? No. Worry was
ever present, and it had a sound all its own, like a car radio in the

mountains when you're driving alone, nothing but that lonely buzz and the occasional voice of a weatherman or park ranger, speaking in numbers. Now, for the first time, she decided not to worry. Mary or no Mary, she would enjoy the walk, find one clear band width, maybe a piano sonata. She closed and locked the door. Peter would be fine.

Minus five degrees, and why was she happy now? Chinook conditions and there was that arch of sky, visible even at night, one enormous and open eye behind the mountains. Tomorrow would be warm, melting and a rehearsal of spring. Tonight would be windy, and by the time she was in bed listening to the windows rattle she would know what would have been said or not and this would be the past, photographed and developed. Why had she not resolved to see Mary earlier? So absurd to put it off, await intervention from whom? A kindly and omniscient lesbian social worker provided cost-free by the provincial government?

First she would walk to the intersection of Avalon Boulevard and Forty-Fourth, where she would cross over onto the residue of Bowness Park, a sweep of grass ending in a steep incline down to the river and along the bike path into the park itself. You shouldn't come here at night in the dark, you could be murdered or raped, but she had been here so often with Peter in the late afternoon and on weekends that she couldn't stir up the electrolytes of fear, try as she might. She would sit on the edge of the drop for a while, collect her thoughts, then see or not see Mary.

Earlier in the day her mother had called. And Julia had answered in a Bonnie half-whisper, thinking it might be Mary.

"Are you all right?" her mother asked.

"Yes, I'm fine." No further explanation offered.

"I'm coming to visit in the summer," her mother said. "Just booked the ticket this very day. Your dad and Stephen are staying here, at my request actually."

"You are?" Her mother? Coming to visit on her own? This was

an odd little cactus of surprise, prickly in her throat. Who would have ever thought that thing would flower?

"I need to get away for a while. Or so Eugenia Wilde tells me. She more or less tells me what to do these days, which suits me actually. She told me to leave the whole operation to your dad and Marcia, get out of it altogether, and she was right. No sooner had I done that than they decided it was all too much work and Marcia and Sven split up over ideological issues and Marcia went back to school in crop science. She wants to farm now, free-range hens and sheep."

"When did all this happen?" Julia asked.

"I began to quit last spring and Sven left in August and Marcia in December. Domino effect, but I would never have predicted it. Stephen works some in the inorganic houses, as they've come to be called. We're all able to have a bit of a laugh about it now on good days. And Eugenia and I are thinking of a venture — a store. Antiques and collectibles. I might get a small-business loan. That's partly why I'm visiting — looking for Western memorabilia, or so I'll tell the accountant."

"Do you ever see Lois?"

"Lois lives in Winnipeg; she comes back maybe once a year. According to Eugenia, she has a girlfriend. I always thought that Lois was a little queer and I guess I was right. Anyway ... "

"But have you seen her, Mom? When she comes home once a year?"

"Not for about five years. Last time I saw her she had her hair dyed red and four earrings in one ear and none in the other, which I guess is what they do, from what I've read. Have signals, I mean. Eugenia and I were just discussing that on the way to an auction. That, and is it genetic because I guess she has an older brother who never married and teaches piano. Anyway, what do you care about signals? I hope early July is a good time to visit. You don't have to take time off. I can entertain myself."

"But Dad and Stephen are welcome to come too."

"No no no. I need to do this. Eugenia's right, as usual. It's for me. When have I ever gone anywhere on my own?"

"Well that's good. Early July'll be fine. I'll take time off … "

"You don't have to."

"But I will. I want to. We can go to the mountains and you can see Katharine's grave and we can take Peter to the dinosaur museum in Drumheller."

"It's all set then. I'd better run. This is going to cost."

"Have you quit smoking?"

"Not yet but I'm buying the lightest brand, which is more like exercise than anything else. I practically blow a gasket inhaling."

It was all set then. All set was a good and enviable state of mind, as if your grey matter had been heated and stirred with coloured sugar and poured into a mould, set and was now gelled. At the moment, Julia herself felt all set and so she should move onward to Mary's house, taking advantage of this lucky convergence of mood, health, attitude and weather. Time was ticking; Peter couldn't be left for long. Although he'd wanted her to leave, he'd also wanted to set the timer on the oven, thinking her return would coincide to the second with the stove's quiet ding in another pleasing assemblage of independence and dependence, but she had said no. That would make her too nervous to enjoy the walk. And so would Mary, truthfully, should she happen to be in, but she wouldn't be. She would be out.

Across the hard grass — there had been so little snow — and onto the grey sidewalk, reptilian in its cold-blooded absorption of the surrounding temperature. The sidewalk in winter was an entirely different creature than in the summer, a frozen skin you hope to traverse without injury. When you're older you might break your hip; you might break an arm or use a walker. You might just stay in and look out your window at a thirtyish woman walking past and think: Maybe she's on her way to see her best friend, the one who kissed her at that party. She looks a little nervous. Because Mary's light is on, and unlike Julia, she would not leave Kristy at home alone even for half an hour, even with the oven timer as a guarantee. But she has twenty minutes and she must make use of them.

She would ring and the door would open and there would follow a gulping, like a wave in her face, washing over her body, breaking on the heels of her feet. "I guess we should have a conversation," she said. And there was Mary, the same as always, only moving in a frame of undivided and hopeful attention.

"I'm just putting Kristy to bed, so come in. Come in and sit down and I'll be right back."

"I'll use your phone to call Peter if that's all right." What if there was no answer?

"Hello," came his voice.

"Are you OK? I'll be there in less than half an hour. Is everything OK? What are you doing?"

"Watching TV."

"Good. So no problems?"

"Zero problems."

Now she'd have to sit for a moment and wait. What to say? She was glad she'd said "conversation" instead of "talk" because the word seemed less binding, the sort of defence one might be able to offer later in a court of law. But I did, after all, say "conversation," your honour.

"I'm sorry about the note," Mary said. She hadn't sat down, hadn't offered tea or a slab of banana bread, was standing in baggy jeans and one-size-too-small T-shirt, looking, there was no other word for it, good. "It was puerile. I've been meaning to call and apologize, but not having heard from you, my motivation was low. Needless to say, I made it all up in a moment of, hmmm, frustration." They were in the kitchen, standing, Julia still wearing her coat.

"So you're not really taking a play-writing course?"

"No."

"Well, I can't stay long. Peter's alone and I told him I'd be back in half an hour. But … I should have called. I'm not good at intimate conversations or even the averagely personal, or so it would seem." Oh, let her talk.

"Half an hour. OK. I'll talk fast. I don't know where to begin. If you're feeling bad about Lenny, I should explain I've known for years I'm a lesbian, probably since I played basketball in high school, and I've discussed it with Lenny for years. It was after Kristy was born that I got more insistent about it all, and finally he got so tired of listening to me, he told me I should go to an endocrinologist; maybe having Kristy knocked me off-kilter hormonally, he said. Animals can start doing weird things after giving birth. Leonard Nordstrom speaking on behalf of the nature of things, as he so often does. So I went along with it, got my hormones tested, which I now see as my last real concession to heterosexuality. Nothing out of the ordinary, was the doctor's conclusion. Why don't we sit down?"

They sat on the edge of the couch, Julia still in her coat, like someone in an arena on a hard bench, wondering why she had come to this particular hockey game. Remembered a time when she and Mary had watched Kristy and Peter play in the five-year-olds mixed league.

"Anyway, after the endocrinologist, Lenny went scientific on me and said how do you know you prefer women if you've never gone to bed with one? I didn't tell him I had, in high school, because I knew where this was heading. The empirical test, as Lenny calls it. So have an affair, he said. Go ahead. You can't make this kind of decision without data. Fine, I thought, carte blanche. But where to locate a woman interested in an experimental lesbian affair?"

"You mean you had an affair right after Kristy was born?"

"Oh no. Time had passed. She was three."

"But you knew me?" Julia was now an unhappy spectator at the game, a woman whose instant hot chocolate had spilled down the front of her coat.

"Of course I knew you. I met you in the hospital, remember? You're not going to get retroactively jealous here are you?"

"No. I'm surprised, that's all. So who was it, if you don't mind me asking?" If you don't mind me asking, a phrase she had loathed and detested from the dawn of time, a phrase Ladonna should use her linguistic influence to have stricken from the English language, erased from all texts.

"Louise. Louise Hornung. I met her at a Canadian Tire store. We were both looking at those little bottles of paint you buy to do touch-ups on your car and she started talking to me, said she didn't want to go to whatever appointment she had and did I want to go for a walk. Now I wonder how many other women she had tried this on, but anyway, she told me she was reading a lot of Simone de Beauvoir and thought every woman should be like her and have at least one homosexual experience. It was de rigueur, she said, without a hint of irony. Perfect, I thought, I'll be one of Louise's experiences. She was older by ten years; she'd been around, I assumed.

"We had lunch together a few days later, during which there was considerable tittering and coy stupidity. Then we checked into a motel, the Regal Inn to be specific, with the intention of doing 'it.' Inside the room, as I was unbuttoning my shirt, Louise let me know in a kind of high strangled voice that she was predisposed to anxiety attacks, hyperventilating."

"Oh no. Poor Louise." Julia's lungs had nothing but sympathy.

"Poor Louise? I had to search the room for a paper bag and found one, fortunately, so she could recover and cry and tell me how unhappy she was with her husband, Garth. With all my buttons rebuttoned, I advised her to seek professional help, feeling like I had entered Ann Landers' secret double life. And that was the last I saw of Louise."

"Well good." Julia wanted to have something further to say, but what might it be? The reference to Louise had bagpiped her lungs into readiness, forced some air up her throat. "Although I must say I can't believe you were doing these things while I was being so conscientiously average and not getting too close to you in Hawaii, worrying I might offend you."

"Doing what things? Sitting in a motel room with an anxious woman? Anyway, these things weren't going on when we were in Hawaii. Nothing was going on then."

"Good. I would hate to think …"

"What? What would you hate to think?"

Dear god, were they going to have a fight? How absurd could this become? Two hockey moms in middle-class fluorescence having a lovers' spat behind the penalty box? "I would hate to think I had gone to all that trouble when you hadn't gone to any at all."

"Well, if it's any comfort, I've gone to quite a bit of trouble. Take, for example, Andrea."

"You mean there was also an Andrea?"

"Well, you might as well hear it all. You do want to hear it all, don't you?"

"I suppose." In truth, Julia's ears, had they the capacity, would have grown dense and woolly plugs, a layer of fibreglass insulation and a soundproof hat.

"Well, Andrea was a flight attendant I met not too long after the Louise debacle. I did learn one useful thing from Louise and that was not to be afraid to make some sort of proposition if things looked promising. I was at a university basketball game — I used to go to them alone all the time — and Andrea seemed to be paying some attention to me, so I decided to use the Hornung technique, as I took to calling it, and asked if she wanted to go for a walk after the game. And so began an actual affair with anger and jealousy and secrets. And after fourteen months of meeting up with Andrea in Calgary hotel rooms and worrying who I'd run into when we stepped out onto the street together, she demanded I leave Lenny.

But I wouldn't. I didn't want to. And he didn't want me to either. It wasn't as if I was keeping secrets from him, or he from me. He was seeing Lucille Demchuk. It was all so Bob and Carol and Ted and Alice, and yet it wasn't, which I guess is what all the Bobs and Carols say."

"I guess." Julia would have to go soon. She was suddenly very tired, worn out from the effort of uttering what? Maybe thirty words. With all this disclosure from Mary, she would never be able to reciprocate and now felt as if caught in an embarrassing banking situation: Miss Raine, I'm afraid you're terribly overdrawn. We suggest you do something about the situation and we suggest you do it now.

"Plus, I didn't have any money, what with my series of part-time jobs in retail and at the newspaper. So I stayed with Lenny. I stayed and made plans. I stopped entertaining the notion of using the Hornung technique at every opportunity and decided to become a real estate agent. Still very Bob and Carol, I suppose. And then I fell in love with you. And then I left Lenny. So that's just a sampling of some of the trouble I've gone to. "

"Oh." Dead silence. Julia's mind was now a dense liquid, moving in slow waves like oil from one side of her skull to the other, splashing against the backsides of her eyes. The room turned a grey colour, blurred like wet newsprint.

"In Hawaii, I knew that." Pardon me? What was that she'd said? A statement both confident and untrue that she hoped might serve as a conversational brake, several flashing red lights on an impassable winter road. Sorry lady, I'm afraid you're going to have to turn around here.

"Yes, that week was the turning point for me. You see, I'm very rational. I wait. I plan. I get myself an income and move out. I have a party and kiss you and you stop speaking to me."

"That's only because I was so surprised. You've been waiting and thinking for years and I've only been waiting. You see the difference? But now. . . . Yikes. Look at the time. I must be going. I can't believe I've left Peter for practically one whole hour. Have you ever done that with Kristy? Not likely. I know, I'll have a dinner party. I'll have a party next Saturday and you come and I'll invite Miriam and Celeste and Harvey and Joan."

"And Peter can come here and stay with the sitter."

"Yes, OK. Now I have to go. The guilt alone, it could shatter the sound barrier. It's travelling faster than me, that's how it operates."

"OK. Go."

~ ~ ~ ~

Next weekend had seemed immeasurably far away, and a dinner party was not the sort of thing she did — its improbability was like throwing molasses into the hinges and levers of time so that really, it would probably never happen. Thursday night the universe would grind to a halt, engines smoking and all belts in need of replacement. Well folks, you can unfasten your seat belts because it looks like we're going to be stuck here for a while. You can forget tomorrow's appointments because tomorrow may literally never come. Freezing rain forever, and until we can get some engineers onto this time-and-space problem, looks like Mary Nordstrom may be showing a house in the far south of the city for some time — whoops there's that word — for the present.

Then Julia would be disappointed, watching Mary being interviewed on television, a casualty of "The Big Stop," as it would come to be known. She'd so hoped Mary could make it. But somehow, magically, without her body. Julia wanted Mary's body to remain elsewhere, resolutely covered in sweaters and underwear, because she did not wish to appear a ridiculous, inexperienced oaf in bed, a smiling head anticipating another Lucas Reef. If only for a while her body could be under the operation of some other head, send this one off to sit in the sun somewhere, let it switch places with Popeye. Basic dog vocabulary was probably enough to get you through most novel sexual experiences: rowf, rowf, that feels good, don't stop, and how 'bout I do this?

She wished her mother would call, if only to remind her that she was not the centre of the universe and that two new constellations had *not* appeared, nor had time come to a halt as a direct consequence of her psychosexual (Harvey's word) dilemmas. Time continued to measure itself away in ticks and tocks so that now it was Saturday and she had to cook. The sitter was arranged at Mary's, which made Julia worry even more.

"Peter can stay the night," Mary had said, a statement Julia repeated an infinite number of times, weighing it for meaning, slicing the syllables into gram-sized portions for analysis. Good thing Harvey was coming, she thought, hoping for some rescue there. But these days his body chemistry was acting up, his bipolarity was wresting itself from the grasp of Joan's surveillance and he was talking up a storm. Julia liked Harvey at all of his poles, but Joan didn't, so heaven forbid they should cancel. Harvey might talk and talk into the night and morning and the sitter would have to go home and a new day would dawn. Mary, maybe we could sleep together sometime but platonically, hold one another through the night, Julia would suggest with a heartfelt hug. Let's not rush things.

"Does Peter want to come over now?" Mary called to ask.

"But it's only five."

"I thought you might want some time to cook."

"Peter, do you want to go now to Mary's? Yes, he's on his way."

"Great. I'll see you at seven-thirty."

Julia couldn't cook. What had she been thinking? She would try for fancy in the main course, but it would be rice pudding for dessert and they'd better be happy with that. All these lemons for the chicken seemed excessive: could the recipe be wrong? Full of typos? No, recipes were never wrong. Just follow the instructions, comply, because there were larger issues to consider. Miriam, for example. How could she persuade Miriam to like her? Or was it a lost cause? And what about conversation? She needed topics. You couldn't invite a group of people over and have nothing to say. There were always current events; she would spend some time reading the paper and jotting down a few notes on the North-South dialogue and the Gang of Four, make a list in very small print to stick to the fridge. She'd come up with five topics and one solid reason to compliment Miriam. What could it be? Her clothing maybe, or the bottle of wine they would undoubtedly bring. Yes. Miriam thought of herself as an oenologist, so she would have to have something intelligent to say about the wine. No. Unnecessary. That's very nice wine, would suffice, along with an appreciative and lingering look at the label.

Now a bit of last-minute cleaning, dusting, changing into a simple black dress, the only one she had, the one she'd worn to the Christmas party, unfortunately, and then she could grab a glass of wine and ding-dong. Someone was at the door. Ding-dong. The entire human race really was under the control of bells and alarms and whistles.

"Hi Harvey. Hi Joan."

"It wasn't a manic episode," Harvey was saying to his wife. "I was just damn sick of my clothes. Honest to god, I have the narrowest road allowance for screw-ups of anybody on the planet. Other people rob convenience stores or build additions to their houses without proper approval from the city. I buy six items of clothing and Nancy Nurse here wants to send me to the psychiatric ward. She has both VISA cards now so we'll all sleep a little sounder tonight."

"Come in and sit down. Oh, I think Celeste and Miriam are here." And then Mary. They all arrived in a chorus of doorbells and mingled and then sat down. Later on, Julia concluded that as such occasions go, it was a reasonable success, though no computer would ever have matched this group according to age, social standing or marital status. Thanks to Harvey, the list of topics remained unconsulted. Miriam responded well to the wine compliment and told a humorous story about wrecking a golf cart. Mary sat opposite Julia and looked great. Doesn't she look great? Julia wanted to say to Celeste, she really is quite something, but managed to pin these sentiments to the blue mats lining her frontal lobes and hold them down for the count. "More vegetables anyone?"

How then did it happen? They were in the living room, the two couples very animated on the subject of Maggie and Pierre, when Mary, with one finger, gestured Upstairs? And examining the four guests for signs of need or discomfort, Julia concluded that now might be an agreeable time to slip away for only one moment, since Mary had suggested it. Julia sought confirmation through mime and hesitation: You mean upstairs? Yes, Mary nodded, and then something let go, as if the elasticity of Julia's garters gave way and they pooled around her ankles, as if all that anxiety were nothing more than a worn-out pair of stockings. Old lisle. Better off without these.

First Julia, then Mary went to the upstairs hall where they kissed, but only for the briefest of times, although Julia wondered about that later. Kissing and alcohol can cause a person to step out of the four corners of the clock and into a sort of stopwatch of time — large moments caught in a round frame: that was when Mary put her hand on Julia's back; that was when she touched her neck, then pressed the flat of her hand onto her breast, hard. She was certain it was only a short while, but when they came downstairs everyone was making motions to leave and she could only think what kind of hostess abandons her duties to kiss a guest of the same sex in the upstairs hall? Don't go, she wanted to say. Get the hell out of my house.

"Thanks, Julia, that was great."

Joan would drive; Celeste and Miriam had come in a cab so she would drive them home as well. Everyone was happy and convivial and disappearing into subarctic coats. And then they were gone.

"Come back upstairs," said Mary, and Julia's face must have said that sounds like a fine idea because next she was being led by the hand into the dark of her bedroom and with one move her dress was off, pulled over her head, and suddenly Julia remembered Mrs. McCracken. Now Mary's shirt, her pants, her bra, then Julia's too, which was when Mary's arms encircled her and their breasts met and Julia was forever rescued from where she stood before that moment, inside some glacial deposit. Avalanche conditions, she said. What was that? asked Mary. Take these off, she said, pulling at Julia's underwear. The instructions were appreciated. Julia hoped they would continue indefinitely, like a manual or reference book that offered the details of an AMA accommodation guide — south off the I-15, take exit number 42, don't worry, you'll be there soon, lie down, lie down, you'll be there soon.

~ ~ ~ ~

Would you call this a sexual awakening? What was a sexual awakening exactly? Would Ladonna be able to provide a definition? Movies and novels were devoted to the subject — with the proper touch, the perfect kiss, her slumbering libido would destroy its glass case, scare villagers, disturb the peace and create more little babies. Julia didn't know. She wanted to call Mary and ask but lived in fear, still, of the direct question, that which Mary might pass back, a hard and rubbery puck. She would say, No I've always been awake sexually but now I'm actually up and walking around, I'm out of my metaphorical bed jacket. What do you think?

There it was, the reciprocity act. What do you think? Julia thinks she's maybe been in school for too long, because to be honest she feels as if she has finally passed all the tests and exams, both physical and mental, the basics. Somebody asked her the times tables and she rattled them off and then she was told her teeth and bones were fine and throughout the whole process Mary was watching. Mary was the judge and the teacher and the basketball

coach who studied the precedents and read the essays and scruti-
nized the instant replays and still chose Julia. Oh this all sounds
stupid. How could you say that every time Mary's voice was on the
phone or at the door, every cell of Julia's body woke up, jumped up,
leapt to its feet, whole organs and glands and the tiniest of capil-
laries, all celebrating as if the war had ended or all of our teams had
won all the cups? She wasn't the type to make that sort of confes-
sion. But still, she couldn't help noticing the astonishing efficiency
of words. The growing body of data.

"Can you go to work a little late this morning?"

"They're going to start wondering."

"I'll just come by for a minute after Kristy's gone to school."

"Peter's already left. Hand bells practice."

And Mary was on her way: the woman Julia Raine could not
resist. She wouldn't go to work late again for the next six months
at least; she'd make a resolution, this was it, but too late now to
change her mind for today. Maybe she loved Mary Nordstrom, but
she couldn't possibly say that yet. Maybe she loved what she
thought of as Mary's entourage, the fact that Mary seemed to bring
with her her own bleachers, trampled grass, the smell of warm canvas, awnings and yards of coloured stripes. The idea of a fair or a
sporting event, the recollection of midway line-ups. What was she
supposed to do? Be on time every day for the rest of her life?

"Julia?"

"I'm upstairs," she replied, a voice possessed of the domestic
assurance of someone else, Donna Reed or Ward Cleaver. There was
Mary removing her pants and shirt, to wild applause from the
spectators between Julia's red ears. Underwear, skin, hair; she was
white, brown and yellow, high-school colours, which could cause a
burst of loyalty, devotion and testosterone. Pom-poms. It occurred
to Julia that Mary was like the girls in the high-school change
room who were not at all afraid to march around in bra and underpants or turn to her and discuss the geography test dressed in

nothing but hard little breasts and a triangle of hair, making her own silly shame more shameful, her own shyness double up on itself like too much of a good thing — watermelon, manners, sun. The result was nausea and that old familiar question: Did she want to be those girls or have them? Seemed this question had been stuck for a long time, thickening behind her breastbone. "Aren't you going to say hello?"

"In a manner of speaking," Mary said, pulling off Julia's underpants, sitting her back into the chair and looking at her. And Julia decided she might be one of those locker room girls after all, one who was thrilled to be seen and in love with her own body. All Mary needed to use was the tip of her tongue. How did she do that? Holding Julia's legs apart, her tongue was harder than the hardest cock. It managed to hit the back of her throat and the top of her cunt and pull them together with a hard cable of desire. And Julia thought: shortstop. There was some form of linguistic shortstop allowing only two words, one thought: fuck me. Oh yes. And the occasional yes. Everything else had stopped. The fans in the bleachers were still watching. Will she come? Yes. A roar. She's never come like that before, one of them says. Or so quickly, says another.

Julia wanted to tell Mary she thought she might be leaving the bleachers and moving into her own body. She wanted to say she had right now at least reached the perimeters of the sheltering canvas. But as the wind carried on, stretching her heart, it knocked all the words off the shelves, like a breeze in a card shop. Which reminded her: she had bought Mary a card. A card with a silly sentimental message, which right now lay in her desk drawer with a handwritten inscription: "You have made a big difference." But now was not the time to make a presentation. Now was not the time.

"It's cold. Let's get under the blankets," Julia said. "Let's stay under them forever."

chapter

The difference is

visual, Julia wanted to explain.
And why not? It was summer-
time, she was at the Stampede
— the greatest outdoor show
on earth — why not make a
public address? Others did, and
on far less interesting subjects
— The Merits of the Landrace
Hog, or Mainstays of the
Kitchen: The Miniature Marsh-
mallow. If masturbation can
result in visual impairment,
Julia would begin, then the
corollary of this truism must
be that a satisfactory sexual
relationship can improve visual
acuity. No, not just acuity,
absence of blur, but the look of
the landscape, the composition

of the view. Corn dogs, enormous fun for Dalmatians, spinning wheels of fortune or blue cotton candy: that which may once have been a little wearying, now is pleasing to the eye.

Come to the Stampede with Mary Nordstrom. Bring your son. Most people arrive in the late afternoon, so you'll need to snake through the midway in a line, checking back regularly to make certain no one is missing. It's a little like a fire drill in the midst of swinging, catapulting machinery you can't trust, since it was most likely in Knoxville or Richmond just last week and has been recently reassembled by carnies. Whom you also cannot trust. The music is circular; everything whirls and begins to light up long before dusk, flashing as if pictures were being taken one after another. Might as well get in line. Ride the boring and slow ferris wheel — the one with the round seats — if only to get a look at the carnies' trailers jammed onto a piece of concrete between the Round-Up Centre and the midway. With their window boxes and lawn chairs, they are an undespairing attempt at home. Take heart.

And expect rain in the early evening. This is when sensation may go olfactory for a time. Rain kicks up the summer smell of dust and dirt, the smell of pigeons, maybe, if you could get close enough or melt them into scented crayons. This might be a downpour so why don't we go into the Big Four building? They always have free samples.

Inside will be a knot of people listening to the voice of a man or woman so confident in their product you will find yourself remembering a certain science or Sunday school teacher. It is the voice of pre-doubt, pre-skepticism, could be Adam himself with a lapel microphone. "You see, ladies and gentlemen, this mop has been treated with a chemical developed in our own research labs, known as Purifium. Harmless to children and pets, Purifium actually lifts dirt and harmful bacteria right out from those spaces between the floorboards. Watch as I use the MopDemon on this space." If you're with Mary Nordstrom she'll put her arm around you, like a friend, but the trained observer will notice some further communication, Braille on the skin of both parties. Kristy wants to see the hypnotist. So does Peter.

The colours to expect outside then are end-of-the-day green, mud and cotton candy. The hypnotist performs on the outdoor stage where already a crowd has gathered, skeptics who love to believe and vice versa. Kids push to the front and adults hang back, although several volunteer to be hypnotized on stage. They're told to think they are Anne Murray or naked or married to a saucepan.

Pardon me? I don't usually encourage audience participation. What was that? Oh. It's the voice of Mary Nordstrom and it's asking a question: "What time does your mom arrive on Saturday?"

"My mom. Right. She's arriving this weekend. I believe the plane gets in around one."

"So what's your thinking today?" This is Mary's way of asking will she be introduced to Julia's mother as a close personal friend, a realtor or the veterinarian's ex-wife.

"My thinking is we've never spent a significant amount of time alone together before. I'm not sure what we'll talk about. So the issue of me telling her about us is somewhat low on my list of anxieties — at least in second or third position."

"Fine, fine. As you know, I hope to meet her."

"You will. You will."

On stage a woman is singing "Snow Bird." Remarkably, or suspiciously, she knows all the words. "This is all so bogus," Mary says. "I don't believe they're hypnotized. This woman has obviously sung 'Snow Bird' in front of her mirror hundreds of times and this is her opportunity to exploit that coincidence. They all ham it up too much to be hypnotized. They're pretending, pretending to be hypnotized, which is a strange set of motivations if you ask me."

"Why would anyone bother to pretend to be hypnotized?"

"Well, because, I don't know. Because they don't want to ruin the show. Disappoint the audience."

"I think they might be hypnotized."

"Nah. They're faking it, overdoing it. Look at the guy on the end. He's slumped over as if he's in a coma. You don't go into a coma when you're hypnotized."

"How do you know? Have you ever been hypnotized?"

"No, but I'm an expert on many subjects and faking is one of them."

"What about comas? Are you an expert on comas?" Mary wasn't listening. "Or the dust virus? Are you an expert on that? You slip into a coma when you have the dust virus."

"Never heard of it. I take it it's an airborne kind of thing."

Julia would like Mary's attention. "Did you ever live in an apartment in Chicago?" Now she has it.

"What are you talking about? Have you been accidentally hypnotized? You're sitting up and talking and yet you're making mention of apartments in Chicago and dust viruses. These are all signs of a genuine hypnotic trance."

"No, I'm fine. It just occurred to me that you remind me of someone I used to know. Her name was Mrs. McCracken. You're a lot like her."

"I hope that's a good thing."

"Oh yes. Definitely."

Now a man is wearing a colander on his head. He is a satellite, a satellite of love the accompanying music suggests to the viewing public. Beneath the music they can almost hear the heat of the stage lights, the forward spin of the carousel.

~ ~ ~ ~

Julia hadn't seen her mother since Marcia and Sven and the basement smoking loge. Frances Raine had aged but at the same time become more lively, as if the accumulation of days had collapsed her old rickety reserve, building in its place something made perhaps of sheet metal — something substantial, suited to all weather conditions. At the airport they embraced, a new convention both would rather have done without, but such was the sociological robustness of the hug, it grew like topsy, Katharine used to like to say. Katharine preferred to shake hands, where you can look the person in the eye. With hugging you never know if they're winking at the next person, rolling their eyes or copping a feel.

On the way home from the airport, Julia asked, "Is there anything in particular you'd like to do while you're here?" In case her mother had no suggestions, Julia had crafted daily rosters of activities, leaving periods of free time open, little doors into anxiety and restlessness. She had gone so far as to highlight those blank spaces with a felt marker, as if the colour would bleed ideas from the page, ideas written in invisible ink. There are some photographs at the Glenbow you might want to see. Or, suggest a game of cards.

Today for example, Saturday, looked like this: 2:45 — Arrive airport. 3:15 — Arrive home, unpack, brief relaxation period. 4:30 — Visit to Stampede grounds (even though I was just there). Rodeo? if desired. Non-nutritious Stampede junk food. FREE TIME. Go to bed.

But her mother immediately threw a spanner into the works by rejecting the Stampede idea in favour of an exploratory walk in the neighbourhood, followed by dinner. Sure that'd be great, Julia agreed, drawing a straight line through rodeo, pencilling in extensive dinner preparations, which were now underway.

"I thought we might go to see Katharine's grave tomorrow — have a reunion like you mentioned once a long time ago. Four people and four generations, if you count Katharine, which I do." But Peter didn't want to go, he'd been enough times and the graveyard scared him, plus he was invited to go to the mountains with a friend tomorrow. "Oh," Julia worried, studying her meager Sunday roster. With Peter there would be a mutual object of interest, a body of flesh for words to pass through, refracting into other sub-jects. "I guess it'll just be the two of us."

"Splendid," her mother said. And Julia wondered: Splendid? Frances Raine did not usually speak in terms of splendid. This was vocabulary she had acquired from Eugenia Wilde. Splendid, she used to say of anything Lois drew or coloured. Gorgeous.

Mary called. "Oh. You're there. So you're not doing the rodeo thing."

"No. Not today."

"Does this mean Kristy and I are invited over for after-dinner mints or coffee or leftovers?"

"Tomorrow might be better, or Monday. One or the other. It's been kind of a long day for Mom with the time change and every-thing."

"Oh no, I'm fine," her mother said, mouthing "Who is it?"

Julia had heard of hysterical blindness; might she be coming down with it at this very moment? The intense pain behind her eyes seemed to arise from optical nerves having had just about enough, prepared to unplug the retinas like two small television screens. But not just yet, not at this moment. The pain passed. Mary said goodbye. Julia's mother turned back to the telephone directory and her search for Corrigans.

"So we're on for Union Cemetery tomorrow."

~ ~ ~ ~

"Kind of an odd spot for a graveyard," Julia's mother said as they parked and began the walk up the hill, across the sprinkler-fed grass.

"I don't think the town fathers back then counted on Macleod Trail turning into a six-lane horror show and the Stampede grow-ing the way it has. They likely thought, how lovely to be next to the sleepy Elbow River. Everyone can have a view. I wonder what they'd have to say now." Midway screams on one side, gearboxes grinding on the other, and in between a long narrow expanse of the peace that passeth all understanding. "But Katharine's plot is down in a little valley so you don't see the traffic, and when the Stampede's not on, there's very little noise. Especially if you come late at night, as I've done a few times."

"Late at night?"

"Yeah. If I've been out and have a babysitter, I'll drop by. There's always a security guard in the little hut. I say Katharine's name and he looks on his list and says 'OK Miss.'"

"A security guard? Now that's what they need in Mesmer and Flax. Somebody's knocked over several gravestones in both places. That might be a good job for me, come to think of it. A little hut with a space heater. As long as I could smoke."

"But you're supposed to stop."

"Once I've found something else to do, that's my first resolution: quit smoking."

"What happened to the store idea? The small business loan?"

"Oh, I've changed my mind. I didn't even sign the papers. The Raines had us as indentured slaves for so long, I just couldn't tolerate the idea of more debt."

"What do you mean?"

"Oh, you know. The damn twenty thousand dollars your grandparents gave Abe to buy the greenhouses. Your aunts and uncles never stopped alluding to that and I was more than a little obsessed with it myself. For years I could only think about paying them back. So when grandpa died and the inheritance came, your dad divvied up his and gave them each four thousand and they are now finally, finally happy. And somewhere in the process I completely lost my stomach for money. Don't want to borrow. I just want to get a job in a drugstore or the egg grading station."

"I guess Sven and Marcia didn't help matters."

"No, Sven and Marcia did not. The switch to organics brought about a dizzying decline in income but I'll say this: it got me out of the whole business and for that I'm eternally grateful."

Julia wanted to ask a question she shouldn't, as it wasn't on the list of prescribed activities and this was not the time to make unscheduled changes.

"What about Marcia?" Julia asked.

"What about her?"

OK, she would ask: a departure of blood from the sinuses, empty places emptying further. "There wasn't anything between Marcia and Dad was there?"

"I don't think so. I mean, there's nothing much between your dad and me, if you know what I mean. Except," she was eating an egg salad sandwich, swallowing but not without some resistance in her throat, "you know, we're at that closer and closer apart stage, as they say. Do you want another sandwich?"

"No thanks."

"In the end it was all for the best. And Sven was good fun. Marcia had her moments too. And I'm free of vermiculite and seedling trays and I feel as if I've started to live, in a strange way. Like I suddenly got to be the pilot, I was thinking on my way here. Not that much has changed, really."

"No, I suppose it hasn't." And Julia saw a hand, somewhere, back at her parents' house in the bedroom with Jannette. Katharine's hand shaking the magic eight ball. *You can depend on it. It is decidedly so. My sources say yes.* Everything that might come to pass, each day's predictions, small and forgettable as chicken bones or last year's seed catalogues.

"Although here you are, in Calgary, with a job and a nine-year-old son and, and … " Fill in the blank, Julia thought, fill in the very big blank. And a boyfriend named Mary.

"Yes," Julia said, "it's really nothing like I thought it would be, back in Flax. Nothing like I thought it would be." And then there was a deep and night-like silence, startling — as if the sound had been switched off, a dire announcement were to be made — but only for a second. Ecstatic new screams from the midway and the roar of the traffic resumed, falling together in a noisy embrace somewhere overhead. "There's iced tea in the thermos, if you'd like."

"I was hoping you'd brought some," her mother said. "So, what should we do tomorrow?"

Marion Douglas' first novel, *The Doubtful Guests* (Orca, 1993), was a finalist for the Alberta Book Award. Her second novel, *Bending at the Bow* (Press Gang, 1996) was the winner of the Writers' Guild of Alberta Georges Bugnet Award. Her short stories have appeared in journals such as *Prism*, *Grain*, *A Room of One's Own* and *the Capilano Review*, and in anthologies such as *Hearts Wild* (Turnstone) and the *Journey Prize Anthology* (McClelland & Stewart). Marion Douglas lives in Calgary, Alberta.

Bright Lights *from* Polestar Book Publishers

Polestar takes pride in creating books that enrich our understanding of the world, and in introducing superb writers to discriminating readers. These voices illuminate our history, stretch the imagination and engage our sympathies.

FICTION:

diss/ed banded nation ~ *by* David Nandi Odhiambo
"Thoroughly convincing in its evocation of young, rebellious, impoverished urban lives … an immersion into a simmering stew of racial and cultural identities…" — *The Globe and Mail*
1-896095-26-7 ~ $16.95 CAN/$13.95 USA

Pool-Hopping and Other Stories ~ *by* by Anne Fleming
Shortlisted for the Governor-General's Award, the Ethel Wilson Fiction Prize and the Danuta Gleed Award. "Fleming's evenhanded, sharp-eyed and often hilarious narratives traverse the frenzied chaos of urban life with ease and precision." — *The Georgia Straight*
1-896095-18-6 ~ $16.95 CAN/$13.95 USA

POETRY:

Beatrice Chancy ~ *by* George Elliott Clarke
Shortlisted for the Atlantic Poetry Prize and the Dartmouth Book Prize. This brilliant dramatic poem is the first literary work to treat the issue of Canadian slavery. "Clarke … carries this story from our heads to our hearts to that gut feeling we all get when we have heard a devastating truth." — Nikki Giovanni

Whylah Falls: Tenth Anniversary Edition ~ *by* George Elliott Clarke
This beautiful edition of a Canadian classic features a section of previously unpublished poems and a fascinating introduction about the writing of the poems. "*Whylah Falls* might be — dare I say it? — a great book … I, for one, am humbled by it, am grateful for it." — Phil Hall in *Books in Canada*

I Knew Two Metis Women ~ *by* Gregory Scofield
Stunning in their range and honesty, these poems about Scofield's mother and aunt are a rich, multi-voice tribute to a generation of First Nations people.
0-896095-96-8 ~ $16.95 CAN/$14.95 USA

Inward to the Bones: Georgia O'Keeffe's Journey with Emily Carr
~ *by* Kate Braid
Winner of the VanCity Book Prize. In 1930, Emily Carr met Georgia O'Keeffe at an exhibition in New York. Inspired by this meeting, poet Kate Braid describes what might have happened afterwards.
1-896095-40-2 ~ $16.95 CAN/$13.95 USA